CHOKE

LISA TOWLES

Rebel ePublishers
Detroit London

Rebel ePublishers
Detroit, Michigan 48223

All names, characters, places, and incidents in this publication are fictitious or are used fictitiously. Any resemblance to real persons, living or dead, events or locales is entirely coincidental.

Choke
© 2017 by Lisa Towles

For information regarding permission, email the publisher at rebele@rebelepublishers.com, subject line: Permission.

ISBN-13: 978-1-944077-17-4
ISBN-10: 1-944077-17-0

Book design by *Caryatid Design*
Cover design by *Caryatid Design*

For Lee

We dance round in a ring and suppose,
but the secret sits in the middle and knows.
Robert Frost

PART ONE

CHAPTER ONE

"Castiglia? Do you have it?" The whisper came in the hushed darkness of San Francisco General Hospital's ICU recovery ward. Nurse Alice Redfield gave an insistent stare as she awaited an answer.

Certified Nursing Assistant Kerry Stine steeled herself against the jabbing pain in the side of her head and gestured toward the bed in front of them. "Right there. And what do you mean 'do I have it'?" She wondered, afterward, if the migraine had colored the tone of her words.

Redfield had already moved on to the next patient. "It's not there," she said without looking up.

Kerry Stine picked up the medical chart from the slot at the bottom of patient Rosemary Castiglia's bed. "Emergency Evacuation Procedures – Part I" was the title on the front page of what should have been, and clearly had been less than an hour ago, Castiglia's medical chart, containing a summary sheet, doctors' notes, lab results, etc. She shook her head and glanced in Redfield's direction. "Who would steal a medical chart?"

Nurse Redfield glared at her over wire-rimmed glasses. "That's the first thing you think of if it's missing?"

This question reminded Kerry that she'd only

been a CNA for six months and most of her classroom training she'd found completely inapplicable to hospital reality.

Nurse Redfield marched toward the exit door and paused. "If you wanted to steal a patient," she whispered, "the best way to do it is to steal their chart first."

Kerry stared at her supervisor. What a strange thing to say, she thought.

"Sure," Redfield went on, " the chart's got the patient's labs, schedule of tests, which then tells you when the patient is likely to be ... unattended. Get it?"

"Not really." The door closed behind Redfield, and Kerry glanced back at the semi-cadavers in post-op recovery – five of them crammed into a small, dark, uncomfortably chilly room purposely set to the temperature of a meat locker for infection control. To her, it felt more like a morgue, except the patients were technically still breathing. Through ventilators.

Rosemary Castiglia, the oldest patient on the ward, was the only one breathing on her own. Miraculous, and no one understood it. Still, with enough morphine to choke an elephant, all the lines she'd previously seen on the patient's face were smooth now – her forehead and eyes looking a decade younger. Sleep, Kerry thought, memorizing the patient's facial features, again acknowledging the pounding in her head. She looked at her watch – ten minutes left on her shift.

"Miss Stine?" The man paused. "Can I see you please?" Hospital Administrator Mark Ferri stood just outside the ICU entrance beside Nurse Redfield. As Kerry approached, Ferri gestured. "In my office." She hated how Ferri talked – pausing at odd times to inject extra importance to his words.

"How's your training class going?" Redfield asked,

looking suspiciously at Kerry. Kerry ignored her and followed Mark Ferri into his large office. Every wall contained a piece of matching chocolate-brown leather furniture. Two stiff-looking chairs, angular sofa, and an oversized ottoman she was sure had never been touched.

"I'm glad to see you taking advantage of our training programs. That's one of the things I'm working to revitalize here." Ferri gave her a 'good work' nod.

She shook her head. "I haven't enrolled yet. I need to stack up as many hours as I can right now. They offer that course again in six months."

The pounding in her temples had morphed into a vice-like squeeze. She felt an almost bouncing sensation when she closed her eyes, as if her head were vibrating. Despite the pain, she was unable to stifle the yawn that crept into her mouth as she sat down.

"Am I keeping you up?" Ferri was in front of her now, leaning back against his desk. She knew the body language – arms crossed to symbolize authority and their distance from each other in the hospital food chain, head lowered to signify interest, even intimacy.

You're not my friend, she thought. "My head ... I'm sorry. I've got a killer migraine."

"Let me give you something for it. I get them too." Don't trust him, her inner voice counseled. "Fiorinal, Imitrex, Motrin with Codeine ... if you ever need anything, help yourself." Now he looked straight at her. "I know what it's like." Ferri handed her a sealed sample packet of Fioricet. She just shook her head and looked at it. "Anyway," he went on, "you're probably wondering—"

"What's there to wonder about? A chart goes missing on Redfield's watch, so naturally blame it on the CNA. I understand the concept of hierarchy. Sir."

Ferri stared, eyes slightly wider.

She crossed her legs and arms, settling deeper into the uncomfortable chair. "Rosemary Castiglia's chart was there at 7 pm, I—"

"You looked at it?"

"No, but I saw it."

"That means you looked at it," Ferri said.

Okay, so you're a freaking homicide detective now. Note to self: watch what you say around him. Kerry rose and walked toward the door, wondering now if he'd secretly locked it. "If you're asking me if I physically picked up the chart and pulled it out of the holder, no. I visually confirmed that it was, in fact, her chart, checked the patient, checked her levels, saw that she was sleeping and moved on." She opened the door.

"Miss Stine, I wouldn't leave right now if—"

The door slammed behind her.

Chapter Two

Second shift at San Francisco General went from 12:30 p.m. to 8:30 p.m. Kerry looked at her watch as she breathed the first whiff of fresh air in eight straight hours. Smells like fall, she thought. Bad day, migraine, a perfect night for comfort food. Tuna melt from Mel's Diner.

This followed by a hot bath, her favorite satin pajamas, and her perfect lumpy lonely bed. It wasn't the thousand-dollar Serta Pillow Top that her husband Bill had picked out for them on their honeymoon. But it was all hers at least – paid in cash.

"Cash," she mumbled, irritated. "My purse." Head pounding again, she grudgingly turned back toward Kansas Street and braced her legs for the twenty-five-degree incline ahead. Two couples walked in front of her, arm in arm, making the hike without so much as an extra breath. Waiting at the crosswalk at Kansas and 23rd, she caught sight of a familiar set of dreadlocks.

As the man came down the hill, she saw more and more of his signature hair and felt her shoulders relax. Jesse Wilkins had a face with a thousand stories but no lines or wrinkles to betray his age or even his race for that matter. Aside from his

Jamaican accent and dark skin, his hybrid features could just have easily revealed Iraq as they could Sri Lanka.

"Miss Kerry," he announced with a friendly grin. "You working tonight?"

"Just got off shift." She stopped long enough to give him an urban handshake that climbed up from the fingers all the way to the forearms.

Jesse's face expanded into a wide smile. "You way too pretty to be so cool, Miss Kerry, hehe ..."

"I think I should thank you, but I'm not sure."

"Oh yes, you should." He winked, with perfect, straight white teeth grinning back at her.

In the awkward pause, Kerry caught her breath.

"Where you headed?" Jesse said.

"I left my purse in my locker. I was just—"

"I go get it for you. You stay here and rest. You got another headache tonight? I can see it in your eyes."

She nodded, the tightening feeling returning to her temples. "They wouldn't give it to you I'm afraid."

"What's that?"

"My purse."

"Where is it?"

"Second-floor lounge."

"You leave that to me, right? Black leather backpack with brown stripes. Right?"

Kerry studied him. He'd noticed how her eyes looked when she had a headache. He knew her purse. Something in her gut called out "Red Alert" but something else made it flutter. Maybe just the idea of someone being interested in her again. How long had it been? A year? Longer? Pathetic.

"If you had a house and a job, Jesse, I might have to marry you."

"You can't marry a man without a job?"

"Nah, my mother would kill me."

Jesse glanced behind them and pointed. "Wait for

me on this bench. I'll be back in no time."
Kerry squeezed the man's shoulder blades. They
felt bulky to the touch, bulkier than her hands
expected.
"Don't talk to any strangers," he yelled back,
laughing, halfway up the hill now.
Jesse Wilkins had been coming to the St. Vincent
de Paul shelter where she volunteered for the past
two years, and in all that time he'd never asked her
for a penny. And there was no part of her that
thought he'd be tempted to take any of the money in
her wallet on the way back down. It was at least
worth noting, she decided. Jesse. Big shoulders.
Kind heart. White teeth. She smiled a tad and let her
lids close for a split second.

Opening them again, she seemed to be walking,
purse on her shoulder, yet she had no recollection of
meeting Jesse again. Panicking, she looked at her
watch – 8:55. That meant she'd dozed for less than
twenty minutes, during which time Jesse had walked
all the way up Kansas and over to Potrero, retrieved
her purse and made it back down again.
Something's not right.
Even the air smelled funny in her nose. Maybe I
should see that neurologist, she thought. Migraines,
she knew from some of her medical training, were
not to be taken lightly and a possible indicator of
something more serious. Brain tumor ... the words
flashed around the inside of her head. My God, now
I'm paranoid.
Heading toward the bus stop at Kansas and 18th
Street, the pain in her temples throbbed harder.
Okay, Kerry, breathe deeply and walk. Just breathe
and walk. In ... out ...
Continuing down the hill and crossing 16th Street,
she kept looking back for the bus but reminded
herself she was only a few blocks from home now.

Not worth the bus fare. The throbbing had diluted her appetite and all she wanted now was that warm bath and bed. Come to think of it – maybe just bed. The streets were oddly bare tonight – almost too quiet from the lack of honking car horns and traffic.

One more block. She could just make out the outline of the Auto Body shop on the corner of her street now. Turning left on Harriet, she rounded the dark corner under the broken street light, past six buildings, then walked up the seven stairs to the main door of her apartment building. A wave of dizziness washed over her body as she jammed her key into the lock and pulled hard on it – too hard, causing her to lose her balance and slip down two steps.

"You okay, Miss?" someone asked, a man she didn't recognize, standing way too close to her face. She felt dizzy. God, please don't let me throw up on a cute guy, she thought, working hard to stand up straight.

The stranger came up the first two steps, sizing her up. "Do you need some help? You look a bit unwell ..."

English accent, Kerry noted, hoping her observation might quell the queasiness in her intestines. The man was pulling her to her feet.

"I'm Damen," he said. "Can I call someone for you? Why don't you sit down a minute?"

Kerry obliged and allowed the stranger to help lower her to the top step. She looked at his face and tried to speak, but just kept thinking if she could only get to her bed and rest, she'd be fine.

"I'll be okay." She stood, feeling sluggish. "Thank you for stopping, though, you're very kind. Do you live around here?"

The man held out something to her. Squinting, she could see it was something small. "It's my card. I just moved into the building on the corner. If you're sick and need help tonight, my cell phone's on here. I'll be up late unpacking boxes, you know how that is."

She glanced at it and shoved it in the bottom of her jacket pocket, offering the merest of nods in his direction. Damn you, Byron, she thought, cursing the elderly landlord who never fixed anything but things in his own apartment, including the elevator which had been broken for three months. She counted the stairs as she climbed. "Thirty-five, thirty-six ..." As she passed the third-floor landing, an eerie feeling slowed her steps – as she noticed something else that was entirely wrong. A light shining from under her apartment door.

And she never left the light on.

CHAPTER THREE

(415) 557-2643. There was no answer, but she kept hitting redial on her cell phone as she tapped one finger on the door to Apartment 166 – Byron, the landlord. She didn't even know his last name. The phone whirred back at her over and over, and she already knew he never retrieved voicemails.

"Byron?" she whispered, her mouth pressed into the crack in his front door. "Byron!"

A noise sounded from upstairs that resembled a door closing – her door. What was the cute guy's name who'd helped her on the street? "If you need help tonight ..." what had she done with that card? Her fingers fumbled inside her pockets, only to reveal the soft, torn fabric she'd vowed to mend months ago.

No one's here to help me, Byron's asleep or not home, and someone's in my apartment. Kerry crept up the stairs and squinted as she rose to the third-floor level. There was no light on under the door now.

No light. Jesus.

Migraines can cause visual and auditory disturbances, I probably saw someone else's apartment and got confused. No light, she kept thinking on the way up the stairs, hoping it would quash the kernel of dread in her belly.

The third-floor hallway was empty. She moved close and tentatively pressed her ear to her front door, then stuck her key in the lock and shoved open the door. Flipping on the living room light switch, her panicked eyes scanned the room. She leaned back against the door before moving, checking in, knowing that if her space had been intruded, she would somehow feel the energy of that invasion.

No one's been here.

"Lavender bath, bed, bath, bed," she chanted, fumbling toward the bathroom to turn on the water, push down the stopper, and pour the cupful of remaining bath salts into the water. Her clothes felt sticky on her body – was she sweating, or feverish? She peeled them off and dipped one toe into the hot bathwater, then a foot, leg, knee, before folding the rest of her haunches into the aromatic brew. Lavender, she reminded herself and drew in a deep breath, and slowly exhaled. She closed her eyes.

A scratching sound came from the living room. Wood against wood.

She drew another quick breath, wondering for the second time today about the sanity of her thoughts. Her body stiffened, and her feet naturally poised themselves for traction – soles facing down. First seeing things, now she was hearing things. But unless the world was suddenly upside down, someone had just stuck a key into her door lock.

"Jesus," a man's voice gasped. "Why's it so bright in here?"

CHAPTER FOUR

"Being a Master Gardener isn't a complicated science," said Grace Mattson, "it's about temperature management."

"Climate control," a young man blurted from the back of the classroom.

Grace nodded. "Monitoring the temperature of the soil, where the growing roots are, so the plant can get what it needs from the environment and, in essence, make food and survive. Water cools and hydrates. Sun heats and dries. There aren't that many variables in this equation but, let me tell you, it's a tricky balance. Good soil with the correct additives for a particular species will help the plant adjust on its own to the outside climate, which is in constant change. We don't want to control a plant but instead control some of the variables to allow it to control its own environment. That's what makes it strong and resilient." Blank faces stared back. "Then apply as needed to human behavior," she joked.

A young woman in the back row snored, in odd contrast to the eyes of the young men in the room which were fixed upon her face. Grace Mattson was not a young woman anymore. What do they see? she wondered. "Merrell?" she cued to the girl in the back.

"Yes. So sorry."

"A Master Gardener has three jobs," she continued. "Number one – *intuition* to determine what you feel the plant needs. If it's not growing, there's an imbalance. Two – *research* to find what the imbalance is. And number three – apply an additive to correct the imbalance and *observe* the changes. Now, someone, what's the treatment for aphids? And what type of plant is most susceptible to their attack?"

Grace softened at the sight of thirty young, wide open faces, and allowed a smirk to show on her lips.

"Okay, to pass this course, you don't need to memorize the names of a thousand species or plant diseases." She took three steps closer to the front row. "Miss Kuan? Are you awake over there?"

The young woman swiftly clicked off her iPhone. "Yes, ma'am."

"I'm not asking you to become horticulturalists," she went on, scaling the room. "A chimpanzee can memorize facts. My job is to inspire your intuition and connect it with your eyes and brain. Use common sense to discover what a plant needs. Does this plant seem healthy to you? If not, why? What does it need? If you can't tell, ask it."

"We should talk to plants?" The young man in the back again. "Do they prescribe medication for that?"

"Mr. Loomis, why do you want to be a Master Gardener? Is my class keeping you out of jail? Or perhaps Mummy's made you come?"

The young man visibly seethed and ran his fingers through dark, unwashed hair.

Grace approached him in the back row. "What can you tell us about aphids?"

The man rolled his alluring brown eyes. "Mostly attack roses, clear soft bodies, capable of asexual reproduction."

Grace stepped backward and folded her arms.

"Surprised?" the boy said, a smug look on his

face.

"Actually, yes. Reproduction's a big word for someone like you. Now," she turned her back and moved to the front of the class. "Ultimately, becoming a Master Gardener is about relationship management. You must become close to these plants, the plants I'm going to assign to you for the duration of this course. You'll all be given three plants to *manage* and cultivate and nurture. Some will be healthy, some may be dying. You must learn to know these plants – be intimate with them, so to speak. Talk to them, listen to them, smell, observe, touch them, and pay attention to the details you observe. Sometimes you won't see the details with the naked eye, but you'll just know – you'll feel them. That's ... intuition." Grace locked eyes with Loomis as he stood up from the small desk. "See you all on Friday," she said.

Chapter Five

Grace checked her phone for the time, secretly touting the fact that she was fifty-five years old and owned a smartphone, iPod, iPad, Kindle, and was more computer-savvy than someone half her age.

There were a few minutes left to check email before leaving for dinner. But first, she performed the typical rituals of teaching in the New Haven County Extension Division office – close and lock the windows, walk the aisles to see who left headphones, iPods and other electronic devices inside the desks. She stood looking down at the desk of the young man in the back. What was it about that young man? Had they met before? Stepping around the desk to look inside, a folded sheet of paper stuck out. She stooped to pull it out when the door creaked open.

"Grace." It was the Office Administrator. Damn. What did she want now? "There's a man in the lobby for you."

"Be right there," Grace replied without looking up.

"I think it's your partner."

Adrian? How strange, he never comes here.

The metal door to her classroom clanged open, bouncing against the rusted hinge. "We've got a problem."

She stopped and took stock of Adrian Calhoun's

taut face, wavy uncombed hair and harried presence. "We?"

"Sorry," he stepped backward and put his palms up. "*I've* got a problem."

"Just tell me if you're canceling dinner because I'm starved."

"No. I just wanted your ... needed your brain for a few minutes first."

Grace Mattson, for the first time all day, sat and listened. Listening was another talent on which she prided herself, not to mention a complete role reversal from four hours of lecturing.

Adrian Calhoun paced the tiled floors of her classroom and repeatedly pushed his hair out of his face. She watched him, hearing him saying something about a disease.

"And it spread."

"What?" she said. "It doesn't work like that."

"Grace, I'm telling you, it's spreading."

"But they're a different species for God's sake. Not only that," she said and then stopped. "The plant's physiologies are completely opposite. Monocotyledons and Dicotyledons have almost opposing susceptibilities to pests and plant diseases."

Adrian looked glum. "I know that."

"And *Solanaceae* are, well, one of the hardiest species on the planet. They're virtually indestructible."

Adrian shook his head, causing tufts of curly gray and black hair to fall into his face. "Not this time."

Grace studied his eyes for a moment. "How many?"

"Three," he signed, "and almost all the orchids are gone. But—"

"My God. But you were only gone for three days. Who was caring for them?"

Adrian was in the hallway now, hands on his hips, peering at her through the narrow doorway, beckoning her it seemed, to crack some unbreakable code.

CHAPTER SIX

Atticus or Chapel Street?" Grace said, walking a few steps behind him through the front entrance of the County Extension Office.

"I've got two or three students monitoring the greenhouse," Adrian continued, while Grace steered them to Atticus Bookstore and Café in New Haven's busiest collegiate enclave. "You know we'll never find a table."

"But the black bean soup is so worth the wait." She glanced at him and winked. "Who specifically was there last week?"

"Hard to say. I've got Kathleen, Kathleen Dwyer, to where she pretty much runs things in my absence, but under her ... it varies," he said. "And sometimes by the hour. Remember when you were eighteen?"

"I try not to."

"Kathleen's trained them to keep pretty thorough observation logs, though. Watering, soil testing, temperature."

"Nothing out of the ordinary last week?"

"No," Adrian sighed in response to the clusters of students swarming around the café. "It's almost as i—"

"Could they have been tampered with?"

"That's just what I was thinking," he said, pointing at her. "You tell me – can you inject a plant with a disease with any level of certainty of the response?"

Once they'd cleared the mob, there were three miraculous open tables. Grace glanced, confused, at her watch and claimed one, folding her Burberry Trench over the chair.

A student approached the table. "Do you guys know what you want or need menus?"

"Green tea and black bean soup," Grace replied and looked at Adrian.

"Same thing but with cappuccino."

"That's what you need, more caffeine. Why do I never see you eat anything green?"

Adrian adjusted his glasses.

Grace knew the meaning of this gesture. "Isn't it odd that we were waited on so quickly and found a table at 5 p.m. when classes get out?"

"You're stalling," he pressed. "I want to know if you can inject a plant with a disease and be sure of the response."

"You mean is it possible to kill a plant through injection?" Grace instinctively glanced around the bookstore and snickered. "You can kill a plant with salad dressing if you use enough of it."

"I'm serious."

"Of course. I've done it," she said under her breath.

Adrian's eyes widened.

"Despite what people say, anyone can be bought." She poured tea into a too-small cup. "That's all I'm saying about it."

Adrian sipped the cappuccino and pointed out the window.

"What?" Grace said, looking.

"It hasn't rained here in over a week," he said, indicating a woman outside the café holding a red umbrella.

"Is it me or is she looking right at us?"

"I don't know." Adrian looked deep into his cup. "Will you come and take a look?"

She nodded. "Tomorrow morning. I'm free from ten till eleven."

Adrian glanced across the street at the umbrella holder, then at Grace with a question in his eye. Grace shrugged. "No idea."

"Do you know her?"

"She could be a hooker, a spy. By the look of her, not very good at either."

The server set bowls of soup, napkins, and spoons in front of them. "Thank you so much," Adrian said and smiled. This reminded her about him. Gentility. Did she still see this trait as a weakness as she had years ago? Or maybe something she wished more for herself?

"What's Neville up to?" Adrian asked.

Neville. She waved her hand. "Oh, you know him. He sent me an email today saying I'd received a strange letter ... that for some reason he decided to leave on the porch. Odd."

"Even for him."

She chuckled. "He's involved in this project and that project, never telling me what they're really about. He could just as easily be a stamp collector or ambassador to a small island nation for all I know."

"Apple doesn't fall far from that tree perhaps?"

She feigned shock. "I am not!"

"Oh, come on Grace, you're the most secretive person I've ever met."

"That's ridiculous."

"It's not a compliment. I don't like it. You don't let people close to you. Even people like me."

Now she saw the wounded expression. She leaned on the table. "All right then. What do you want to know about me?"

"Really?" Adrian's face brightened. "Twenty questions?"

"How about one or two."

"Neville's father for one. Have you ever been married?"

"That's two questions. Once, and never to Neville's father." Grace noticed that the Umbrella Woman had crouched down, talking to a homeless man lying on the concrete across the street from them. "Okay, six-month green card marriage to my best friend in college – a lovely gay man named Rodney."

"My God, I never knew ..."

"Of course you didn't, I'm bloody English. Anyway, enough small talk." She wiped her mouth and took a last sip of tea. "I'm off." She rose, slipped her jacket under her arm and leaned over to kiss Adrian's cheek.

"That's what you call small talk?"

"See you in the morning."

"Neville's father?"

Grace laughed aloud.

"You think you're pretty sneaky."

She leaned in close. "You have no idea."

CHAPTER SEVEN

Two new classes of fresh faces, the chilled air of mid-autumn, and her favorite cable knit sweater. There was something, Grace thought, about the comfort of a familiar sweater on a cold day, the symbolism of warming your shoulders, your back, like a young mother coddling an infant. Was her sweater telling her that everything would be okay, that Adrian's tobacco plants hadn't been tampered with, and that the woman with the red umbrella wasn't about to indelibly change all their lives?

Something Adrian had said today went beyond his usual paranoia. His eyes, normally clouded by fear and anxiety, had a resolve in them now. He knew something or felt something. That someone had found him out, perhaps? The possibility was inevitable, and she had said as much at the beginning of the research. *Their* research, as once upon a time it had been her dream too. But the world had changed since then, hadn't it? In more ways than one.

A biting gust, typical of New England October, startled the bare skin beneath the holes in her sweater and angled the limbs on a red maple along her path home from Atticus. Maple tree. Grace narrowed her eyes. *Acum.* Necrotic spots. The first sign of maple anthracnose. Sad, she thought, such a beautiful specimen otherwise. Ten steps ahead – victim number two, a Japanese black pine with signs of pine blight. Was she incapable of just enjoying the view of vibrant foliage instead of constantly diagnosing their biological defects?

She peered cautiously at 147 Kensington, in the bohemian part of New Haven – near Yale, Bishop Tutu Corner, the chaotic nucleus of academic life and free thinking, perhaps the only free thinking in New England. She could see it from the street. On the white wrought iron table on her front porch was a long, sealed black envelope held down by a large stone. Where had the stone come from? Did the woman bring it with her? And, for that matter, how did she instinctively know that the Umbrella Woman had left it? Beside it was a handwritten note written on white printer paper. She recognized Neville's script.

"Letter dropped off by a woman this morning. Is it raining?"

In her five decades on earth, Grace Mattson had learned to pay attention to instinct. And right now hers was telling her not to touch the envelope sitting beside Neville's note. Instead, she gazed upon it, using her powers of perception and everything Sherlock Holmes had taught her about the observation of details. The most significant of which, however, was the churning feeling in her stomach.

"You're right to be cautious." The female voice startled her. "I would be too."

Grace noticed the umbrella even before seeing the woman's face. It was a smooth, sculpted face with mistrust woven into its elegant features. "I can't decide whether to invite you for tea or sick my Doberman on you."

The woman blinked, revealing dark blue eyes. "I

would prefer tea with an English woman than death by an invisible dog."

Grace allowed a momentary smirk. "I don't suppose I look like a dog-person."

"No."

Something about her, this woman with impeccable taste in clothes, fashionable without a hint of overstatement, and her steely voice, caused Grace's heart to thud inside her chest. The blue eyes stared evenly, and Grace's palms felt clammy. What was this about, and why had this woman watched her and Adrian at Atticus?

"Come in then," Grace said finally, "we'll have tea in the garden." And I hope I live through the experience.

The woman followed her inside, and Grace unlocked the back door. "I'll boil some water. Please, make yourself comfortable." She pointed to the back yard, to a vine-covered trellis, under which sat two Adirondack chairs adorned with flowered pillows. She hated those pillows. A gift from Neville, she'd wondered if they were Neville's way of making her more soft or feminine, somehow.

"We're interested in your research," the woman said after Grace came out to meet her.

"We?

"What I mean is ...very interested," the woman went on, ignoring the question. Her voice was flat, monotone, controlled, without a hint of inflection or emotion. Was she an android? A highly functioning artificial life form such as she'd seen on the SyFy channel so many times? The woman's face looked as though it hadn't ever cracked a smile. The skin was beyond smooth and the eyes looked hard, almost menacing. Just as if the woman used her voice simply to deliver instructions, rather than the sharing of communication.

Grace fondled the sealed black envelope. "And

this is to offer me a million dollars for it?"

"It's an offer ... of exchange, yes."

"Who's we?"

"Me and ... my employers."

"And who are you, exactly?"

The woman slowly crossed her legs. "You can call me ... Beth."

"Well, I could call you a lot of things. But that doesn't answer my question."

"I'll say it again – my employers are *very* interested in your research."

"What research are you talking about exactly? I'm a retired ethnobotanist, I teach gardening classes and breed rare species of plants. It's not very exciting, I assure you."

"Orchids. Isn't that right?"

"Not *only* orchids. But yes. You want to know how I do it? Come to my greenhouse, I'll show you."

"We've been to your greenhouse."

Grace's palms felt slick with sweat; she reminded herself to breathe.

"In fact, we've been going there for the past six months. It's not there."

"Excuse me? You've been ... what's not there?"

For what felt like a long time, neither of them spoke. Not one single bird chirped, no traffic sounds, pedestrians, car alarms, or sirens.

"We're prepared to pay for what we want."

"That's very kind of you," Grace joked.

"We're not in the business of kindness, I'm afraid."

"No?"

The woman sighed, uncrossed her legs. Then crossed them the other way. She looked uneasy, as if she were about to launch a different tactic. "The decisions we make affect the economy, on global levels."

"Really? You don't look like a banker."

The woman smiled and looked toward the house. "Water's boiling. Pardon me, I'll be right back."

Grace returned with a bamboo tray containing a pot of tea, two cups, a pitcher, and tiny bowls for milk and lemon.

"Royal Doulton," Beth commented with what seemed like admiration. But Grace knew already that she was not what she seemed.

"It was my mother's," Grace said and swirled the brew around in the teapot and then poured.

Beth held the cup and stared intently into the liquid, glanced at Grace, and returned her gaze to the cup.

"I'm still not clear on what research you want."

"You know what we want." The woman sipped the tea.

"Careful, could be poison," Grace said and stared.

She watched the woman take two more sips and then soundlessly leave down the side walkway toward Kensington. She continued watching her all the way out toward Chapel Street, and then slowly opened the envelope. On one heavy sheet of stationary paper appeared a single typed sentence.

The research in exchange for your partner's life.

Adrian, my God, she thought. What have you done?

CHAPTER EIGHT

The unmistakable sound of groceries tumbling from a paper bag sounded from the front door.

My front door.

Kerry felt something clench inside her belly. She rose from the tub and wrapped a towel around her dripping body, working to process this reality.

Someone's in my house.

Dripping, she peeked around the wall to see the door entrance and, instead, caught the peering gaze of a man's eyes. Creepy, hazy blue eyes. She muffled a scream with her palms.

"Who's there? I-I-I don't have any money! I'm calling the police!"

The man stared back unmoved.

"You are here to rob me, right?"

The strange man raised his head and chuckled. She could see his whole face now – long, angular bone structure, short receding black hair, unfriendly crooked nose.

"What are you ... and how did ..." She looked at the man's hands. "How did you get in here?"

The man raised his right hand to display a key in response.

Kerry blinked and wrapped the towel tighter around her body. The man wasn't moving toward her. He wasn't moving at all.

"You ... have a key." Something welled in her body.

The man held up his palms. "I ... have a key to *an* apartment. I was told this was vacant. I didn't mean to startle you."

"Told? By whom?"

The man sighed and glanced at the ceiling. "The guy who gave me the key."

Kerry shrugged, taking one baby step toward the living room.

"Bill." Pause. "Bill Stine."

Kerry's mouth opened involuntarily. "What did you say?"

"So, what, he's your ... landlord or something?"

Shaking her head, "Um ... sorry ... I ... who was that again?"

The man raised his eyebrows, then sighed. "I told you, Bill Stine."

"When did he give you this key?"

"When?" The man laughed.

"Yes, when!" Get a hold of yourself, she thought.

"I don't know, a year, maybe ten months ago."

Kerry laughed and shook her head. "Are you crazy?" She felt her feet moving two steps toward him and watched the man back away toward the door.

"I'm just leaning down to put these groceries back in the bag, and then I'll be on my—"

"Who ... what the ... who are you?" she stammered. Stay calm, she thought. You're in a towel, and there's a strange man in your house.

"I'm Jim Rex."

Pause. Long sigh. "How do you know Bill? And how did Bill come to give you a key to *my* apartment when I wasn't living in it a year ago?"

"Well, obviously *he* was living in it then, yeah?" The man tipped his head to the side as he said it.

"Wrong answer," she shouted in a voice she didn't recognize. "Bill and I were still married a year ago and were living together ten miles from here."

"Oops." The man grimaced, mocking her.

An ambulance siren screamed past the building. Kerry rubbed her temples and examined the man's eyes again. "So how do you and Bill know each other?"

The man shrugged. "We met at a conference."

"Bill doesn't go to conferences."

"Well, I guess he went to that one, didn't he?"

"Where?"

"Dallas. It was an NAS conference."

Kerry's brow lofted.

"National Association of Stockbrokers."

"*You're* a stockbroker?" She chuckled. "You look more like a lobster fisherman," she said, then remembered the flimsy towel around her naked body.

The man snickered, nodding at her comment. "I'm a Pit Trader. It's not unlike … lobster fishing."

"Bill's an analyst."

"I know. I met him, I mean I knew him before the conference, but we saw each other there too."

Kerry shook her head and closed her eyes. This wasn't happening. This strange man in her house, her encounter with Jesse, and then Damen, the new neighbor from down the street. They had to be connected. What else would explain this turn of events? The pulsing in her temples climbed upward in her head. She felt her lids close a half inch. "Bill never went to conferences."

"Look, lady—"

"He can't fly. He's terrified of air travel."

"I sat next to him on the plane. He was fine."

"What? I've been on flights where he had to be escorted from the plane before it even took off."

"Look, ah, what's your name?"

She looked at him now, a full-eye, full-face look. His wasn't a nice face; she'd seen the type before. The kind of face that knows how to look nice, but only has teeth and grit and sand beneath the surface. "Kerry."

"Okay, *Kerry,*" he mocked, "it's *obvious* there's been a mistake and this apartment is not vacant, so *obviously* I'm not gonna stay here." He bent down and picked up the grocery bag. "Buh-bye."

"Wait a minute!" she shouted, louder this time. "You can't just ... I need to know what's going on here! Why ... how did Bill have a key to this apartment when I only moved in here six months ago?"

"I don't know, how'd you find this place?" He set the bag down and leaned against the wall. "That'll tell you something right there, right? Newspaper ad? Craigslist?"

Kerry stared back, reminding herself how to breathe.

"In other words, was it totally random or did someone you kn—

Oh, God. "Bill's sister told me about it, she's ... friends with the landlord."

"Then you know what that means."

"What?"

"You've been set up."

Kerry remembered the gun she kept in a dresser under her sweaters. It was twenty steps away. "Krista ... what did you do?" she said under her breath.

"Krista? Yeah," the man nodded, "his sister, the clothes designer, yeah, I know her. Works for Calvin Klein."

"Jesus." Kerry ran back into the bathroom and slammed the door shut. "Don't move, I'm just getting dressed. And I keep a loaded gun in my bathroom."

"That's normal," he mumbled.

Kerry turned the faucet on high, dropped the towel to the floor, pulled her dirty clothes back on and grabbed her cell phone off the sink. She pressed redial. "Come on, Byron, pick up, pick up, pick up!" Her hands were trembling. While she waited, her fingers fumbled around the medicine cabinet searching for her Imitrex bottle.

"Hello? Kerry?"

"Byron, thank God," she whispered, hoping the water would conceal her voice. "Are you home right now?"

"Not exactly, no. Are you all right?"

"There's a man in my house."

"I can't hear you, dear. What did you say?"

Kerry jerked her head toward the window and covered her mouth. "There's-a-man-in-my-house," she enunciated. "I need you to come up here."

"A man? Who?"

"I don't know who the fuck he is! He just showed up here and ... like completely out of nowhere with a key—"

"You don't mean Rex—"

She didn't speak for a moment, working this new information through her brain. "What?"

"I got a message from him this morning, never had time to call him back."

The pounding in her temples rounded to the fronts of her eyes. She grabbed onto the radiator to steady herself, glancing out the bathroom window. "*You* gave him the key? Is that what you're telling me?"

"Kerry, calm yourself. He already had a key. He contacted me to make sure the flat was empty."

"Empty? Are you mad? Did it ever occur to you to wonder *why* he had a key to my apartment?"

She heard Byron clear his throat, and seemed to be rustling clothing. "I'm sorry, dear, what was that?"

"Why didn't you call me? Why didn't you tell me, at least give me a head's up that—" Kerry felt her eyes fill up and vision blur. There were no sounds coming from the other room.

"Well," he laughed, "I assumed you knew of course."

"Why would I?"

"Because he's your brother-in-law?" he said, more as a question. "Sorry, ex-brother-in-law."

"Wha ... what do you mean? What are you saying?"

"He's family, so I assumed you would have known about his visit before I did. It really never occurred to me to tell you."

Kerry rolled back on her heels and sat on the bathroom floor, water running out of the tap, about to spill over because of the broken drain, her temples feeling like they could split apart at the seams.

"That ... man ...is *not* Bill's brother," she said softly.

"Oh, sure he is. I can see the resemblance myself."

"Byron, listen to me carefully. Are you listening?"

"Yes, I'm listening."

"Bill doesn't have any brothers."

CHAPTER NINE

"Why don't you lie down, you're obviously upset," Byron suggested.

"Have you ever even met Bill?" Kerry demanded, pressing her mouth harder into the phone. "I only moved here six months ago, and Bill's never been here."

Byron sighed. "Of course he has – he put the lease in your name, not to mention paid the first month's rent."

Tears fell from Kerry's eyes, and the room seemed to be spinning. How could this possibly be true? Was she going crazy? Bill knowing Byron, Bill having a brother who, in four years of marriage, he never thought to mention?

"I signed the lease, Byron," she said grabbing a bath towel. "Me." She held it close to her mouth to hold back a row of sobs starting in her stomach. "Don't you remember? It was pouring that day, I was wearing my glasses and looked like a wet rat because I'd left my umbrella on the bus."

Silence.

"You made me a cup of English Breakfast tea that kept me up till three in the morning."

"Kerry, Bill's had this apartment for the past four, five years or so. I assumed it belonged to both of you, or that you at least knew about it. Of course you would ... why wouldn't you?"

An outbreath of shock escaped her lips. "Four or five ... *years?*"

Okay. She steadied herself to this obvious pack of lies. Bill has a brother I never knew about. Bill was never afraid to fly. Bill kept a secret apartment for five years during our marriage ... What in God's name had he done here, and what had he used it for? She looked at the walls in the bathroom, the bathtub, wondering who else had bathed here, slept in the bedrooms, stored clothes in the closets. Oh, my God, she thought, her stomach roiling. She leaned over the toilet and vomited, still conscious of the strange man in her living room, or what she'd thought was her living room.

"Look, I don't see why you're getting so upset. Rex said he was passing through for a couple of weeks ... I don't see what the—"

"Weeks?!?" she shrieked. "He told me a few days. I don't even know this guy, and I live in a one-bedroom—"

"All right, all right, do you want to come downstairs and sleep on my couch while he's here? Will that make you feel better?"

"No, Byron, it won't, because this is my goddamned apartment!!"

Chapter Ten

The main floor of San Francisco General Hospital buzzed with the typical flurry of morning activity. The din of voices, the chorus of milk frothing and coffee beans grinding at the Java Hut coffee stand.

The Adult Medicine department had been added onto the primary care wing of the main hospital building in the 1970s and comprised floors two through six. The lower level and first floors, though, had the look of a nineteenth-century institution – concrete floors, interior brick walls, matte steel and chrome creating an atmosphere of austerity, impervious to the whims of more modern design. It looks like a prison, Kerry thought, keeping her eye on the menu plaque at the coffee stand.

She eyed a woman with cropped blonde hair polishing the chrome shelves above the Java Hut flat screen computerized cash register. She liked the smell of this place – somehow always infused with a mix of dark roasted coffee and fresh lemons. It represented everything she didn't feel right now. Fresh. In the past seventy-two hours, her world felt as if it had veered down a rabbit hole. Was there more chaos waiting around the next corner, or would there be comfort out there somewhere?

"Still deciding?" a girl behind the counter asked,

for the second time.

"Caramel cappuccino." A perfect cocktail of sugar, caffeine, and adrenaline.

"Hey," said her colleague, Shannon, in an inappropriately perky voice. "Are you awake?"

Kerry, at the front of the line, pulled her chin up in response to the familiar voice. "Barely."

"How's it going?"

"Fine."

"Is that the short answer?" the woman asked, impolitely staring while tearing open three sugar packets.

"There's a strange man in my house. I slept in my car. Long story."

Shannon stopped moving.

"Double espresso," Shannon announced. "Slept in your car? Here, in the parking garage?"

Kerry surveyed Shannon's face, realizing it was too shiny for this time of the morning. "Like I said, long story."

"Now that you mention it, when I came in a few minutes ago from downstairs, I heard two security guards talking about you."

Kerry turned her body to face Shannon. "Me?"

"I sort of forgot about it until you just mentioned the garage. Yeah, one of them said 'a CNA named Kerry Stine.' I'm sure of it. You'd better check in with security."

Absolutely, she thought. The minute hell freezes over.

Stairs are more anonymous than elevators, she thought, especially this time of the morning. She made her way up to the third floor, pulled open the heavy steel door and peeked her head around to view the reception desk. Two security guards. Dammit, she thought.

Concealed in the darkness of the hallway, she

spotted Kathy, the morning receptionist, who by some kind of Jedi radar, spotted Kerry right away in the doorway. Kathy didn't point or gesture – she didn't have to. The guards saw her notice something and turned. But by then, Kerry had recoiled silently back into the stairwell.

One, two, three, four, five, six, seven, eight, she whispered, counting each successive stair to keep her heart from racing out of her chest. Down one floor then another. Then out through the parking garage, the familiar shape of Hospital Administrator, Mark Ferri, materialized from behind a pillar. Did he have cloaking technology?

"Going somewhere, Miss Stine?"

"In fact, yes," Kerry replied calmly, masking her internal flinch. "I left something in my car." She kept walking.

"Like a body perhaps?"

Now she stopped. And turned. "Excuse me?"

"Come with me, please." Ferri stepped aside and opened his palm, signaling Kerry to walk ahead of him.

Kerry stood still and crossed her arms, taking a moment to consider his expression, body language, and to scan for the two security guards.

Ferri raised a brow as if to say *now.*

She stepped into the elevator and seemed to understand that there would be no talking until they'd reached his office. Once there, he again leaned against his desk, arms crossed over his chest. "Sit down, Miss Stine."

Kerry pulled out her *bored* expression and pulled a strand of hair out of her eyes. "What is this about?"

"Security guards, for one thing. Perhaps you noticed them when you tried to creep up to the third floor from the stairwell." Ferri paused. "Jogging your memory yet?"

"What am I, wearing a tracking implant? Don't you people have anything better to do?"

Ferri blinked and tried not to smile.

"I've already told you I don't know about that missing medical chart."

"We've got bigger problems than a chart. Rosemary Castiglia is missing."

"Um ... from where?" She almost laughed.

Ferri blinked back at her with judgment in his eyes. "There's an empty bed in ICU where she used to be lying. Got it?"

"Since when?"

Mark Ferri didn't answer right away. Instead, he moved from in front of the desk to the expensive leather chair behind it and sat. "How about I ask the next few questions? Like where were you at 3 a.m. this morning?"

"Where I usually am at that time of night. In bed," she lied.

"Alone?"

She closed her eyes. "For God's sake."

"That was the last time Rosemary Castiglia was logged in by the third floor nurse's station. I don't suppose you know anything about that."

"Can I use your restroom?"

"No."

Kerry raised a brow.

"I think you know what happened to that patient's medical chart, and I think you know something about her disappearance as well. Now, the restroom's right through there," he pointed down a short hallway. "Why don't you spend a few minutes and really think about the next thing you're gonna tell me. Because your career, or more than that, could depend on it."

Kerry's mind wandered while Ferri was still talking. Gina Varga. Elementary school. Her best friend in the world. They hadn't talked now in –

what? – two or three years.

Would she remember the code?

As kids, they developed a code for emergencies, or at least what comprised an emergency to eight-year-olds: Call the other person, let the phone ring once and hang up. This signaled the recipient to check their mailbox, where they would inevitably find an empty Pepsi can with a secret note coiled inside containing one of three possible numbers:

SOS Levels:

1 – Normal

2 – Urgent

3 – Life or death

And from that code came an accompanying location, though this part had never been written anywhere – only remembered.

1 – The tree house

2 – Japanese Tea Garden in Golden Gate Park

3 – Safehouse

The tree house was located, and specifically erected, precisely equidistant between their two houses in the woods behind Lincoln Street. The Tea Gardens were for more urgent matters and offered more privacy and, as such, involved a fifteen-minute walk to get there. The safe house ...

"Nurse Redfield said that Castiglia's medical chart disappeared on your watch," Ferri continued.

"On Redfield's watch, you mean."

He blinked but said nothing. She hated how he did that, as if a strategic pause brought more importance to his words.

"She's my supervisor," Kerry added, "so she's ultimately responsible for what happens on her shift. Right?"

Ferri looked uncomfortable. "She's being questioned as well. I think you're missing the point."

"Really? What is the point you think I'm missing?"

"You know, for a junior staff member you've got a

smart mouth."

"I'm trying to save my job, sir. I'm coming out of a devastating divorce, and this job is my anchor right now. I haven't missed a single shift or arrived one minute late since I started."

"To balance that," Ferri replied, "I've gotten reports that you're argumentative and you question the decisions of your superiors."

"That's my right as a human being. If Redfield doesn't like it, she should've hired a dog, not a CNA."

"You're on very tentative footing at this hospital, Miss Stine. Unless you've got some answers up your sleeve, I'd get my affairs in order."

Gulp.

"I've been instructed to escort you downstairs, where Security's waiting to question you about the missing patient. Got those answers for me yet?"

"I need the restroom."

"Feeling sick all of a sudden?"

"A bit, yes," she replied.

I hate that guy, Kerry thought, automatically turning on the faucet to mask the sound of her phone. She pulled her smartphone out of her handbag and found Gina Varga in her contacts. She typed a text message that read S_O_S and waited. She flushed the toilet, and a second later felt her phone vibrate. Wow, she remembers. Thank God.

The text message read: Go.

In trouble, need help, she frantically typed, eyeballing the doorknob.

Specifics.

Getaway car.

Im in Palo Alto – r u @ SFGH rite now?

Y

Will check on Plan B – sb…

SB – stand by. My God, she thought, how long had it been? Kerry inhaled deeply to calm her nerves, washed her hands three more times, and heard Mark Ferri on the phone, probably calling Security. Or the police.

Blue car will be at the San Bruno loading dock, will wait for 20 mins, driver Rick, #6504286298

TY
NP
MY
MT

Turning the door handle, Kerry remembered the wall outside Ferri's office.

CHAPTER ELEVEN

For the past hour, Grace Mattson had paced the polished wood floors of her Kensington Victorian while pressing Redial on her cell phone. Pacing always seemed to center around the freestanding fireplace – up one side, across and down the other, shaped as it was like an odd little peninsula jutting out into the expanse of her living room. Adrian loved that fireplace, frequently alternating his own pacing by plopping down on the surrounding smooth black ledge. What was this strange feeling in her palms, suddenly, that he'd never again sit in front of that fireplace, or anywhere else for that matter?

"Adrian, pick up the damn phone," she opened with on voicemail number four. "Where the bloody hell are you?" She sighed and slapped the fireplace mantel. "I need to hear from you, that you're okay. I have a feeling you know wh—"

The vibration of an incoming call interrupted her message. It had to be him.

"Just tell me you're all right," she demanded.

"Grace, listen carefully." His voice was too calm.

"You're not at your apartment. I've been calling you for over an hour—"

"I know."

"That woman, standing outside Atticus, was—"

"I know," he said.

"You know what, exactly? Do you know her? And if you do, can you guess what was in the envelope she left me?"

Silence.

"What's going on here? You told me a story this morning about someone sabotaging your plants. To be honest, I didn't really believe it. And now—"

"She wants something I have," Adrian said.

Grace masked a heavy sigh.

"But we can't talk about it now."

"Why not?"

"Remember Daniel Glynny?"

She remembered. One of Adrian's colleagues suspected of creating bio-weapons in his chemistry lab. Phones tapped by the police. She found herself glancing out of the windows now, wondering if she'd locked the door behind the woman after she left. Had she?

"Do you remember where we saw that rare *Dendrobium* specimen last summer?"

Their campus tour of endangered orchids. "The—"

"Go there. Can you meet me in an hour?"

Yale's Battell Chapel. "I can be there in five minutes," she replied.

"All the better."

Chapter Twelve

They've been in my greenhouse, she narrated on the short walk from Kensington through Bishop Tutu Corner and onto the grounds of Yale's historic Battell Chapel. Research. Greenhouse. Touching my plants. My greenhouse. Dammit.

She entered the long, arched walkway from the grass expanse that separated the chapel from the school of math and sciences. A figure stood at the end of the walkway at the chapel's entrance. Adrian. He pointed down, then vanished into a shadow.

Battell Chapel had no formal lower entrance that she knew of. So why had he pointed down? Two students with book bags walked behind her across the lawn.

"I'm starving," the young woman said. They must be headed to the Student Union, Grace thought. Wait, the grad version of the SU had an underground entrance that must lead to the chapel basement. Ah! Now she remembered – a day care center in that basement and a kitchen for after-service receptions. She'd been there once after a piano recital.

Grace veered from the grass to the smooth concrete walkway. Children's voices bubbled up from below. The entrance narrowed as she stepped down the last few of the thirty-seven steps. A young girl, maybe five, appeared out of nowhere handing her a slip of paper.

"Stairs twenty steps ahead," in Adrian's left-handed scrawl. She looked up and the girl had gone; no sound of her footsteps anywhere. How cloak and dagger. Okay, she thought, advancing a few steps. Taped to a concrete exterior wall up ahead was a hand-drawn arrow pointing to a staircase winding to the right.

"Grace," Adrian whispered halfway up the stairs. "Here," he motioned downward. Grace peered at the right side of his face. The skin looked darker than usual.

A small door ahead, illuminated by sun through extraordinary stained-glass panels above, led to the main chapel – a symbolic portal between the secular and vernacular worlds. She stared for a blank moment, knowing there was no time for a decision. Or that some part of her had already made it.

"It's dark in here," she whined.

"Better that way."

"I can barely see you." She reached out and fumbled with his shoulder. He flinched. "My God, what's the matter with you?"

No response came, only the taut buzz of pure darkness. As her pupils dilated to adjust, she realized she was standing behind him now – both hovering between two tall pillars in the rear part of the Chapel. Adrian turned toward her, his face still partially in shadow.

Grace reached up to touch his cheek. "What happened to you?" she said gently probing the skin around his black and bloodied eye.

He flinched. "They want something. I told you." His voice was flat, monotone, as though he was barely awake.

"What? What is this research that woman talked

about? And why does she think it's mine?"

Adrian hung his head and sighed. "It's where we started, Grace. It's how we first met."

"You're hurt – can we attend to that first?"

He pulled away. "I can't tell you everything."

"You mean you can't tell me anything, don't you?"

"I, listen to—"

"And your apartment's been breached. I went there."

"I'm trying to tell you that I don't want you involved in this."

"Don't want me involved? Then what are we doing here hiding in the back of a church? Involved in what? Did that woman mean *my* research, like my plants, growing techniques, breeding notations? Who of any importance would be interested in that? I mean who in her circles?"

Adrian turned around and crossed his arms, shaking his head.

It's where we started – it's how we first met, Grace replayed his words.

A botanical conference. Adrian was working in New York doing a residency in a microbiology lab during medical school. He'd told her he was interested in medicinal plants. She had called him another Albert Schweitzer.

"How could plants affect the global economy?" he'd asked a group of people – an accidental reverend at the pulpit of a hotel lounge. The bar crammed full of conference participants, all drained from three days of stodgy lectures, he had them in the palm of his hand. And she'd been no exception. Who is he? Grace had wondered, vowing to meet him by the final dinner.

"So did anyone answer your question?" she said later that night at the ice machine on the top floor of the Hilton Garden Inn, each of them in bathrobes.

"Excuse me?"

"Your economic speech at the bar."

"People were either too fried or drunk to care."

She didn't need to ask Dr. Adrian Calhoun if he was on his way to the pool. She just knew. And he seemed to instinctively know that she didn't really want to swim. So they walked past the pool, talking like that, strangers with an inexplicable familiarity, till 3 a.m.

"What's an ethnobotanist exactly?"

"An investigator. I study medicinal plants, and use humans as my control group," she'd replied.

"Ever hear of the theory that plants are extraterrestrial life forms, far advanced beyond us, that came here to study us? To study humans?"

She'd loved, back then, the width and elasticity of Adrian's mind – probing into thorny topics, stretching them out to present alternate views. Had he been the smartest man she'd ever met? And what did that mean for her, for them?

The next morning, as if part of the same conversation, she knocked at his door at 6 a.m. "Ever hear of Alex Shigo?" she said.

Adrian got dressed right in front of her without a hint of self-consciousness. "The tree biologist, yeah. I know of him."

"He thought," she said, "that every tree was actually a limb on one gigantic cosmic tree turned on its side. Earth being the cosmic tree I suppose."

"Planets as trees." He'd nodded. "It's not a new concept by any means. Almost every ancient civilization, from the Celts to Native Americans, believed that the Tree of Life motif signified the planet, or God, as a large tree. Why couldn't God be a tree?"

In the shadow-striped landscape of the Chapel basement now, Grace relived these moments, half-looking into Adrian's crazed, bloodshot and swollen eyes, the bruised temple. Her mind wove together the strands of this new epiphany – strings of a truth from their earlier life together. That earlier version of herself. How could plants affect the global economy? – he'd never answered the question, not then and never since. Had the Umbrella Woman, somehow answered it for her: Global economy?

Adrian had spent the past two decades studying tobacco plants. Jesus, no, she thought, jarred by a sudden chill in her spine.

He was watching her intently, though still fidgeting every few seconds. Could he see this new truth on her face? Just like their first night together, did he just know?

Grace gently eased away from him, step by step, angling her body to resemble pacing, but yet sliding into the lengthening concrete shadows surrounding them. Don't look for me, she thought. Don't come.

And then she ran.

CHAPTER THIRTEEN

Houses and storefronts raced past in her peripheral vision too quickly. The surprising speed of her legs matched the frantic flutter in her chest at this new realization. Slow down, she thought. Pace yourself.

Just a block from Kensington, now, Grace spotted the edge of Neville's nondescript, government-looking black sedan in the drive, edged as always close to the fence so as to appear as invisible as possible. The sight of it gave her a strange comfort.

She jammed her key hastily in the front lock and before she'd even turned it, the door pushed open.

Unlocked.

Neville never came in the front door.

Grace stood shaking in the foyer, panting from overworked lungs, taking stock of the smooth wood floors, the reflection of scant afternoon light filtering down through the skylight at the top of the stairs. It was a house full of beauty and mystery. She sat on the bottom stair and looked at the door.

"Mother, is that you?" Neville called from the kitchen, clanking what sounded like her good bone china.

"No, it's the maid you scared away two years ago." Without even hearing his approach, she stared up at his abnormally large hands awkwardly gripping her most fragile Royal Doulton cup and saucer.

"Looks as if you could use something stronger," he said.

She took the cup and gratefully sipped his crude American version of tea. "What're you doing home this time of night?" She stressed the word 'you'.

"I live here. Remember?"

"We share space, Neville, you don't *live* here," she corrected. "I really don't know where you live. The Syrian Embassy, perhaps? Amtrak station?"

"My car, mostly."

"Wouldn't doubt it." She handed back the cup and saucer, eyeing his hands again. "Thank you for that."

"Are you all right?"

"Your concern is touching, really."

Neville sighed. "I care about your well-being," he argued.

"Since when?"

"Since that mannequin came to drop off your mysterious envelope. To be honest, I'm afraid for you, Mother."

She nodded. "Quite."

"Have you opened it yet?"

Grace shook her head, rose to meet her son's gaze and walked past him through the dark house.

"Neville? Are you still here?" she called out from the upstairs loft, half expecting him to bring her more tea.

"You left me there, Grace. You just left."

Adrian. Her hand slapped her chest. "Jesus, you scared me." Grace moved to the edge of the loft and looked down, gripping the rail. "I thought you were—"

"I wasn't finished explaining—"

"Guess I was finished listening."

Adrian moved three steps closer, walking across the smooth, wood floors of her living room toward the bottom stair. "There's not much time left."

"Not here," she whispered, exaggerating her eye movement toward the kitchen. She motioned toward the greenhouse and moved quietly down the stairs, touched his elbow and led them down the narrow walkway outside. Leaving the overhead light off, she snapped the button to the heat lamps.

"I need—"

Grace raised her index finger and pushed the button on her boom box. Brahms Symphony No. 4 in E Minor. "They were here," she said in a regular voice now, stuffing her sweaty palms into the pockets of her long sweater. "In my greenhouse, my laboratory. With my plants." Unexpected tears filled her eyes.

"Who?" Adrian looked around, squinting. "This lighting's a bit romantic," he joked.

"Why not? I don't have a lover right now – these plants are what I nurture instead. I guess that's how we're different."

Adrian's eyes turned downward. "We're not so different."

"We didn't used to be," she replied.

Adrian chuckled and touched one of the orchid stalks. "You were intimidated by me at first."

"Well, you had such frightful, nervous energy, hovering over people like you were going to bite them." She refused to smile as she said it, knowing that whatever controversy he had set in motion would erase any reverence she'd ever held for him.

"Are you ready to h—"

"Hear why you sold out?" She turned and crossed her arms. "Sure."

"Sold out? How could you say that?"

"That letter I got was meant for you."

"Grace, I may have developed the most significant contribution to cancer research since World War II."

"With *my* research, no doubt."

"Your research *methods,* yes, were a contributing—"

"Methods? You didn't even know what a bloody cultivar was when I met you. You didn't know a thing about cross-breeding plant species." She felt shaking in the center of her body and her throat tightened.

"You want credit? Is that it?"

"I want ... a normal life." She added in a softer voice, "It's what I always wanted."

"Which means what?"

"Anonymity. I'm a researcher and a teacher. It's satisfying work. It feeds me. You always had to be a rock star, seeking controversy, newsprint for your name in big letters."

"I've wanted to make a lasting contribution, yes. There's nothing—"

"Fame, that's what you wanted, say it!"

Adrian turned toward a row of perfect orchids.

"Your ego—"

"*My* ego?" He turned sharply. "Really. Do you know what I've developed, Grace?" He paused, staring her down.

"I've been afraid to think, to be honest," she whispered. Then she wondered how much Neville had heard of their exchange. She grabbed Adrian's arm and pulled him to the opposite corner of the greenhouse, gesturing into the house. She motioned him to her, then leaned against the wall and slid to crouch on the cold floor. Adrian crouched beside her, their knees touching.

"Do you know?" he whispered now. "Do you get what all this is about?"

Something thumped near the back door of the house. It had to be Neville leaving.

Grace nodded. "Of course I know. You've been trying to do it since your mother died twenty years ago." She glanced up at the darkness surrounding the structure. "You've developed a cigarette that cures lung cancer."

They both let the sentence hang in the air for a few moments.

"Haven't you?"

"Well, wouldn't you think that would be worth the risks?"

"How have you confirmed your findings?" she said, ignoring his question.

Adrian glanced around and sunk lower onto the floor. "We had a control group of thirty people."

"Who?"

"Elderly people, all dying from lung cancer."

"A private control group?"

He just looked at her.

"In what way does that constitute a clinical trial?"

Adrian shook his head and looked away.

"And what's your FDA approval status? Have you published yet? Applied for a patent?"

"Are. You. Insane?"

"Look—"

"How could I possibly do that? I don't think you fully appreciate what this means to the world as we know it, Grace. Go ahead and say I've got a Jesus complex if you want. I don't care."

He was right. Grace took a few breaths to form her thoughts, to wrap her mind around an unthinkable construct. "I know what it means," she said somberly. "If you've really done this, and if your findings are partially confirmed, you've become a hazard to the pharmaceutical industry and probably one of the greatest liabilities to global commerce."

"That's a little grandiose," he argued.

"Do you know how much cancer medications cost? Some of them are a hundred dollars a pill. Think about how many pills people buy in one prescription, compounded by the hundreds of thousands of people who buy them."

Again, silence. Crickets cheeped outside the greenhouse in a chorus all around them. The thud at her back door nagged Grace's curiosity, probably the neighbors. He could sell the idea to Big Pharma, but more likely they'd steal it and dispose of him. "They'll kill you, you know," she whispered.

"They'll try." He pointed to his jaw. "They already have."

"I'll bet you don't make it to your next birthday."

He glared at her. "You don't sound too disappointed."

"Of course I am – where does that leave me?"

Adrian grabbed her hand. "Will you help me?"

"Help you *what*? You can't undo it now. The snowball's halfway down the slope."

"This is all I can tell you right now. I have to go. Yes or no?"

"Yes or no what? What are you asking for?"

"Your help, your alliance. Your confidence."

Grace shook her head. "I ... I don't know. How will I contact you?"

He was walking out the door before she got her answer.

Chapter Fourteen

"One, two, three, four ..." Jim Rex counted with a motion of his finger staring into Kerry Stine's cavernous linen closet. "Sixteen pink bath towels." He laughed. "Pink." His cell phone vibrated in his pocket.

"Yeah Dave-O," he answered the gruff, familiar voice.

"What's your status? Are you there yet?"

Jim Rex continued to move around the apartment, opening drawers, counting the handbags in the back of her bedroom closet, learning Kerry Stine. More like re-learning. "Yeah, I'm here, in the apartment ... so to speak."

"Clarify, please," replied Dave Rothman in his characteristic monotone. "Is there a problem?"

"Not specifically, other than the fact that she was here."

Pause. "I thought you'd arranged all that, some fucking training or something."

"Let's just call it an unanticipated variable."

"You took care of the problem?" said Rothman.

"Not like you would, I'm sure, but the situation's under control."

"Have you retrieved the item?"

During the pause, Jim Rex calculated his odds.

Find something in Kerry Stine's apartment that she's "supposedly" had in her possession since childhood. Where would she keep something like this? In an unlikely place, like the refrigerator, or under her bed? And that's assuming that she still even had the item and attributed to it any sense of sentimental or commercial value. This, in his mind, was a stretch. Dave Rothman was midway through a sentence of signature threats.

"Yeah, I know, Dave-O, it was a long time ago. But I know a thing or two about how the female mind works." She remembers, he thought. She has to. Her life depends on it. So does his.

CHAPTER FIFTEEN

The *dong* of the left elevator sounded as Kerry followed Mark Ferri out of his office. She glanced quickly at the wall to their right as Ferri motioned for her to follow, navigating through a sudden sea of medical staff, students, and patients. Just ahead, the right elevator arrived and a young couple exited holding hands, now walking toward them.

Now.

Without thinking, Kerry slipped her foot under the stride of the young man. He fell sideways and then forward, letting out a loud groan as his tall body hit the floor. The young woman bent to pull him up, and Ferri turned to help.

The left elevator was closing. Kerry took two strategic steps backward and slid in between them with only a second to spare, Ferri's wide eyes fixed on her as the steel doors united.

"Yes?" a man's voice replied into her cell phone.

"Is this Rick?" Kerry whispered. "I'm Kerry. Gina said you'd be—"

"Where are you now?" the man said in a powdery voice.

Her hands trembled. "Elevator."

"Do you know how to find the loading area?"

"I'm going to the basement—"

"Don't – it's the most obvious place. Get off at the second floor. Is it too late?"

She pressed "2" on the elevator's wall panel. "No, I got it."

"Don't get off at two – just wait a second, then press G."

"Are you insane? G's the lobby, security's on that floor and they're waiting for me!"

"Look at the buttons. B basement, L lobby. G is Ground – that's the cargo floor, for loading freight and accessing the freight elevator. Take it."

Kerry obediently pushed "G" and noticed the thud of her pulse beating in her chest and throat. What the hell am I doing, she wondered, barely recognizing herself. G level lit up at the top of the lift car and Kerry tried to remember which way the exits were on each floor. Just then her phone rang.

"Turn left," a voice instructed. Creepy. How did he know where she was? And was this even the same voice as before?

"Now, a quick right and go down the short staircase ... should be six steps." It was. "Follow the hallway and come outside. No one's out there."

Kerry took the stairs and peered out the doorway. Indeed, it was deserted. And this entrance faced the woods. "Um, where am I? This doesn't even look like the hospital anymore."

"It isn't."

Before she could reply, a white SUV screeched around the corner and stopped short a few feet in front of her. "Get in the car, Miss Stine," the voice on the phone said.

The sky had an odd arrangement of orange stripes and smears, uncharacteristic of winter in San Francisco. The sun, hanging too low, told her something. A message. Get in the car.

Kerry took two steps forward and stopped.

"We're in no hurry, Miss Stine," said an older

man, English, with a gravelly voice. He leaned cautiously out from the SUV's back seat. "You, on the other hand ..." and the man's voice trailed off as he glanced behind her. Footsteps sounded on the stairs leading to the street. Kerry jumped toward the car and climbed in beside the man in the back seat.

Chapter Sixteen

Inside the SUV, Kerry's brain kicked into emergency mode.

"Are you quite comfortable, Miss Stine?" the older man said.

Right away, she hated his voice. "Quite," she mocked.

Observations: one young man in the driver's seat, poorly dressed, messy hair, likely a student. The older man in the back, impeccably dressed, English accent, private school, city. "Are you Rick?" she said to the driver.

The driver mumbled something to the Englishman.

"Okay ... how about telling me where we're going?"

Again, no answer. She calmly reached for the door handle, though the car had to be traveling at more than eighty miles per hour. As her fingers touched the chrome, the older man lunged over her and clamped her right wrist.

Kerry forced her mind to concentrate. Potrero Hill. Near AT&T Park. Car not obeying stoplights, suggesting an urgency in reaching their desired destination. Driver, Caucasian, but spoke a foreign language. Russian? The SUV's all-leather interior was spotless. Not one speck of dirt on the floor mats. Old man wore a Movado watch; young bohemian student – no watch, no sunglasses, shifty eyes. He feared the older man – that was obvious in the first few seconds. But the older man did fear something. He wants something, she decided, something he thinks he's not going to get.

"Miss Stine," the man swirled to face her. "Listen to me, and listen closely because this information is vital to your survival and it will only be revealed to you once."

"Pull over," he yelled into the front seat. The car slowed but didn't stop. The old man glanced at the driver's head. "I'm not sure you quite appreciate the gravity of your situation," he continued.

"What situation is that?" Kerry said.

Another empty stare.

"I'm in trouble with my boss, last I heard."

The old man cocked his head.

"Okay, a patient is missing, and I may have been the last one to see her chart."

Now he shook his head and sighed in disappointment.

"What?" she shouted. "What am I not getting?"

"Rosemary Castiglia is dead, Miss Stine, and you are being held accountable for her murder."

"Murder? W— She's ... dead?"

His eyes fearful, the young man looked at the older one.

"I don't believe you," Kerry said. "I'm calling Shannon." She slipped her phone out of her pocket, predicting it would be yanked from her hand.

"Go ahead," the old man said, gesturing to the driver. "Call your friend. Shannon ... Burke, isn't it? She's standing at the third-floor reception desk at this very moment, talking about you no less."

Kerry stared into the silver-haired man's ice blue eyes, wondering. Shannon's voice pulled her to attention.

"Hey, I'm here," she replied.

She heard Shannon speaking to someone in the background. "Hold on, Mom," she said into the receiver. Mom? Who was she hiding Kerry's identity from?

"Dude, I'm in the bathroom," Shannon whispered. "Where the fuck are you? Do you have any idea what's going on over here? I – when I saw you this morning, at the coffee stand, I ..." she paused, "I guess I didn't realize ... any of—"

"Shannon, wait a minute! Nothing's happened, it's all a big mistake. I didn't—"

"You didn't kill that woman?" Shannon sniffed. "I knew her. I treated her one time while she was in ICU. I can't believe she's—"

"Listen to me. She's not dead," Kerry interrupted.

Two pairs of eyes stared at her in the back seat.

"Well, there are a few people here who disagree with you, like Mark Ferri, security ... the police ... do you get what I'm saying? They've all been here today, questioning all of us about where you are, when you last saw the patient ..." She sighed and stopped. "Where are you right now anyway?"

"I'm—"

The older man held out his hand. Kerry instinctively handed him her phone.

"Miss Stine will call you another time, Miss Burke, goodbye." He pressed the red button and looked out the window.

"Who do you think you are?" she shot back.

The old man pointed out the window and smiled.

She'd already surmised that they were getting on the Golden Gate Bridge, headed toward North Bay, Marin County, possibly Sausalito. She clenched her sweaty palms as a wave of nausea moved upward from her stomach. Breathe. In. Out. In. Out.

"Do you trust me?" the older man asked her.

She rubbed her hands on her stomach. "You've got to be kidding."

"Smart girl. I must earn your trust. And I will."

"I doubt it."

He turned slowly and laid his silky hand on her forearm. "You've got two choices now," he said coolly. "Trust us, or go it on your own. You'll be found, of course, because they know where you'll run. Found and tried ... for murder."

"Who knows? And who's they?" Kerry demanded, then moaned from a sudden pain in the back of her head.

"There's more." The man aimed his head closer to her ear. "You lost something precious to you a long time ago." For a moment he didn't speak. A sound came from the right rear tire on the SUV. And a strange smell floated through the inside of the cab.

Lost something precious ... long ago.

"You remember, or some part of you does."

Tears spilled strangely from her left eye – only the left. Her stomach roiled from a sourness that seemed to come from nowhere. And her head in a vice, squeezing together her temples, pushing at bone and flesh.

"I'm in a unique position to help you find ... what you've lost."

"What are you talking about?" she shouted, her voice trembling. "I didn't lose anything."

"Or so you've convinced yourself, yes. But you'll start remembering. And when you do, you'll need help. In particular, mine."

"You don't know anything about it," she cried out, her voice and resolve caving in. "Where are you taking me?"

"You'll have a lot of questions, and I can answer those for you. But you must come with us now, and trust everything I tell you."

Lost something ... "I don't trust anyone," she

replied.

"If not us, then who?"

"Why do you care what I do or think or feel? I've never met you before, either of you."

The two men exchanged quick glances.

"Were you visited by a stranger recently, in your apartment?"

"Visited?"

"Were you?" the old man insisted.

She blinked back. "More like descended upon."

The older man nodded. "Yesss, that's his style. He announced himself as Jim Rex."

Kerry squinted. "How could you ... know this?"

"He aims to kill you, Miss Stine."

Kerry's eyelids flexed open.

"Did you recognize this man?"

"No."

"You can't remember, not yet. You will. This man, Rex, believes you have something that he desperately needs."

"What?"

The SUV screeched around a corner, shoving Kerry into the side door. The old man pulled himself from her and shot a look at the driver. "Where are we?" he shouted up front. "Nico – what's happening?" Another dangerous sharp turn, this time in the other direction.

Kerry glanced out the window, and somehow they hadn't gotten on the bridge.

"Nico – what's happening?"

"Back there," the driver replied, gesturing behind him.

"Tailed? Impossible. Who?"

Kerry stared at the old man – his words strange and heavy in her ears. "This man, Rex. What does he want from me?"

"Information."

"What informa—" A loud *pop* shuddered through

the SUV, shattering the rear windshield. The old man's heavy frame heaved right, mashing Kerry against the right door as the vehicle fish-tailed across four lanes. Using her shoulders, she wrestled herself out from under him and noticed, in a surreal moment, how she saw too much out of the front windshield. Where's the driver, she thought calmly, and then her eyes saw him slumped sideways over the front passenger seat with blood on the side of his face.

"Get up," she screamed, "your driver's been shot!" But the old man didn't move. She shook him hard and kicked at the older man's legs. No one moved, she was trapped underneath the old man's body, and the car was steering out of control.

CHAPTER SEVENTEEN

The brakes.

In one of those unthinkable moments, when the ticking of time slows and dancing images pass surreally before your eyes, Kerry reacted on pure instinct. She bent awkwardly over the driver's seat, reached her right arm toward the steering wheel and yanked it downward, thrusting the briskly moving vehicle to the right. The car was moving too fast to control it.

Somehow, she needed to thrust her leg between the two front seats and stretch forward to hit that brake. No sound or movement came from the other passengers. Jesus, she thought, am I the only one left?

In a fit of pure adrenaline, she maneuvered her hips to the right of the driver's seat and tried to slide her right foot down. Lower, lower, come *on*, she thought! She needed just two more inches to make contact with the pedal. Then again, when it did, from this angle her head was likely to smash into the steering wheel. The edge of her shoe just touched the brake pedal now. She used her toes to finesse the movement and slow the potential for total disaster. And in a new moment of panic, she realized that the SUV wasn't slowing down.

"Ohhhhh," she grunted, creeping over the old

man's heavy frame and crouched awkwardly over the driver's body to access to that brake pedal. Her head pressed into the roof of the car and her feet still barely touched the pedal. Both hands on the steering wheel now, she pushed the brake as the car started down a mild incline toward Lombard Street.

Nothing else mattered right now but those brakes. Keep it straight, she counseled herself. Breathe.

Gently angling to the right, the brake responded and slowed them down. "Okay," she narrated, "corner of Lombard and Fillmore." She scanned the sidewalk for the open parking spot that never exists in San Francisco. "Wait, over there ..."

A familiar blue car paralleled her on the road as she veered further toward the sidewalk. The blue car angled closer, nearly touching the SUV, then lurched forward and cut her off. Kerry slammed the brakes and jammed the gears into park. "Who the fu—"

Before she could finish, someone pulled open the driver's side door.

"Get in. Hurry." Gina said calmly, looking into the car and then up and down the street.

Kerry gestured to the bodies in the car, noticing now that the younger man had blood on the forehead. "What about the—"

"There's no time, Kerry. Now."

Kerry Stine watched numbly as images moved past her field of vision. A young girl wearing what looked like her old favorite pink pajamas. An older couple running, rubbing their eyes. A gray house, barely visible behind a thick wall of dark smoke.

"Kerry?" a voice called out.

More smoke. Grass seared to a crisp before her eyes.

"Come on, Kerry, wake up."

Her vision moved, rocking slowly back and forth as if ... wait, it was her head moving. Kerry blinked a few times, slowly, sensing that she was returning from someplace else. Where?

"Are you awake?"

It was Gina's voice. "I feel like lead," she managed, noticing her words felt wrong in her mouth. She looked into Gina's eyes. "What's wrong with me?" Kerry glanced out the window. "Where are we?"

Gina pressed her hand on Kerry's shoulder. "Lie back and relax. I gave you a sedative. You had quite a shock back there."

The SUV. The two men: the driver dead.

"I'm making tea. Get up when you're ready," she heard Gina say from the other room. But their current location bore no resemblance to Gina's Palo Alto apartment that she'd been to a hundred times.

A bright room. Soft sheets, thin cotton blanket, where were her shoes? Kerry sat up ninety degrees and pressed her stocking feet onto a hardwood floor. It felt strange, not like a floor should. Spongy. Gina was watching her. Even Gina looked strange.

"That man. His driver," she sighed, remembering now what had happened. "What time is it?"

"His name is Nigel Watson," Gina replied setting a cup of tea in front of her at the small, kitchen table.

"You look different," Kerry noticed. "You dyed your hair. When did you start doing that?"

"He's been watching you for a long time."

"Watching me? Why?"

"Not just you."

Kerry sipped what smelled like Earl Grey. She hated Earl Grey and Gina knew that. "What does that mean?" She swallowed the bitter liquid.

Gina settled in the chair across from her. "Are you ready to hear this?"

"How do I know? Hear what?"

"What you should've heard a long time ago."

PART TWO

CHAPTER EIGHTEEN

Kathleen Dwyer felt beads of sweat dripping down the back of her neck and face as she struggled to lift another box.

"Oh … my God." Panting, she dropped the file box from a standing position and let it clunk heavily on the concrete floor. She looked up to survey the detailed roadmap of what had been her every waking moment for the past week. An orderly grid of circles, squares and lines tacked to the wall in the main cavern of the warehouse space – file boxes filled with medical charts, dry tissue samples, dry-iced fluid samples, cultures, beakers, Petri dishes, microscopes, and tools.

She'd had a life once, six months ago, maybe more like ten months; had a cute guy to eat dinner with; friends; a social network; until she first heard the stories of him – the renegade who once had an office on campus and taught classes in his bare feet, pacing back and forth like a captive polar bear.

"He does experiments on live humans, I heard."

"Well, I heard he's a healer, like a modern day Albert—"

"He's a botanist, isn't he?"

"Not exactly. He's a pathologist who used to work at Yale Medical School."

"What happened to him?"

"I heard he got fired for forcing his patients to smoke."

"Weed?"

"No."

"He's a doctor, right? Why would he do that?"

Something cracked outside, like a table snapping violently in half. Keenly aware of the sound, Kathleen kept her eyes on the floor and used her foot to maneuver the twenty-pound box of files against the back wall of the warehouse. I'm close to Bridgeport, she thought, and I'm here alone. Great.

Without any ventilation and the only window in the front door, the air felt thick and stagnant in the cold space. Okay, she thought, no wind, no cars. So what was that sound?

Walking warily toward the only door in the room, she felt a tightening in the pit of her belly. Her cell phone rang in her pocket. "Jesus!" she muttered, fumbling for it.

"Yes," she said without looking at the caller, "this is Kathleen."

"Hey, Kath, where we at?" the familiar voice said.

"I heard a—"

"Are you all moved in over there?"

"For God's sake, Adrian, I just got here," she shot back. "I've got the PCs and server set up but—"

"What about the lab? Is the water turned on? Gas and electric? You scheduled them for today, right?"

Something thumped from the hallway. Closer this time.

"Monitors up and running, yes, water's on—"

"Gas and electric?"

"Well, I just said monitors are up and running, so—"

"Look, Kathleen," Adrian interrupted, with a heavy sigh.

"No, you look. I'm all you've got, Dr. Calhoun. You'd better be nice to me."

Pause.

"Do you realize the magnitude of what we're doing here? What I'm doing? Moving a nightmare of a lab and eight years' worth of data files across a complex network, across town, and I'm doing it alone and in like three or four days. So before I go any further, let me just ask you again if this is what you really want."

"What does that mean?'

Kathleen eyed the door. "I mean, before I finish unpacking everything and basically build this center for you, am I doing it in vain?"

"We had to move," Adrian replied *sotto voce*. "You know that. Exposure is lethal in a case like this, and that puts our patients in danger. We needed mobility because we must ensure their safety."

"Mobility? Meaning what, like a, a van?" She laughed. "Yeah, that's a great idea."

"If you've got a better idea I'm all ears. If not ..."

"I do."

Silence.

"Don't set up anything," she said.

"What?"

"Why do you need to move an entire clinic and years' worth of research?"

"What do you mean, like quit?" Adrian replied.

"For God's sake, no. You've already achieved what you set out to. Nine out of ten patients are healing! Do you hear me? Their. Cancer. Has. Stopped. Growing. What more do you need?"

"Proof," he said. "And I can't go public with my findings or publish until we conclude the last cycle. Two months, that's all I need. Eight more weeks of data, tracked, documented findings and the FDA is sure to—"

"The FDA? Have you completely lost it? Get your head out of the sand, Adrian." Kathleen steadied herself on the counter and plunked down on two file boxes. "You can never go public with this, and you can't publish anything. You know this."

"Not without a lot of trouble, anyway."

"No, not without putting your life in danger, not to mention the control group, and me. Don't you see what's happening?"

"Yes, of course, that's why we're moving the lab," Adrian replied.

"And not without putting all our lives in danger."

"So you're worried about your own neck then?"

"Yes, and you should be worried about yours," Kathleen replied and noticed a long shadow moving past the hallway door. "Adrian," she said in a softer voice, "did you tell anyone I was here?"

"No, of course not. Why?"

"There's someone in the hallway outside."

"That's impossible. Only we and the landlord have a keycard to that space. Listen to me …"

But Kathleen had already put the phone in her pocket and moved closer to the door. I'm in a warehouse in Bridgeport, she thought, it's getting dark, and I'm alone here. The safety of her boss seemed somewhat less important than the sound of a door being jimmied open.

The laboratory door had a window positioned as the center panel, with a heavier locked door on the other side of it leading to the hallway.

"Kathleen, answer me," she heard Adrian mumble from the muffled earpiece.

"I'm here," she whispered, creeping behind a short wall of boxes stacked unopened near the door.

"What's going on over there?"

Three quiet knocks came from the door. Kathleen eased down and crawled on all fours toward the back of the space that led to a small storage room. Now, out of earshot from the door, she leaned up against the wall and drew the phone to her mouth. "Adrian."

"I'm here."

"Where's your gun?"

CHAPTER NINETEEN

Kerry blinked to help her gauge a sense of place. Now she was sitting in another part of Gina's living room. "What's going on here? I thought I was sitting—" She stopped and suddenly looked with suspicion into her teacup. And what is it about your hair, she kept wondering about Gina.

Okay, they drugged me with the tea, then picked me up and moved me to another part of the room. Note to self: remember you're sitting in the armchair now.

"What do you remember from when you were ten?" Gina spoke in a careful voice, still sitting in the same place but facing a different direction, still with her hair all wrong.

Kerry's awareness clicked back inch by inch, certain that the tea in her cup had been laced with barbiturates. "When I was ten? Why? I never think about it, to be honest."

Gina glanced at Rick, who stood by the window with his arms crossed, monitoring the street. Rick, the scruffy young man driving the car, the one who was supposed to be dead.

Had he been feigning death, or just knocked out from the collision?

"Kerry?"

"Yeah, sorry, when I was ten. Um, nothing really. Went to school, hated all my teachers."

Gina shifted her legs underneath her body on the couch. "Who was closest to you back then? I mean, besides me," she added with a chuckle.

Kerry felt a throbbing again, this time directly behind her eyes. "Ohhhh."

Gina edged closer. "Kerry, listen to me."

The faint sound of a cell phone pinged from the bedroom. "That's mine, "Kerry said. "It's in my ..."

Rick disappeared into the bedroom and returned with the phone. He handed it to her, still ringing.

"Who is it?" Gina said.

Rick bent down toward Gina's ear. "Ferri."

"Damn, I need more time!" Gina whispered.

"Don't worry about it, I'll take it," Kerry said. "Let me just ... find the ..." but the ringing stopped by the time her finger touched the green button. With her phone in one hand and a cup of tea in the other, Kerry sat up and appraised the situation. Gina, her best friend. Rick, a stranger, who apparently knows her boss. "What's going on here?"

The phone beeped, indicating a new voicemail. Rick reached toward it, but Kerry pulled the phone from him, standing quickly – a move that rushed too much blood from of her head. She went to her Calls menu and selected voicemail. Still wobbly with the phone outstretched in one arm, she pressed the volume key down but didn't catch it fast enough. Mark Ferri's voice sounded as she jerked the phone to her ear.

"...Stine, it's Mark Ferri. I'm not calling as your boss, though I should inform you that you're suspended from work as of today, duration indeterminate." She wondered if Gina and Rick were hearing this. "Mainly this is a courtesy call, because I thought you should know that a warrant's been issued by SFPD for your arrest in connection with the disappearance of Rosemary Castiglia. I suggest you contact me when you get this message, with answers that will no doubt affect more than just your job."

"I need to get to my apartment, now. Can you help me?" she asked, directing her question to Rick.

"You've still got your key, right?" Gina asked.

"Rex could have changed the lock, that's what I'm worried about. Especially now."

Gina, glancing at Rick, said, "You can take care of this, I trust?"

"I think so."

"Good," Kerry replied. "So you're verbal after all, and a criminal to boot."

"Rick will take you, then. I've got something to take care of here."

'Something to take care of here,' Gina had said. The words echoed eerily in her drug-fogged brain, a phrase that the Gina she knew would never have used. And now her signature dark hair was streaked with crude, punk-rocker pink down one side. And this didn't look like Palo Alto. Something didn't feel right about this. Then again, what *did* feel right in her life?

"You and Gina grew up together?" Rick asked en route to Harriet Street.

Kerry took in the landscaped views, rolling green hills near where 84 intersected with 280. "Not here, we didn't," she replied. "Palo Alto's not exactly my style."

"You live on Harriet?"

She nodded, sluggish, blinking, brain cells still incapacitated. "Near ... um ..."

"Don't worry, it'll all come back in an hour or so," he replied.

"And why was I drugged in the first place?" Kerry demanded.

They passed Thai Ginger restaurant and then turned onto the 280 entrance ramp. She looked directly at Rick now, whose eyes scanned nervously left and right while he drove.

"Did you hear me?" she pressed.

"As a precaution."

"Against what? Or whom?"

The sound of the motor silenced her question into one of many with no definable answer. She almost felt accustomed to the pattern by now. The car clock read 1:50 p.m. Perfect time to travel north.

Thirty minutes later, Rick veered the sedan into an alley facing the back of her apartment building. Kerry looked up at the fire escape. "Guess we can't go in the front."

"I'll go," Rick announced. "Tell me what you need, I'll only have five minutes."

"No," she grabbed the sleeve of his worn black jacket. "I'll go. I need some personal things."

Secret things.

Rick stepped out of the car and scanned both entrances to the alley, then nodded with a tacit 'go now'. Kerry climbed one creaky stair after the other, ignoring the gaps between them and the open dumpsters beneath her feet. Rick, five steps behind, held a small, black pistol in his right hand. Kerry stopped.

"Move," he said without looking at her. She didn't, still staring at the gun, and he pressed one hand into her left shoulder blade and squeezed.

Do exactly as he says, she counseled herself, moving forward toward the kitchen window. She tugged upward on the window frame. "It's locked."

Rick jerked his head to the left and she moved aside two inches. She watched him lift his jacket in the front and pull what resembled a miniature Slim Jim from his waist. He jerked it into the gap between window panes and when he pulled upward, there was a *pop*, followed by a piece of metal flying off the jamb.

"I'm guessing you're not from Palo Alto either."

"Get in," he motioned, holding up the window with his back, his legs straddling the opening. Kerry followed directions and climbed, or more like tumbled, into her kitchen and then stopped.

"What is it?"

"Cereal," she said appraising the five boxes on the counter. "How much muesli can someone eat, anyway?"

"Never mind that," he said. "Technically you don't live here anymore anyway. Get what you need, we have three minutes." The *blip* of a police siren sounded from a few blocks away. "Make that two."

One hundred and twenty seconds to grab what she thought she might need over the next few days, weeks, months. Okay. Emergency cash and credit card from the envelope under her nightstand drawer, then clothes.

"One minute," Rick bellowed from the kitchen.

Jacket, underwear, T-shirts, she thought, digging into the dark closet, then fumbling on the floor for the small gym bag she took to work. Where was that thing?

"Come on," Rick said, grabbing her elbow and pulling her into the kitchen.

"Two seconds, I need some cosmetics from the bathroom!"

"No time." He physically pulled her by the elbow to the kitchen window. "Wait," he blocked with his arm glancing out the window at the neighborhood. "Go now."

Kerry moved down the clanky fire escape stairs, angling the duffel bag on her shoulder and keeping an eye on Rick, who was three stairs above her. Then she realized that she should have been looking down.

"Step down, miss," the police officer instructed and moved to the bottom stair.

"I live here," Kerry protested in a purposely soft voice.

"Forgot your key, right? Of course you did."

CHAPTER TWENTY

"Sylvie?" the man said, jamming his finger on the gray button on his phone. Where is she now? "Sylvie?"

"Yes, yes, Mr. Cabot, what do you need?" a meek, sleepy voice answered.

"I need you to be available when I call you."

Pause. "I am available, sir, I mean I was, I mean—"

"Would you come into my office, please? No need to use technology unnecessarily."

A moment later, a young woman emerged wearing a dark gray skirt, light blouse, long black cardigan fully buttoned, black tights, and black running shoes. A nun, he thought. All she needs is a huge silver cross hanging from her neck. The girl stood at attention ten feet away from his desk concentrating all her focus, it appeared, on the wall behind his head.

"Let me say it a different way to make sure you understand. Okay? I need you available, immediately, when I call you. Not after ten minutes, or ten seconds."

"I understand."

"Can you do that? And please consider the question's full implication before answering. Because if you can't, it would benefit us both to learn this now, rather than later."

"Yes, of course, Mr. Cabot. I'm very sorry I kept you waiting. Now, what was it you ..."

Cabot rolled his eyes and gave a "go away" motion with his hand. "Get me George Fernandez," he said as she walked away.

"The State Department, sir?"

"That's where he works, yes."

"Right away, sir."

He couldn't be certain, but there seemed a tinge of defiance in her 'sir'. He could see it in her eyes too – the latent 'fuck you' dangling from the end of every sentence, in her last step out of a room, the resigned rebellion that no more cared about advancing her career than she did the pigeons in Central Park. Swiveling his Italian leather chair toward the panoramic view of Manhattan's Upper East Side, Cabot scrolled through the contacts on his iPhone to find Pamela Grieves. He pressed the icon beside her name and waited.

"Jules Cabot," she answered in a knowing voice. He hated her voice.

"Hello, Pamela."

"What's wrong, Jules? Don't tell me we still didn't get it right."

"*You*, Pamela, *you* still didn't get it right." Cabot remembered his first impression of Grieves. This would be the third, no fourth Executive Assistant in five months, who had disappointed him. But he'd thought Grieves had that ever-rare quality of accidental glamor that he'd only ever seen once before. In his dead wife.

"Jules?"

"I'm sorry. She's just not that all there, if you know what I mean."

"Tell me everything. This will help me when trying to place her elsewhere."

"You were supposed to be screening these ...

young ... whatever they are ... things."

"I did, and I do," she defended. "We thought she was excellent, well mannered, polished."

Cabot sighed. "Okay, yes she's very good at saying 'Yes, Mr. Cabot, no, Mr. Cabot.' I don't want a damned robot. I want someone who can think my thoughts before I think them myself! And I'm willing to pay handsomely for that."

"Oh well, *that* should only cost ten dollars," she mocked.

"Excuse me?"

"Sure. Open your phone book and look up Tarot Card Readers."

After firing his fifth Executive Assistant in six months, Cabot stared for a while at the compacted sea of cars ribboning New York City's streets, darkly-dressed hoards moving across Broadway, and again considered the same thought he'd had over and over.

It's not supposed to be like this.

Cabot shuddered from the sudden shock of his desk phone ringing. My landline, he thought. No one uses that. Still staring at the mottled sky, he reached back and awkwardly grabbed the receiver.

"Yes."

"Turn around, Mr. Cabot."

His breathing stopped. "Pardon me?"

"I'm the answer to your prayers."

The voice on the phone was within earshot. He shuddered and turned his chair.

CHAPTER TWENTY-ONE

"Yo, Stanton, your girl's here."

"Good, stick her in three. I'll be right there. And Reno ..."

"Yeah?"

"Watch her!"

Detective Pete Stanton looked at his watch and shook his head. Damn, he thought. Stanton had a silent agreement with the SFPD that he played racquetball every Monday at 3 p.m. as a form of job-related stress therapy that allowed him higher levels of performance and focus. He peered in at the suspect waiting in interrogation room #3 and again looked at his watch: 2:55.

"Miss ... Steen is it?" he purposely mispronounced. "Twenty-seven years old—"

"Stine."

"I'm from Human Resources and I'd just like to welcome you here to the police department and see if there's anything I can get you. Coffee, a veggie burger perhaps ?"

"How 'bout a lawyer?" the girl shot back.

She's quick, Stanton thought, unflappable. He slowly circled the room. Early-mid twenties, somewhat refined, low maintenance which, to him, meant no manicures and from the look of it, no makeup either. Significant. Fifteen years with the PD had taught him that the flash observations in the first two minutes of interrogation were more important to establishing a case than a forty-page psych profile.

Stanton sat opposite her and slowly removed his badge from his wallet. "Okay, let's start over. I'm Detective Pete Stanton," he said earnestly this time. "Do you know why you're here?"

"Sure," the girl replied, "for breaking into my own apartment."

"That's what you've said, yes. Do you have any documentation to show that it's your apartment? Your lease?"

"Do you walk around with a copy of your lease, Officer? Or the Promissory Note on your mortgage?"

"It's Detective. But you knew that already."

"And you knew my name wasn't pronounced Steen. So now we're even."

Stanton nodded. A worthy adversary. Interesting.

"Would you like to see some of the dirty underwear in the laundry hamper in my bathroom?" the girl said.

Stanton smiled to himself. "There's a warrant out for your arrest in connection with the disappearance and now the death of a patient at San Francisco General. Are you aware of this allegation?"

"She's not dead."

Stanton raised a brow. "Who?"

"The patient. Rosemary Castiglia. She's not dead."

"How do you know that?"

"I can't say."

Stanton tapped a finger on the desk. "Can't or won't?"

Kerry stared, unmoving.

"Okay ... can you tell me where she is? And let me add, before you reply, that your answer to this particular question will greatly affect your ... how shall I say this? ... quality of life."

"No."

"No, what?"

"I can't tell you where she is because I don't know. And I wasn't even the last person to see her."

"Right."

"Nurse Alice Redfield, my supervisor, saw her after me. All I did was note that her chart was missing."

"Her chart. So this chart disappeared on your shift then?"

"Not necessarily. I just noticed that it wasn't where it was supposed to be when I was monitoring the patients in ICU."

"What did you do?"

"Told Redfield."

"And what was her reply?"

The girl shook her head and smiled. "She told me that stealing someone's chart would be a great way to make someone disappear."

Stanton doodled something on his notepad to simulate interest in her last statement. But he wasn't really interested in Nurse Redfield or even what this young woman was telling him. He felt more interested in what she wasn't saying.

"How old are you, Miss Stine?"

"You just read it. Twenty-seven."

"Married?"

Pause. "Divorced."

"How long have you lived in your apartment on ... Harriet Street is it?"

"Less than a year."

"And where did you work before SF General?"

The girl drew a deep breath and sat back in her chair, arms crossed in front of her.

"You got your bachelor's in biology from UC Santa Cruz and you were enrolled in the pharmacy program at UCSF, weren't you?"

The girl didn't move.

"You were in your second year when you dropped out."

"Dropped out? That's the information you gathered from your research?"

"You're saying you didn't drop out?"

"I couldn't pay a mortgage and school on a single income."

"So you're working as a CNA now."

"That's right. Guess that's what they mean by 'from scratch'."

"Sorry?"

"Are you married?" the girl asked him.

"I'm asking the questions here."

"Whatever," she replied.

But Stanton liked the question. "What was the patient being treated for? And how old was she?"

"Was? She's not dead, you know. Why does everybody think she's dead? Do you have a body? No."

"And how is it that you can confirm this information?"

Kerry looked down at the table.

"So the patient was in her bed when you noticed her chart missing?"

"Yes."

"In ICU recovery."

"Correct."

"Isn't it typically dark in ICU recovery? Dark and cold, that's what I heard."

"You think I only *thought* I saw the patient and it was someone else?"

"Isn't it at least possible?"

"No."

"Why not?"

"'Cause I'm not a moron, that's why. When do I get to ask questions?"

Stanton was being careful. Talking quietly,

probing gently enough to appear kind, but deep enough to irritate her. It was a practiced ploy, he admitted. Good cop. Always the good cop, never bad cop. Catch more flies with honey.

"Go ahead," he replied. "Ask."

"So are you planning to question Nurse Redfield? The chart did disappear on her watch."

"No comment."

Stanton watched her lean forward and put her elbows on the table, rubbing her face with her palms. "And what about Jim Rex?"

Stanton stared across the table.

"You think it's normal for someone to show up at your house with a key and pretend they live there?"

More silence, during which time Stanton wondered about this procedure of breaking down suspects. Was it humane? Was he toying with the fragility of the human psyche? This girl was under duress, no doubt about that, and he was causing her to unravel even more. "He's here right now," Stanton said at length, in almost a whisper.

"You arrested him? Good."

"Actually, he's filing a report that you were illegally trespassing in his apartment while he was away on bus—"

"What?"

His subject rose and her chair toppled back, making a loud clang against the floor.

"Do you ... realize what you're saying?" she asked, wiping sudden tears from her eyes. "He just showed up here two nights ago with a bag of groceries and—"

"Miss Stine ... Kerry ... can I call you Kerry?"

"Look, I can provide tangible evidence that I've lived in that apartment for the last seven months."

"Dirty laundry that's seven months old?"

She picked up the chair. "You wouldn't understand," she said with her back turned. "But I'll bring it to you. Unless of course, you intend to hold me here. Am I a threat to society, Detective?"

"You called me Detective. Our relationship is advancing."

"Fuck off."

"On second thought ..."

"You have no actual evidence against me. You know you can't hold me here."

"You're right," Stanton replied.

"And furthermore, you— What?"

"No, you're exactly right. I don't have direct evidence that can prove that you stole a patient. We've been to your apartment, there's no body there. All I have is a report that an old lady's missing and you were one of the last people to see her before she disappeared. The way that this has escalated so quickly just proves that you've got some enemies at work. Be careful over there."

"So ... you're letting me go?"

"Do you take out your landlord's garbage?"

"Pardon me?"

Stanton lowered his head. "Garbage? You must do something nice for him, this guy named Byron. He's posted bail for you and vouched for the authenticity of your residence. Glad you've got someone in your corner."

"Really? Why do you care?"

Stanton shrugged. "I don't know."

"I can go then?"

"Let's just say I'll be in touch. Leave your mobile number and email address with the officer up front."

The young woman nodded and looked at the door. "Thanks."

Stanton waited ten minutes, during which time he poured fresh brewed, cheap grocery store coffee into a Styrofoam cup and swirled it around to cool it off. Paper-clipped to his 'Stine, Kerry' file was a slip of paper with the mobile number and email address from her hospital work record: (415) 268-8587 and *ks998@hotmail.com.*

In the time it took for him to walk down three hallways, the coffee had cooled.

"Smit, how's it going?" He circled around the officer at the dispatch desk.

"Cute girl," Smit replied.

"Yeah. She leave her mobile number and email address with you?"

The officer looked down at his log. "Ah ... yeah right here. (415) 999-9999, and. *kerrystine@biteme.com*"

Sonofabitch, Stanton smirked. Never think below the waist.

Chapter Twenty-Two

Fifteen minutes later, Kerry stood at the edge of the SFPD public parking lot on Bryant. Byron would be swinging by to pick her up in a minute, which gave her no time to consider where Gina met people like Rick and Nigel Watson, what she and the old man had been trying to tell her, and what information Jim Rex was trying to squeeze out of her. She didn't even bother touching her head this time when the pain circled back.

Byron beeped the horn on the ancient Toyota Corolla, leaning a bristly face out the window. "Can you stay here with the car? I need to run in and use the restroom. You know, the organs are aging."

Kerry nodded and sat in the passenger seat, looking at the keys in the ignition.

Keys.

Was this an unforeseen opportunity? She'd been bailed out, happily, but for what purpose? And, worse yet, where would she go? The lock on her apartment door would likely have been changed by the intruder who was, no doubt, filing a police report that she had broken into *his* residence.

Leaning left, she turned the ignition key. The engine lurched and sputtered. Stick shift. "Damn," she whispered and climbed into the driver's side. By her estimate, she was seven blocks from her apartment. For the second time today, she pulled herself behind the wheel of an unknown car and sped off.

Passing 5th and Bryant near the block-long St. Vincent de Paul compound, her phone buzzed in her pocket. She blinked and let it ring. Two, three, four times.

"I'm sorry," she answered.

"This is the man who's just paid a thousand fucking dollars to bail you out of jail!"

"Okay, okay, I am terribly sorry for taking your—"

"Stealing, Kerry, it's called stealing. And let me gently remind you that I'm still standing in the bloody police department parking lot. Hadn't thought of that part, had you?"

"I need to get into my apartment, and there's no time left for a song and dance, Byron. I'll leave your car in the parking lot and your keys under the mat."

"It's an eight-block walk from here, and I'm old."

"Um, didn't you run the Boston Marathon last year?" She veered down the alley leading to Harriet Street.

"That's not the—"

"And the year before?"

"Ah. Well, see ..."

She hit the red button, scanned the alleyway, and for the second time in one day climbed her fire escape stairs.

The space smelled damp and felt cold. The third floor was never cold. She moved around, scanning the windows every two seconds like an escaped convict, flinching at every street sound. Nothing looked necessarily out of place, but nothing seemed quite right either. She stood still in the middle of the kitchen, surveying her pots and pans hanging from their designated hooks over the butcher block, the same three navel oranges in the tiered fruit stand near the sink. Her desk untouched.

In five minutes, she managed to fill the duffel bag with clean underwear, gray socks, jeans, T-shirts, makeup, saline solution, extra contact lenses. Reaching into the linen closet for a single, clean bath towel, she shuddered. The screeching train whistle outside pulled her attention for a split second, but couldn't muffle the thudding of her chest. Every single one of her pink bath towels had been replaced with black ones. Brand new, fluffy, neatly folded bath towels. Black.

In the bathroom to splash cold water on her face, her movements again stopped dead when she lifted her gaze to the mirror.

You remember it, don't you? was the first line scrawled in a ragged slant script on the medicine cabinet mirror in red lipstick.

I don't even own a red lipstick.

Falling back two steps, Kerry dropped the duffel bag and grabbed the shower curtain rod overhead. Breathe, she thought.

Then written below it in all caps, *THE MIZPAH.*

Mizpah. That word.

She blinked slowly, and could almost hear an echo of giggling voices. The soot of cigar smoke, no, not cigar, something else. A clamor of confusing sounds. Where was ...

Her eyes snapped back to the medicine cabinet.

Third line: *Kezar underpass at Golden Gate Park, 10 pm, bring IT. You have one chance.*

CHAPTER TWENTY-THREE

Grace Mattson fumbled with the toggle button on her down parka before stepping into the slick chill of New England Fall, once again making a call she didn't want to make. She'd gotten a text message from Neville about a Fedex envelope left for her.

"What do you want me to do, Mother?" Neville asked in a strained voice.

"Where was it?" Grace said into the cold air, headphones connected to the phone in her pocket.

"The porch."

"A box?"

"Envelope," he replied.

"Well, what time did you leave?" she pressed now, hell bent on extracting as much information as she possibly could about the Fedex envelope.

"One o'clock, or thereabouts."

"Really."

"For God's sake ..."

"What, Neville? Must I walk you through every step of deductive reasoning? When did you leave, when did you bloody well return and how long were you gone?"

"Three hours. There, I was gone three hours. Satisfied?"

She didn't bother asking where he'd gone. That

question never came with an answer.

Okay, she thought. Someone dropped off a FedEx envelope between one and four o'clock, and the airbill contained no information from the sender.

She'd been to Fedex enough times to know their policy – no tracking information meant no accountability in the event of a loss. Therefore, they'd never ship an envelope with no sender information. So the airbill had obviously been removed ... and replaced with a blank that contained her name and address.

The chill beginning to penetrate even her long, heavy down coat, she moved quicker to her car parked across the rectangular Yale faculty lot. Her breath left frozen clouds in the air in front of her face.

"Neville?"

"Yes, Mother," he mocked.

"Check the airbill, please. What's on it, exactly?"

"I told you already. Nothing."

"Nothing at all? On the whole slip?"

During the pause, Grace could hear Neville's shoes clicking against the wood floors back to the foyer where he said he'd left the envelope. "Aren't you on your way home?"

She knew this meant that she was wasting his time.

"All right," he said after a moment. "Nothing in the Sender section other than today's date, your name and this address in the Recipient box, Priority Overnight, no value declared, and the sender apparently paid cash. Will that suffice for now or would you like the police to dust for fingerprints?"

"Open it, please," she said in a different voice.

"I will not, it's yours. Besides—"

"Let me guess – you're going out."

"Mother, don't you—"

"Why do you even pay half the mortgage, Neville?

All you do is—"

"Address, Mother. For what I do, I need a viable U.S. residence address." Click.

Well, isn't that an interesting phrase, she thought. Residence address.

"A-a job?" Jules Cabot stammered, still shaken by the intrusion and the woman's startling appearance. Platinum blonde hair, white silk blouse, suit a dark shade of fog-gray that matched the color of her eyes. An Arabian among mere quarter horses. "And why would you want to work for me, Miss ...?"

"Carrera. Martina Carrera." She realized, just then, that she'd forgotten to use 'Beth', her tradecraft name. How could she have forgotten this? Now she would have to kill him.

"I'd bet my life that's not your real name."

Actually, it is, she thought. "Do you care?" She feigned disinterest. "I'm your dream come true, Mr. Cabot, the ... answer to your prayers. I'm so good, I'll be thinking your thoughts ... before you even think them yourself."

Cabot shoved his chair back and rose. "Tell me who you are. Now."

The woman remained perfectly still. "Why not ask me what you really want to know?"

Cabot stared, feeling once again the humiliating certainty that he was unqualified to relate to the cryptic female sex. He hated them, he'd admitted to his therapist, hated how a certain class of them seemed to incapacitate him, even choke him if confronted. This was the class he most feared and despised. He could handle the Sylvies and the Pamela Grieves of the world. But this breed, the Arabian show stallions, possessed everything a man could ever want without even trying.

"Well, go ahead, ask," she chided. He watched her lower herself evenly into the chair across from him.

Cabot kept staring, blinking, wondering.

"I need a job," she said in a different voice now. Yet another in her litany of practiced voices, he knew.

"Why me? Shouldn't you be working at the American Embassy in Qatar or something?

The woman, in her menacing gray suit and silk blouse, smiled the smallest of smiles and crossed her bare legs. Cabot didn't dare look at them, and there was no point. He already knew everything he needed to know about her. Silk underwear, matching tops and bottoms of course, probably purchased at Bloomingdales or Saks, silk pajamas, professional manicures, spa every Friday, tennis lessons twice a week, drives a BMW. Probably reads during sex.

"I might be more regular than I appear, you know," she said, again reading his thoughts.

"Doubt it."

"I take out my own garbage."

"That's because you're too proud to allow your servants to wait on you. But you and I both know you have them. Two or three, I'd guess."

She blinked and smiled.

"Education," Cabot continued, "Yale, Princeton, something?"

"Okay, you have me there," she said with a broad smile. "Princeton. I'm a Jersey girl."

"Uh-huh, sure," Cabot replied, wondering how long this would continue.

"Why don't I start with a cup of coffee? It's my job to simply *know* how you like it."

The woman rose. "I even brought a special kind with me. It's brewing now." She turned and slowly walked into the reception area, closing the door behind her. Sitting behind the reception desk, the woman felt her phone buzz in her pocket. Checking the text message, she typed a short reply. Yes. I'm in.

Your cover safe?
No.
Can you make it work?
I'm working on it.

Setting her phone back in her handbag, she envisioned Cabot's ordinary, somewhat worn, middle-aged face and right now hated these assignments. She knew she needed Cabot's office for its strategic vantage point overlooking the busiest parts of university traffic – and the most likely point from which to spot her prey. And the only way to ensure occupancy without potential exposure would be to eliminate the witness. She knew there was no other way.

Martina slid a tiny dropper bottle from her jacket pocket, squeezed two drops into the bottom of the mug, pulled a small container of Half and Half from the paper bag she'd set on the desk on her way in and poured some into a dark mug on the counter. She stirred precisely one-third of a teaspoon of raw cane sugar into the cream and slowly poured the freshly brewed Jamaican Blue Mountain coffee over it. She knew her serum was odorless and tasteless and, without stirring, she knew the heat from the coffee would naturally melt the sugar and blend in the cream by the time she turned the knob of Cabot's office door again.

She set the cup in front of him, sat, crossed her legs, and smiled.

Cabot looked deep into the cup and inhaled. "Well, it smells like coffee."

"Would you like to see the container it came in, and I think I still have my receipt from that place on ..."

Cabot looked up eagerly, hoping to God that she would stumble. Some minor detail or mistake, something to make her at least slightly human.

"Here, give it to me," she reached out a long arm. "I'll take the first s—"

Disgusted by the gesture, Cabot grabbed the mug and took one sip, held it in his mouth for a moment, closed his eyes and swallowed. It was by far the best coffee he'd ever tasted.

Watching him take three more sips, all with his eyes closed, the woman mentally counted back from twenty and, by the time she got to ten, she rose. With one hand, she applied two fingers to Cabot's neck, confirmed no pulse, then pulled her phone from her pocket again to type another message.

It's done. And then assembled the telescope by the window.

CHAPTER TWENTY-FOUR

With Byron's car parked securely in his favorite spot by the staircase, keys under his doormat, duffel bag in hand, Kerry remembered the cell phone charger still plugged in behind the TV. Damn it. She looked at her watch, and glanced up at the kitchen window through the fire escape stairs. Was there time to go back? Would Byron be here by now blocking her entrance or, worse, Jim Rex, or Rick? Where was Rick in all this?

Flinching at the sound of a bicyclist heading down the alley behind her, her stomach growled, a faint reminder of the necessity to eat. How long had it been?

The hospital was out of the question by now, even though Detective Stanton had let her go for the moment. She remembered a Verizon store near *La Boulangerie* on Market Street near Union Square Park. She spotted the Muni bus two blocks down 6th Street. She ran, keeping her eye on the bus the whole time. There, it made a stop, buying her a few extra seconds.

Another police siren behind her now. Jesus, she thought, was it coming down Harriet? Who even knew about her street? The bus inched its way down 6th, and the siren got louder behind her. Was it coming for her? This time, the siren made two short *beep beep* sounds, as if to get her attention.

She didn't look back.

Closer to the bus now, she jogged across Howard Street, passed McDonald's and hovered behind two nervous old ladies at the bus stop in front of the car wash. The squad car slowed, sliding into the McDonald's parking lot. She could just make out an officer's face scanning the parking lot.

Was he watching her? Or was she just paranoid?

The bus stopped in front of the carwash, and Kerry rudely wedged her body between the two old women, who clutched their purses tighter to their chests. I'm not gonna rob you, she thought climbing the bus steps, feeling even more like a criminal. As the bus tooled away, the officer stood outside the squad car with the door still open, staring in her direction.

He's here for me.

The bus stopped at Taylor and Market. Before getting off, she checked both sides of both streets, spotted the quickest path to the Verizon store and felt comforted by a swarm of pedestrians. A tour bus double-parked on Taylor emptied clusters of seniors onto the wide sidewalk. Kerry stood frozen outside the bus, surveying the scene. Two blocks, maybe forty steps. And the Verizon store looked nearly empty, something else to register on her list of oddities. No one needs a new cell phone today, or a new headset? It was nearly dinnertime, the end of the work day. It just didn't make sense.

"Can I help you?" a young man said as she went through the door.

Talking, waiting, pacing, her eyes didn't leave the Verizon store windows for an instant. With no one in line, buying a new charger took all of three minutes. As she stepped cautiously outside two minutes later, stuffing the new charger in her duffel bag, she heard a man's voice behind her.

"Miss Stine?" The screech of bicycle tires. "Delivery."

She jerked her head behind her to see a man on a bicycle with a helmet and a bag slung over his shoulder. He stopped, reaching into the sack.

"Excuse me?"

The man held out a small package. "Walgreens delivery," he said.

A trap. Someone purposely diverting her attention from her surroundings. She looked left and right and scanned the crowd behind Bicycle Man and the Powell Street BART.

"I don't have all day, miss," he said.

Bending her neck down slightly, she could see her name printed on the pharmacy receipt stapled to the outside of the bag, and the word Fiorinal.

Butalbital. Her migraine medicine. Why would it be delivered? And, more importantly, how did this stranger know who ... and where she was? "Don't I need to sign for it or something?"

Bike Man didn't flinch and kept the bag in his outstretched hand. "I was instructed to deliver this to you." He slid his sunglasses to the top of his head. Blue eyes, early twenties. "It's obviously something you need," he added and pressed the small, white bag to her chest and sped off.

The Metreon on Market across from the Union Square center had a Starbucks, Kerry remembered. In one hundred forty-five steps, she had crossed the street and stood at the counter asking for the restroom code. "2-4-6-8."

Methodically, she locked the door, hung her duffel bag on the knob, and leaned against the wall. Tearing open the package, she first shook the bottle and heard pills. Then she scanned the label, barely remembering the pharmaceutical label template from her program at UCSF. N for narcotic, C for controlled substance. What did "0#0" mean? A sample? Not for distribution? Slowly, half expecting a soft-fabric coiled snake to burst out, she removed the lid. Blue and white capsules lined the bottom, with a folded slip of paper flat along the wall of the container.

Someone knocked on the restroom door and pulled the handle. "Someone's in here!" she shouted over the screech of the cappuccino frother.

Sliding her index finger into the jar, she dug her nail on the edge of the folded paper and pulled. Something buzzed in her pocket – her cell phone. Leave me alone, she thought, heart pounding, fighting back tears of frustration. Who was watching her to the extent that they would know she'd exit a bus on 6th and Market at the precise moment that it did? Was she a rat in a cage being observed under a mega-scope?

After capping the bottle, with one hand she unfolded the page and held it up to the light. And with the other hand, she pulled her cell out of her pocket. The note contained small, typed letters in three centered lines:

DON'T GO TO GGP TONIGHT
JESSE KNOWS WHERE MISSING PATIENT IS
BE CAREFUL

There was no time left. She flushed the toilet, washed her hands, and quickly exited the windowless room. A woman sighed and shoved past her. The aroma of coffee woke her to attention. How long had it been since she'd had a real cup of coffee, a cup of anything for that matter? And there was no one in line now.

"Tall latte and a plain croissant," she said pulling her phone into view.

The envelope icon displayed on the home screen,

showing a new text message. From Rick. The message read, Checked your apartment lately?

"Double or single?" asked the barista.

Kerry's fingers managed a Why? into the keypad. She looked up a moment later and made note of the girl's orange-dyed hair. "Oh, um, single."

"Four fifty-seven," a man, this time, announced behind the coffee counter. Kerry peered behind the man, looking for the orange-haired girl, but then the phone buzzed in her hand with what she knew was an immediate reply. The man stared behind her. "Ma'am?"

Don't call me that, she thought, yanking the slim wallet from her purse. She withdrew a five-dollar bill and set it on the counter, quickly returning her gaze to the text thread, which read, There's a dead man in your bathroom.

CHAPTER TWENTY-FIVE

The sound of clunky shoes against hardwood floors reminded Grace of her empty house. Eerie in the late afternoon, she'd always thought, with long, diagonal shadows spilling gray streaks across the living room floors. Occasionally, she stopped pacing to gaze down at the unlikely Fedex package. A cell phone – obvious enough by the feel and shape. She could probably make a call without even opening the envelope. A howl of wind shrieked past her windows at the same moment that the tea kettle whistled two rooms away.

She'd been trained, by three generations of example, to respect the gravity of tea as a cultural artifact rather than an arbitrary beverage. "There's a magic that happens when you apply the correct form to things," her mother had taught her, a proverb she summarily dismissed as hogwash. My tea, my way, she thought, spooning a heap of East Indian Assam into a strainer. Water poured over it, she watched the browning liquid fill the mug while a slightly nutty aroma filled her nose.

Open it, her conscience nagged.

She stood in front of the sink silently counting to thirty – thirty seconds for the freshly poured tea to settle – before taking three quick sips. The pull tab tore across the width of the envelope, and an older model flip phone dropped into the stainless steel basin. The note taped to the cover read, Just press '0'. The gritty side of her knew what this meant, or at least implied. She went straight to her computer and clicked to open Google Chrome. While she waited for her weak WiFi signal to connect her, she clicked on her locked horticulture file, titled Amazing Grace. Her log-on screen opened. She typed "obregoni189" in the username field and "stymyx" in the password. A rotating hourglass let her know that the system was logging her on. Her fingers tapped the wooden desk while she waited. It never took more than two seconds to connect to a file that resided on her computer. Something was wrong.

Just press 0.

She backspaced to erase both the username and password entries and started again, this time entering each character slowly. A new error message read "Please contact your Administrator if you would like to reset your username and password."

"What?" she said aloud. "I am the bloody Administrator!"

Elbows on the desk, she grasped her head and ran her fingers through her hair with this secret knowing in the pit of her belly. Eyeing the alien cell phone, she clicked the "Back" button and entered the password again, and again, knowing the ugly truth. Bank accounts, she suddenly wondered. Jesus, Adrian, what have you done?

"Ms. Mattson," a woman's voice answered. Grace knew that voice. "Thank you for calling."

"Did I have a choice?"

"Of course. Call or don't call."

"Who is this?" Grace demanded.

"You know who it is. We met in the last twenty-four hours."

"Look, is there something I can do for you, Miss—"

"Oh, you'll be doing many things for us. But for now, it's what I can do for you."

"How about unfreezing my files, for one thing."

Just silence. Then, in the background, she heard voices and a sort of

muffled, low-pitched moan.

"Yes, I did anticipate that this would be ... confusing for you."

"Oh, for God's s—"

"Why don't I let you talk to someone who can no doubt clarify things."

In the silence, Grace noticed her palms sweating. The sun had receded, and dark shadows shrouded all but the kitchen table, leaving an unnatural orange glint against the dark wood. My files, my research, she kept thinking, until a familiar sound came from the receiver.

"Grace. It's me."

My God, she thought, could that possibly be Adrian? "What have they done to you?"

"Listen to me," he said, slower this time.

"I'm here."

"They want ..." he groaned, trying to clear his throat. She heard a scuffle on the other end, a wrestling sound, Adrian moaned. Jesus, she thought, helplessly.

"No, please. She'll find it. I know her."

"Adrian, find what?"

"The formula," he replied in a more lucid voice this time. "I don't know it from memory but it's in my files. They're password protected, but Kathleen knows the code."

"I don't ... quite ..." She shook her head. "Who are these people and what have they got to do with your research?" No answer came, so she continued. "I suspect they've got a lot to lose if your findings are published."

Again, only silence.

"Who's to say that you're the only one who has this formula, if there even is one? What if you, for example, gave it to—"

"Grace, they're holding me here until they get what they want. Please, go to Kathleen. Tell her I sent you. She'll know what to do."

"What does that mean? You're not making sense."

"I'll put it to you this way. They want the formula for what I've been working on for the past fifteen years. And they'll kill me if they don't get it in the next three days."

Chapter Twenty-Six

Early morning sun cast diagonal lines across the walls of the boathouse. The girl murmured from the makeshift bed. He watched her from his perch in the corner – a perfect vantage point for watching the steady stream of yacht owners and fishermen flood the pier preparing for the day's work.

The drug had about four hours' worth of potency left. That meant there wasn't much time, and Jim Rex had never been good at waiting.

The girl turned, her hands struggling from the bindings, no doubt to rub her head. "Ipp ... noll," she muttered. "Rnn ... nol."

"Just rest, sweetie. That's all you gotta do right now is rest and stay outta my way."

The girl cleared her throat and opened her eyes. No, Rex thought, shaking his foggy head to attention. Could it have worn off already?

"Was it good for you?" the girl mumbled, eyes wide and scanning the floor.

Rex laughed slightly. "I already told you. All you gotta do is keep quiet and stay out of my way."

"Yeah, but was I any good?" She sat up now, propping her upper body on her elbows. She rubbed hair from her eyes and looked square at him. "Rohypnol," she enunciated clearly now, sitting up.

Rex shook his head with a wry smile.

"The date rape drug."

"I gave you a sedative."

"Valium's a sedative. Flunitrazepam, also known as Rohypnol, is an active phenotype in rat poison."

"How would you know that?"

"I'm a pharmacist, you blockhead. You didn't know that?"

Blank stare.

"You just, what, pick up random women on the street and subject them to ..."

Rex watched as the girl rubbed her eyes, combed strands of hair out of her face, and surveyed the condition of her body under the thin, stained sheet. "Sounds like you didn't perform the required research before taking this job."

"Job?" he mocked, standing over her.

"Or do you just blindly do what your superiors tell you and take the money?"

Rex dragged the chair over to the bed and sat, just inches from her now. "I was told not to harm you and I didn't. But that can change."

"I've no doubt you're an excellent soldier."

"Look, as I said in the car, I need one thing from you."

The girl shook her head. "She doesn't remember me. She was too young. Too much happened."

"Oh, she remembers, and ..." he looked at his watch, "few more hours and I'm gonna prove it to you."

Chapter Twenty-Seven

I just need time to think, Kerry narrated, pacing the large square tiles of the underground BART platform. Irregular patterns of students, businessmen, and last-minute shoppers charged down the escalator, bags clanking, parading toward the open train doors. There's a dead man in your apartment, the text had read on her phone. And whatever that meant, if even true, was secondary to the issue of ten p.m.

Kezar Underpass, bring it with you.

If she recalled her scant knowledge of Yiddish, a mizpah was some kind of jewelry that earned its significance through the recipient. That's right, she realized only now, a halved necklace worn by two people that share a certain connection. Lovers. Friends. Kerry searched her mental archives while visually scanning her surroundings. No one looked familiar or threatening here. That was the great thing about BART – it could help someone virtually disappear.

How can I find out what's waiting for me at Kezar without actually showing up? Then it came to her.

Jesse.

That's it, she nodded. Be there without being seen, be there by being ... someone else. Okay, I need binoculars. They were in her apartment. Negative, she thought. Just then, an old woman in a feathered hat turned and made eye contact, seeming to coax her thoughts. Right, she thought, responding to the cue – a disguise.

Digging her phone from her tight pants pocket, she pressed the human figure to access her contacts list. Jesse Wilkins. Two, now three rings. Damn, Jesse, I need you!

Where would Jesse Wilkins be this at this time of day? Outreach, of course. It was his pet project: Finding homeless people who weren't hooked into one of the shelter communities. He'd referred to them as 'fringe' before, a list of souls too lost to ask for or accept help from anyone.

Nearing 8 p.m. now, Jesse would be in one of the corners of Golden Gate Park, where the fringe congregated after dark. Perfect, really – shaded corners of soft grass, hidden by lush trees, hills, and embankments. She'd met him there before, so she knew the place. She exited BART at Civic Center and pushed through a throng of people at the top of the stairs, enjoying the concealment of a graying sky. About a two-mile walk from here. Uneven gusts of cold, damp air rushed against her face and hair.

"My girl Kerry – is that you?" Jesse was heading down a grassy hill to the footpath near Stanyon and Kezar. His skin was so dark she could barely make him out, save for the shape of his untamed, signature dreads lit up by a street lamp.

He was smiling at her. "You couldn't see me in the dark, could you? Admit it."

Kerry held back a laugh and wrapped her arms around his body and squeezed, tighter than she meant to. A faint sob escaped from her lips as she pressed her face into his bare neck.

"Feels good, no? Human contact and all that?"

Jesse kept his clench around her frail body as he said it. She felt frail too, maybe she'd never felt so frail as this. Then unchecked sobs spilled out. Her whole body shook, and Jesse's large hands slid up from her back to gently cradle her head. "I got you now, my girl Kerry, you let Jesse hold you. That's right."

"Can't you just get a real job so I can marry you?" she joked, or at least half-joked.

"You sure you'd want to be married again?"

She pulled away to see his face now. Jesse understood things, the weird dynamics among tangled paths, things she hadn't taken the time to explain to him. So it was a sound question.

"Maybe not, then."

"Come with me," he said and climbed back up the grassy hill. He turned and grabbed her hand to guide her in the dark. It was nearly pitch black under the dusky sky and thick canopy of trees. He sat down in a patch of tall grass and motioned for her to join him.

"Tell me what you're doing here, Miss Kerry, this time of night, looking ragged, like you've been chased by the police or something. You're not on your shift?"

"There is no shift," she admitted. "No job. No apartment."

"What's happened?"

The story felt somehow like a movie or at least somebody else's life. A story that couldn't possibly be true, not for her.

Jesse listened. "And this man, Rex, he's meeting you here? At ten o'clock tonight in a place like this? That doesn't feel good to me. Not good at all."

She nodded, soberly. "Is it still open then?"

"The tunnel? Sometimes they close it at eight, other times midnight. Usually eight on the weekend. You can imagine what goes on in there with this crowd."

"So it should be open tonight then." She felt a tingling stir in the pit of her stomach.

Two hours later, hard blades of Bermuda grass poked into her from the holes of a thin blanket. Kerry fumbled with the earpiece connecting her to Jesse by a wireless signal fifty feet away.

"Can you hear me?" Jesse asked.

"So, like, where did you get expensive surveillance equipment like this?"

"Hehe ... I know people," Jesse replied.

"I can hear you fine. I can hear you breathing. I can hear hair growing on your face," she joked.

"How about ambient noise?"

"Not so much." Kerry paused to assess. "Some street noise, traffic."

"Click it up to eight."

From her prostrate position on the grass, Kerry reached down to pull the plastic volume control from the wires wrapped around her wrist.

"You got it?"

"No. I can't see."

"Okay. Push it up a little and I'll test it out."

During the pause, she heard him breathing heavier than before, grunting almost, or struggling.

"You okay over there?" she asked.

More ambient noise on the other end. Car horns, a woman yelling, no, laughing. "Jesus, Jesse ... where are you?" she said in a loud whisper. There was clicking on the other end, and what sounded like the rustling of clothes. What the hell was he doing?

"Jesse!"

Bending down to reach for her watch, her movements stopped at a familiar sound.

"Um ... Jesse can't come to the phone right now."

Chapter Twenty-Eight

That voice, she thought. *Jim Rex.*

"And even if he could, it would be pointless, see, because Jesse probably couldn't talk right now anyway."

"Don't hurt him. I'll give you what you want."

Laughter. "Now before you go giving me orders, I have two questions. One, did you actually bring the object with you?"

"What's two?"

"Answer the question!!"

Kerry paused to think. If he was this intent on getting the object, she had a ball in her court. He wants something from me, she decided. "I have it," she lied.

"Good." Kerry heard him exhale. "Now, question number two," he chuckled, "why ... WHY ... are all the towels in your apartment ... pink?"

That last question, somehow, implied a mental instability that she hadn't quite put together before. He probably didn't take medication for whatever the mania was, bipolar, schizophrenic. Towels.

"Well?"

A rustling somewhere close shook her back to the reality of her location. Golden Gate Park, dark, and now completely unprotected. She knew she had about ten seconds to get out of there.

"Pink," she stalled some more, struggling to get up without betraying her movements. Pulling her legs out of the tangle of wrappings one by one, she scanned the area and saw a light illuminating a concrete walkway up ahead. "What's wrong with pink?"

"It's just that it's, how shall I say it, incongruous with the rest of you," he replied. The ambient sounds behind him were changing now, which meant he was on the move. Less traffic, more voices, crickets, footsteps. *Footsteps.* Jesus! Where is he now?

She was about fifty steps from the lit walkway leading up to Stanyan, her hands completely empty of the blankets that protected her, as well as her backpack. Her backpack was her only means right now. Money, cell phone, ID.

"I want to talk to Jesse," she said, gathering her thoughts. In ten seconds, she was almost back to the blanket, only silence on the other end. Then came a long sigh.

"Huhhhhhhhhh, Kerry Kerry Kerry. I don't negotiate. It's not my way."

She cleared her throat and shook herself to attention. The backpack was visible ahead – a small lump sticking up from the rumpled blanket. "I want to hear Jesse's voice right now, and then I'll give you the object."

Now laughter. "How 'bout I shoot Jesse and come and get it myself?"

Would he do it? She had a feeling about people, sometimes, but there was no reading this guy – a man who in one day took possession of her apartment, had somehow influenced the unraveling of her job, and her life as she'd known it. Would a man like that kill Jesse, an expendable stranger? Now she heard another man's voice in the background. Jesse? And was he about to die right now because of her?

A loud yelp followed a quick *pop.*

"No!!" she screamed and grabbing the backpack, scrambled forward, toward the lit walkway near Stanyan Street. Weird shapes appeared on each side of the path, but there was no time to scrutinize safety. Jesse, she thought. Fifteen steps away now, she heard the traffic, car horns up ahead, a movement in the brush beside her to the right. She twisted to acknowledge it, and when she turned back, there was a large body standing firm in her path. A man, black T-shirt, no jacket.

That smell. I know that smell.

"Hello, Kerry."

Bill Stine. How could he be here? She just stared momentarily, while the shape in the brush to her right rose into the shape of a man. Jim Rex.

"What's going on here?" she said in too loud a voice, tears forming in her eyes. Jim turned quickly, gauging the effect of the commotion, then muttered something to Bill.

Bill raised a hand and grabbed hold of her elbow, pulling her into the Kezar tunnel. It was late. Way too late to be in there, in the dark. But she couldn't think straight now, not anymore, not after so little sleep, so little water, food, and trust. And what about Jesse? Had that been the shot that Rex fired? She was dizzy, too much to consider in too short a timeframe. Gina and Rick both crossed her mind in the few steps toward the tunnel. Jim Rex behind them, Bill kept a grip on her elbow and seemed to notice the tears involuntarily dripping off her cheeks. Kerry stopped walking and yanked her elbow back to look him square in the face.

"Bill? Come on, how could you be here ... with him, that man?"

"You mean with his brother?" Rex piped in with an exaggerated tone.

"Is it true?"

Bill Stine just stared back at her.

"What are you doing here?" she begged.

"No, Kerry, what are *you* doing here?" Bill leaned his face in closer to hers and grabbed her elbow again. "Why didn't you go to that training? Why?" He sighed. "You could've avoided all this, we planned it months ahead. No one was supposed to get hurt. Especially not you."

Kerry wiped more tears from her eyes. "Why do you care what happens to me?"

"Personally, I don't," Rex cut in.

"Because now ..." Bill paused, "you have to disappear."

CHAPTER TWENTY-NINE

A hum from deep in her ear vibrated down the length of her body, fingers, feet, and elbows. She felt strange, a sort of inbetweenness, the way consciousness unfolds in layers when awakening from a deep sleep. The hum grew louder in the form of a rhythm, a pulse, steady as a heartbeat.

A machine, she thought. The engine on a machine. But why was it so loud? I must be close to it, she decided. Or how else would the sound vibrate her whole body? And why was her right cheek so cold?

I'm lying on the floor. Okay, go through the basics. Am I breathing? Check. Move fingers and toes? Check. I can open my eyes, but there's very little light. Next, am I injured?

Slowly, Kerry inched up from the floor, pressing the concrete with one palm and balancing on her left hip. Pain immediately shot down to her wrist and her hip. Looks like that was a yes.

Lying back down again seemed like a sound idea. This time she just opened her eyes, rolled onto her back and surveyed her surroundings. The first light of dawn was sliding in from long vertical openings opposite her about fifty feet away. But the shapes were all wrong to be windows. The air was thick and damp, laden with the odor of chemicals. A warehouse smell. Come to think of it, her right cheek perceived a wetness on the concrete floor.

Oh, God, she thought. Blood? She wiped her cheek with her hand, but it was dry. Was I dreaming?

Am I still?

Chapter Thirty

Grace walked her creaking bones to the clanging phone wearing only a bathrobe, trying not to skid her wet feet on the wood floors.

"Yes?" she answered with an unfriendly clip.

"Gr ... Grayy," someone said. Adrian. "Gracccce. Listen."

My God, she thought. What have they done to you now?

"Have you found her?" Adrian insisted, strain wrapped around each labored syllable.

"Who?"

"Kathleen."

"For God's sake, can you give me ten minutes to take a shower?"

"I *need* you to find her."

"Where you are right now?" she demanded.

"I've told you about her."

Okay, he's ignoring me. Is there a gun pointed at his head? Is he being restrained? "Yes, your prized assistant," she replied, unhappy with how bitter the phrase came out. "I know of her. Where does she live?"

"Ah ... I—"

"Adrian, if you want me to find her, you need to tell me where she is."

"Those flats west of Tutu Corner. The ones with the—"

"Yes, I know, the tacky blue shutters. We've walked past it a hundred times." She sighed. "I'll find her, one way or another."

"You know that guy, Indian Jo, with the terrible cough?"

Pause.

"We bought him lunch that time at Atticus, Number Two Special. Do you remember?"

"Yes." She had no idea what he was talking about, which gave her a sudden certainty that he'd been drugged. "What about Jo?" she pressed, playing along.

"Kathleen lives next door."

Less than an hour later, Grace climbed the blue-painted staircase. Horrible, she thought. Who in God's name would apply blue paint to stairs? Probably the same person who painted the banisters red. Like a bloody American flag.

She fumbled her gloved fingers in her pocket to retrieve the envelope. Kathleen A. Dwyer, 457 University Avenue, Apartment 1103, New Haven, CT 06511.

Up one more staircase and down another, a door stared back with a mini version of a Tibetan prayer flag string tacked across it. Hmm, she thought. Maybe not a complete waste of time after all.

The door clicked open after two polite knocks.

"My God, you're bleeding. What happened to you?"

"I'm okay, just cleaning up," Kathleen replied, both sizing each other up. "I just—"

"How did—?"

"Yes, yes, come in," Kathleen stood back and motioned, "I know who you are." Staring again. "And I have a feeling I know why you're here."

Grace nodded and removed her gloves.

"How did you find me exactly?"

Grace held up the envelope. "Your paycheck was on Adrian's desk." Grace watched the girl take the envelope and took a moment to survey her face. One eye badly bruised, with a crust of dark red blood sealing her left eye closed, another on her left temple and also the corner of her mouth. "Do you need help getting cleaned up? Are you dizzy or anything?"

"I'm all right. Make yourself at home, be with you in a moment."

"Mind if I make some coffee?"

"I just put some on, should be brewing now. Help yourself."

CHAPTER THIRTY-ONE

The blinds, thought Detective Pete Stanton, a thought that scratched at the inside of his brain every time he came to this place. To this particular conference room, within the San Francisco Police Department's third floor, and to this place in an investigation. The juncture where facts, circumstantial or otherwise, failed to prove the truth and incited, almost summoned, the supposition of the impossible. He glanced at his phone, which should have been ringing by now.

"Estevez!" he shouted while banging flat-palmed on the conference room door. "Can't you do something about these blinds?"

The young officer entered a moment later with a stack of files in his arms. "I'm not the Facility Director."

"Who would that be, then?"

Twenty-four-year-old Officer Ricardo Estevez plunked the files on the conference table and stood back a ways from Stanton. "I know, sir. The sunlight glare obscures your view of your whiteboard so that—"

"Can't you just ..." Stanton awkwardly manhandled the bottom and sides of the dry erase board.

Aside from being an overt smartass, Stanton had always thought Estevez was everything he would never be. Sharp-witted, smooth-talking, apathetic, well dressed, and unyieldingly competent, even in the most meaningless situations. Preparing a witness statement or bringing a sobbing woman a cold drink, for someone like Estevez, there would always be a clean glass and chilled water.

"I don't know why they're nailed down, sir," Estevez answered, sitting and arranging the files. "Are you ready to go over these now, or are you not quite finished complaining?"

"Hey!"

Stanton over-gestured toward the white board and shook his head. "How 'bout a drink? Is it five o'clock?" Then he looked at his phone and noted again the call that had not yet come in.

Estevez looked up and shook his head.

"Watch it, Estevez, I'm your superior officer." Estevez had a micro grin on one side of his face. Stanton pulled out the chair next to him, turned it backward, and sat. "I don't need you to spend the next hour reading to me from old police reports."

"So you know what's in them already? Then why was I given this assignment?"

"Because you're new to the department and we like to observe a buddy-system he—"

"Chief Madreas is forcing you to babysit me. I don't need any more friends."

"I'll betcha a hundred bucks that's not true."

Estevez smirked. "And you nurture a lot of close friendships, do you?"

Stanton sighed. "My dysfunctional social—"

"Non-existent?"

"Fine, my social life is none of your concern."

"Don't think you were *my* first choice, either. You're not what I'd call a role model."

Stanton rose and paced past the whiteboard, upon which he had created three columns and four rows. "Partnership, Estevez, is the very essence of police work. I really don't mind mentoring you, and I really don't care how you feel about me. Think of it as if we're just two brains, each looking at a certain scenario from our unique personal perspectives, and then sharing information to reach our desired outcome. As you aptly point out, I've got a jaded view of humanity, and you're just out of college." He put his palms up. "There. We can help each other."

"I don't drink at three in the afternoon, sir," Estevez said, arranging the files in front of him alphabetically.

"What? I don't—"

"Neither do most self-respecting members of society."

Stanton feigned wounding from the drinking crack. But secretly, he liked the attention, and he could feel Estevez's affection for him. Not admiration, certainly. No one here did. Yet he still felt Estevez liked him deep down and hated himself for it.

Stanton slid out of the conference room, filled two cups with stale coffee, and returned to the whiteboard. "What do we got?"

Estevez had laid four 8 x 10 photographs side-by-side on the rectangular conference table with their accompanying file folders. "Four missing."

"From?"

"Here."

Stanton sighed and closed his eyes. "What parts of the city?" He started erasing the white board.

Estevez fumbled with the files. "Ah ..." he mumbled flipping through the first file, "Potrero, Soma, Dogpatch, Potrero."

Stanton thought for a minute, then drew four new columns, writing the neighborhood names at the top of each. "Ages of each victim?"

Estevez piled all four file folders on top of each other. Quickly flipping pages, he scanned with his finger. "Sixty-two, sixty-five, seventy-three and sixty-nine."

"Respectively?"

"Excuse me?" Estevez looked up.

"Are those ages respective to the neighborhoods you just told—"

"Oh, sorry, yeah. That's right."

Stanton recorded the numbers beneath each neighborhood. Then on another part of the white board, he set a small inset city map he picked up from the conference table with a black magnet holding it up. He drew dots on the four neighborhoods.

"What are you doing?" asked Estevez.

"What else do we know about the four?" Stanton paced in front of the board. "Potrero, Soma ..." he mumbled to himself.

"Um ..."

"Who reported them missing?"

"The Potrero woman, reported by her husband. Soma, granddaughter. Dogpatch, wife, and the second Potrero, daughter."

"Okay, so we got four people, three men, one woman, all elderly, all reported missing on the same day." Stanton put his hands on his hips. "That strike you a bit strange?"

"No."

"Really?" Stanton folded his arms.

"People disappear all the time from San Francisco. It's a freakin' melting pot of every conceivable culture and ethnicity, travelers, students—"

Detective Stanton shook his head and ran his fingers through his tangled curly hair. "What's the mean age in an average missing person's case, Estevez?"

"I don't know, most are under the age of twenty-one."

Stanton smiled and lowered his head. "Most are under the age of ten, sadly. What I'm saying is that the unlikely coincidence that four elderly residents of San Francisco all disappear from the same general area of town on the same day is noteworthy."

Estevez examined the wood grain on the conference table. "You think they knew each other?"

"In a sense." Stanton was pacing again.

"What are you thinking?"

"What do you think of when you think of old people, Estevez?" Stanton snapped his fingers. "First thing that comes to mind."

"Nursing homes ..."

Stanton nodded. "Hospitals. The human body gets old and falls prey to age-related degeneration. Brittle bones, respiratory ailments, clogged arteries." Stanton stepped up to the whiteboard and pointed at the map he'd tacked up. Folding his arms, he peered at the four blue dots on the map corresponding to each missing person. "Betcha a hundred bucks there's a hospital in the middle of those four points."

Just then, Stanton's phone lit up. "Finally," he picked it up and eyeballed Estevez. Estevez gestured toward the door with a question, to which Stanton shook his head.

"Detective, this is the Medical Examiner Administrator from the OME's office. I'm returning a call you placed to the chief pathologist."

"Great, thank you for calling. Do you have the status on our autopsy results?"

Silence. "What kind of *status* were you looking for?"

Stanton glanced at Estevez. "Um, internal examination, external examination, toxicology, lab tests, and maybe even something that we detectives call 'cause of death'?"

"No need for sarcasm, Detective. I was just wondering what additional information you were looking for. We sent the autopsy results over to you two days ago. You should have gotten them by now. Yesterday, in fact."

Stanton laid his palm over the phone mouthpiece. "Estevez," he whispered, "any word on that autopsy report I've been waiting for?"

"Yep, got it right here," Estevez answered without looking up from the files. A moment later he looked up. Stanton was shaking his head, palms facing up. "What the fuck?" he lip-synched to the officer. "Um, sorry to keep you on hold. We've had a mix-up here at the precinct, and it appears that we did receive the results but they were routed to the wrong department. I think we've got it all cleared up, though."

Another pause. "I'd be happy to email an unstamped duplicate copy to you, Detective."

"Won't be necessary, thank you very much." Stanton disconnected the call and held out his hand. "File."

Estevez pulled an interdepartmental folder with a manila envelope out from the bottom of his stack with a 'whatever' expression.

Stanton sat opposite him. "What ... exactly ... were you doing with *my* autopsy report?"

"Reading it."

"Reading it," Stanton echoed.

"I'm new to the department and wanted to learn what's in it. What's the big urgency, anyway? The woman's dead, isn't she?"

"So you didn't read the report?"

"I did read it."

"Were your eyes closed? Because the report's inconclusive. We don't know at all whether Rosemary Castiglia's dead. Someone brought what they were calling her body into the ME's office and gave her name, but the person refused to leave *their* name and the dental records were inconclusive. Nothing's tying that particular body to the name Rosemary Castiglia, or not yet."

Estevez closed the file in front of him. "So someone died, but we have no idea who it is?"

"Not conclusively, no." Stanton was reading the report.

"So what's the big rush then?" Estevez asked. This time his face looked more sincere than surly. Stanton made a note of it, took note of the fact that Estevez wasn't always an asshole.

"In a typical case, not that we have any, the timing of the ME's report can be critical. Why? Because building a homicide case is like building a house, and the foundation's set in stone within twenty-four hours after a body's found. The timing of an autopsy report showing cause of death, for example, relates to evidence we find at the scene, and all that relates to our ability to get a court order to search, for example, a defendant's residence. If a toxicology report shows the victim was a drug addict, then we can look for evidence of drug use at the crime scene, in their home, whatever. Any fact that we can match up with a piece of evidence, our house, so to speak, will be airtight."

Estevez had sat back in his chair and blinked at him. "So what's in the Jane Doe report?"

Stanton had his finger on a line on the last page of the narrative. "She was seventy-two years old," he looked down at the page, "and had advanced stage lung cancer."

Estevez nodded with a slight smile. "Did she live—"

"Yep. Kansas and 18th. Potrero Hill."

"Want me to add her file to our list?"

Stanton rose and nodded. "I'm gonna head down to the residence, see if I can get a statement from any family members." With his hand on the door knob, Stanton looked back. "And Estevez?"

"Yeah?"

"Stop opening my mail."

CHAPTER THIRTY-TWO

"Tell me again," Kathleen Dwyer insisted. "His exact words if you can remember."

"Oh, I remember," Grace nodded.

"Hold on," Kathleen rose from the flowered sofa. "My roommate's got a whiteboard in the office."

"That's perfect."

Grace watched Kathleen refill her mug and admitted to herself that she'd been pleasantly surprised by the strong brew. She rose and picked up a marker and wrote in neat, blocky letters:

Indian Jo with the terrible cough
We bought him lunch at Atticus, the #2 Special

"That's it?"

"Well," Grace. snickered, "he said you lived next door as if that was the reason why he was saying it."

"Are you sure it means something else?" Kathleen studied the white board. "Go see your friend Indian Jo, bring him some cough syrup and take him to lunch. And who's Indian Jo?"

Grace shook her head.

"Well, you said you thought he'd been drugged, right?" Kathleen said.

"Even so, he was communicating something very specific in that precise moment."

"I know where the formula is too," Kathleen

added.

"In his safe, right?" Grace assumed. "Did he tell you the combination? He never told me."

"He couldn't remember it himself half the time because he changed it every week, and every time he used it he hid the code someplace else."

"Lord." Grace thought and closed her eyes.

"Refill?" Kathleen said, startling her.

Grace studied her while the young woman poured more coffee into her cup. "I never liked you, you know," she said, uncaring of how it sounded.

Kathleen kept pouring.

"I hated the idea that Adrian might need you more than me."

"You don't beat around the bush, do you?"

"Life is short, and there's even less time to waste than you think."

Kathleen replaced the carafe on the burner and moved to the couch in front of where she'd positioned the whiteboard. "Well, in that case, it looks like you've got a decision to make."

"I've made it," Grace shot back.

"You're giving them the formula?"

"No, of course not," she whispered. "But it will look like the formula."

CHAPTER THIRTY-THREE

Grace pointed to the trickle of blood sliding down Kathleen's right temple.

"Damn it," Kathleen said heading for the hallway.

"Don't you think you should tell me what happened?" Grace bellowed down the corridor toward what looked like a single bedroom and bath. A moment later the girl returned holding a washcloth to her head. She perched uneasily on the edge of the couch.

"I'm in the middle of moving the lab."

"Why?"

"Security. Adrian said it wasn't safe to keep everything there out in the open. So he rented this warehouse in Bridgeport."

"Bridgeport? No wonder you were attacked."

Kathleen shook her head. "It wasn't a thug or something random. The man who broke in knew I would be there, addressed me by name and said I'd been informed to give him something." She gestured with open palms. "I didn't recognize him."

"What was he looking for?" Grace watched a slight smirk crawl across the girl's face. "What?"

"The safe."

Grace nodded.

"I knew the formula wasn't in there but I

pretended to put up a fight to make the man think it was."

"Good girl."

"He found the safe, threw me across a few tables, and walked back to me with a gun pointed at my face."

"Jesus."

"I told him I didn't have the combination ... and I don't. So he took the whole thing with him."

"Just walked out carrying a fifty-pound safe?"

"Probably weighs more than that," Kathleen nodded.

"Was there anything of value in it? Anything Adrian might need? You already said the formula wasn't in there."

Kathleen shook her head and smiled again. "A loaf of wheat bread."

"He keeps bread in his safe," Grace mumbled.

"And specifically wheat bread," Kathleen added. "It turns moldy faster than anything else."

"Indian Jo. So East Indian? Native American?" Kathleen said, watching Grace at the white board.

Grace contracted her lips into a pucker, forcing herself to focus. "I don't know," she admitted. "But ultimately it's all about plants or he wouldn't have given it to me this way."

"Why do you say that?"

"I'm a botanist. Plants are the language I know best."

Kathleen exhaled and crossed her legs. "What if Indian refers to India? Like Ayurvedic plants?"

"That could be," Grace considered, "but I don't think so. It's the word 'cough'. Coughing is an involuntary mechanism of the lungs."

"Okay, how about a Native American herb then? Like feverfew for headaches ..."

Grace nodded. "Or maybe it's not a Native

American herb at all. Maybe just a domestic herb used to treat pathology of the lungs."

"Mullein?"

Grace smiled and raised a brow, starting to comprehend Adrian's faith in her. "Very good. Though I was thinking more along the lines of *Lobelia*."

"I've heard of it. What's its significance?"

Grace leaned forward. "Oh, it's significant. The common name ... is Indian Tobacco."

"Tobacco." Kathleen nodded. "And Jo?"

"Coffee."

"That's what I was thinking."

"Chicory," they said in unison.

Grace picked up a marker. "And it's a stimulant and nerve tonic."

Kathleen gestured toward the board. "What've we got so far?"

Grace started writing:

1. Indian Jo - terrible cough
Lobelia, chicory
2. #2 Special at Atticus

"Is that the BLT?" Kathleen asked.

"That's Number One. Number Two is half a turkey sandwich with a cup of asparagus soup."

Kathleen turned up her nose. "Eww."

"It's highly medicinal," Grace argued.

"In what way?"

Grace folded her arms to think, glancing around the tidy apartment. "Bladder and kidneys, as I recall."

"How does that relate here?"

Grace exhaled. "I'm not sure."

Kathleen changed positions on the couch. "So nothing about asparagus root could treat Indian Jo's lungs?"

"Indian Jo's lungs," Grace whispered. "Guess we haven't yet considered *Indian* asparagus."

"Which is what?"

Grace smiled. "It's what you suggested earlier. Shatavari is an Ayurvedic preparation of wild asparagus root."

"Does it treat lung disorders?" Kathleen queried, wide-eyed.

"Oh yeah ..."

"Okay, so that's three then," Kathleen gestured toward the white board. "Lobelia, chicory, and Shatavari. What does that leave?"

Grace folded her arms and gazed at the board. "Turkey. A half turkey sandwich." She shook her head.

"I need more coffee, be right back."

"Twenty-two hours."

"What?" Kathleen shouted from the kitchen, peeking her head around the corner.

"We've got twenty-two hours to figure this out or Adrian—"

Kathleen put her hands up. "Don't go there, we're being productive and thinking clearly right now. We're simply going to outsmart them." She returned a minute later with the coffee pot and spoons. "What about L-tryptophan? It's in turkey, right?"

Grace nodded, staring at what she'd written on the board.

"Can we relate that to plants somehow?"

"Well ..." Grace tilted her head, "tryptophan's a sedative. That could mean valerian or something, but why even *say* turkey?"

"He didn't," Kathleen clarified. "What he said was Number Two Special.' I'm sure he only meant to point us to the asparagus soup for the Shatavari."

"I'm not sure of that at all."

Kathleen sank to the sofa. "Why not?"

"Because I've known Adrian for twenty years and he's not someone who wastes time on things he doesn't need. He's the most impatient person I've ever met. What's that?" she asked, looking at the bookcase. "What's that book?"

"North American Plants, just a big pictorial index."

"Good – pass it here," Grace commanded and flipped immediately to the index. "T ... let's find three or four medicinal herbs beginning with T ... *Tropaeolum, Tulbaghia...*" she looked up.

"What?"

"Turkey tail mushroom."

"Mushroom? Well, it's a spore, not a plant." Kathleen sipped. "Could that be part of it?"

"Well, of the other two, *Tropaeolum* is," Grace scanned the dense paragraph, "anti-fertility and treats minor skin eruptions. And *tulbaghia* is an aphrodisiac and ... gastrointestinal aid." She sighed and looked around. "Turkey tail mushroom, on the other hand, has anti-tumor and anti-inflammatory effects ... specifically on the lungs!" Grace slammed the book shut. "He's a bloody genius."

"So ..." Kathleen said, uncapping another whiteboard marker. "*Lobelia*," she wrote and said aloud, "Chicory, Wild asparagus, and Turkey Tail mushroom spores."

Grace glanced at the list. "Let me," she said and stood by the board.

Lobelia: Sedative, anti-tumor, lung tonic

Chicory: Stimulant

Shatavari: Anti-tumor

Turkey tail mushroom: anti-poison, anti-inflammatory, anti-metastasis

They heard a helicopter overhead, in combination with honking horns, outside Kathleen's apartment. They both sat back for a silent moment taking in their discovery.

"Is that it then?"

"You'd know better than me," Grace admitted. You administered the formula to your control group, didn't you?"

Kathleen shook her head. "I never knew what was in it, and Adrian said he'd sack me if I ever tried to find out."

"Bloody paranoid. Well, looks like it's true then."

"What?"

"A cigarette that cures lung cancer."

Kathleen looked at the floor. "Shouldn't we go to the police?"

"And tell them what, exactly? I'm being chased by a ninety-pound killer with a red umbrella whom we believe to be part of the pharmaceutical mafia?"

"Pharmaceutical companies make medicine. Their function is our safety," Kathleen said. "Isn't it?"

Grace coughed as she tried to swallow a sip of coffee. She glared at Kathleen and smothered her condescending comment. Of course. She's young, she thought. "You're correct, of course. But forces are at work here. Bringing the police into the mix might endanger Adrian even more. No, it'll be just me out on this limb."

"It'll be both of us, then."

Grace nodded in relief. Then without responding, she grabbed her coat and moved toward the door.

"Where are you going?" Kathleen asked in a desperate voice. "We've only got about twenty hours left!"

"I need to do some research on how to fake a formula that will effect Adrian's release and give us enough lead time before they discover the truth and come after us. I'll be back in an hour, hopefully with more answers than questions." Grace erased the information on the whiteboard before she slipped out the front door.

CHAPTER THIRTY-FOUR

Kerry detected footsteps and heard the creak of the rusted door. Blinking a few times, she saw a pair of shoes she recognized. Bill.

"So where do you keep your glass eye?" she muttered.

"Excuse me?" the man said, bending down slowly.

"Your glass eye. And do you have a wooden leg?

"Why ... are you delirious?" The man almost laughed. "We didn't give you that much."

"You're not a pirate? Maybe you're a woman, then."

"Maybe."

"Well, why not? Everything else you ever told me was a lie."

"Kerry, look. This really has very little to do with you."

"If that were true, I wouldn't be lying on a concrete floor right now. What did you use the apartment for, anyway?" Kerry sat up and squinted against the light behind Bill's shape. "I mean until the part of your plan that included leaving me and letting me think I'd found my own place."

"Not a day went by that I didn't—"

"And the whole lie about flying? How could you have faked that?"

"I didn't."

Kerry lowered her head back down to the concrete. "Just leave me here, I don't care anymore." She rolled her body so it was facing the opposite wall.

"Not everything was a lie," the man replied, and left through the creaky door.

PART THREE

Chapter Thirty-Five

Malik Sharma had always given special attention to the act of hand washing. This was long before he'd even considered going to medical school. How could I be cleaner, he always wondered. Cleaner hands, cleaner thoughts, cleaner past.

"Go wash that filth off you," his mother would say, standing at the sink in the dingy childhood kitchen of Natick, Massachusetts. Yellow, nicotine-stained wallpaper, gray linoleum tile, those 1950s chairs with chrome frames and green vinyl tufted seats.

"The lab's set up for you, doctor," Sophie whispered in the crack of the door of OGI – Ox Group Incorporated – San Francisco's most cutting-edge pharmaceutical laboratory. Malik nodded absently, quickly drawing his attention from her reddish hair back to the milky froth of antiseptic soap rolling happily around his palms. "Have you eaten today?" Sophie asked.

"I'll tell you what he's eaten," Robert, the project lead, chimed in. "Three cups of Oolong tea with two heaping teaspoons of sugar each. That's almost a quarter cup of refined white sugar before breakfast. You'll have no trouble living to at least ... thirty-five. Thirty-six if you're lucky." Robert lowered his head back to the microscope lens.

"Your point?" Malik said.

"I'm your 'buddy', remember?" he said winking at Sophie. "It was Mommy's idea."

"I should think you'd *want* to mentor our young scientists," Sophie replied, then turned to Malik. "Don't listen to him."

From the vantage point of the large metal sink, Malik could see through the large windows into the entire second-floor lab. Robert Yamamoto, his seasoned partner and mentor, had the beginnings of a dowager's hump from perpetually leaning over a microscope, and had hair he was sure had never seen a brush. Four or five lab assistants milled around the front of the lab near Sophie, trying to look busy to keep their prestigious OGI internships. Sophie ran the department and seemed to have intrinsic knowledge about money, salaries, stipends, and grant allocations. Robert was right – Sophie was his mother now, and these people were his family. Maybe the only family he would ever have again.

"Mentoring, right. What is it we were talking about last night?" Robert asked.

"Nothing compelling, I'm sure."

Robert looked up and moved silently toward Malik's workstation.

"The efficacy of process," Malik returned verbatim, "depends entirely on one thing – where the money's coming from."

Robert nodded and smiled, sensing Sophie's disapproval. He turned his back to her. "You're damn right," he whispered. "If someone's paying for a clinical trial, they've got a say in the outcome."

"And if their say contradicts the findings from the control group data?"

Robert raised a brow. "You figure it out."

Malik went to the main computer and jiggled the mouse. "Not while I'm here," he mumbled.

"Let me tell you about someone else who felt like," he stopped, shoo-ed Sophie into the next room, and moved closer to Malik. "Felt like bringing more truth to the process. Lars Stegens. Danish fellow. Had some kind of an accident where he ended up with a bullet through the back of his head."

"Jesus." The grin, Malik noticed, had gone from Robert's mouth. "What am I getting into here?"

"I'll put it this way, buddy. If you've been hired to work for our division of OGI, it's not so you can be a ... scientist."

CHAPTER THIRTY-SIX

Neville Mattson pushed through the glass door of The Daily Grind coffeehouse in New Haven, viewed the line of about twenty people, and instead settled into the only available table. He ceremoniously removed his long, wool coat and sat with a folded newspaper, watching. The paper was really just a prop, he acknowledged to himself, to pretend he felt fine drinking coffee alone in public. To his right – a table of young girls with too much makeup, purposely talking and laughing too loud. On the left – young lovers holding hands. Depressing, he thought. Was he destined to drink coffee alone for the rest of his life?

Looking up, he caught the outline of a handsome woman wearing a cashmere scarf, and if he wasn't mistaken, that was a Burberry coat.

"What a surprise, Mother. I wasn't sure you knew your way out of Bishop Tutu Corner."

Grace leaned over the flimsy chair across from him. "I know how you like to be anonymous, my dear, but I'm afraid the jig is up."

"Pity."

"I know, for example, that you come here every day at 3 p.m. sharp, pretend not to notice the girl in the dreadlocks with the big hazel eyes but draw pictures of her on paper napkins."

Neville blinked.

"And you'd like everyone to think that you work for, what, CIA, MI6? There," she turned and pointed to a four-story glass building across the street. "How's the insurance business?"

"Am I to believe you've got nothing better to do than spy on me?"

Grace lowered her eyes to the marble table, pulled out the chair and sat. "No," she said quietly and looked down. "I need a favor."

CHAPTER THIRTY-SEVEN

"Venti mocha."

"Two or three?"

"Sorry?" Robert Yamamoto replied, squinting.

"Shots."

"Three."

Neville Mattson rubbed his hands together standing behind him in line. "Two of those, please."

"On the same check?" the barista asked.

Robert turned back to see the origin of the voice.

"Separate." Neville squirmed forward an inch to see the man's face. "Sorry ... you work for OGI actually, don't you?"

Robert narrowed his eyes. "Who wants to know?"

"I was behind you in line yesterday and saw you go into that building. I, sort of, wanted to ask you a question."

Robert raised his brow now. "About OGI?" He almost laughed.

"No, no, not about the company. That's all probably confidential," Neville said in a strategic voice.

"On the contrary," Robert Yamamoto crossed his arms and took a step back. "It's all public record. We're just not allowed to talk to anyone about what we do."

"Of course," Neville said.

"Who are you?" Robert asked, in a not-unfriendly tone.

Neville looked down. "Nobody."

Robert chuckled. "I'm sure that's not true. You're interested in science. That automatically makes you somebody," he said with a sly grin now.

"I'm in awe of scientists, to be honest." Neville shuddered under his overcoat and pulled the collar up higher. Feigning discomfort, part of the act.

"Do you work in the—"

"Insurance. Far from science."

"We all make a living somehow."

"Venti mocha three shot, and another ... venti mocha three shot," the barista called out. Robert and Neville both pushed carefully through the crowd to the bar on the left. A police whistle screamed suddenly behind them.

"Jesus," Robert said, squinting. He looked at his watch. "Okay, you've got three minutes," He tore open two sugar packs and poured them into the froth.

Neville cleared his throat. "How much difference does the number of atoms make to the molecular structure of a compound?"

Robert stopped stirring. "And you're a ... claims adjuster?"

"Long story," Neville replied, "but I'm interested in biology, strictly as a layperson, and in particular the biology of plants."

Robert snickered. "Well, that narrow subset could account for, say, all life on earth."

"I suppose, yes."

"Are you a horticulturist?"

"Working on it."

"Where?" Robert took the first sip.

"The county extension office offers classes that you can use for college credit."

"Changing careers midstream?"

"Believe it or not, it's a popular choice. I'm thirty-three, and I'm the youngest one in the class."

Robert nodded, seeming to assess the story.

Neville's stomach tightened when he sipped the over-roasted flavor. He sipped anyway, then took another. Just fit in for God's sake.

"Which plant in particular?"

"Well, orchids. They're a lifelong passion, and I'm trying to cultivate them."

"Cultivate? You mean breed with another species?"

Neville nodded. "Something went wrong."

"Well, in a molecule of water, you need two hydrogen and one oxygen atom. So if you switch the two, meaning one hydrogen and two oxygen, it won't make water, but it'll certainly make something."

Robert looked at his watch. "Three minutes. Here's my card. Maybe we can talk more tomorrow." Robert zipped his jacket.

Neville offered his hand, and when Robert shook it, he noticed the skin was warmer and rougher than he expected.

The card read: Robert Yamamoto, Senior Chemical Pharmacologist, OGI/San Francisco.

Neville poured the coffee out into an open trash can watching Robert climb the stairs toward OGI's main entrance. His hands broke into a sweat as he heard an ambulance siren round the corner behind him.

CHAPTER THIRTY-EIGHT

First, the clothes. Classic gray suit, starched white button-down blouse, white lace push-up bra, flesh stockings, brown croc pumps. All came off in a whoosh on the floor as if she'd been splashed with toxic waste. With deft hands, the woman pulled on black yoga pants, a black zip-up cotton sweater, dark gray socks, rubber boots, and folded the gray costume into a duffel bag. Next, a watch, wire-rimmed glasses, Beretta .9mm semi-automatic pistol, and she sat on the edge of the desk to screw on the silencer.

What have I touched, she asked herself. Umbrella Woman went through an inventory of surfaces while snapping on a pair of cream-colored rubber surgical gloves, which she knew were perhaps the most essential element of her tradecraft. White coffee mug, file folder, door handle, victim's hand, victim's neck, edge of the chair in front of the desk. She pulled a folded cloth from her pants pocket, a mini spray bottle from the side pocket of the duffel, and sprayed the cloth four times. Finishing the sanitization task, she peeled off the rubber gloves, sealed them in a Ziploc bag, and took out her phone.

"Yes?"

"It's Martina Carrera. I'm ready."

There was a pause, during which the woman knew the dispatcher was calling in another specialist, like her. Well, not like her exactly, but a trusted member of their cadre, another nameless soldier. There were so many.

"Are you in place?"

"Yes."

"Is it clean?"

"Yes," she replied, glancing around the perimeter of the room again. It was getting dark, she reminded herself, and pulled out the mini Mag-Lite from her bag.

"Five minutes."

"All right. Will there be a need for an additional resource?"

The man on the other end of the phone cleared his throat, obviously an indication of his displeasure at the question. "Why would that be necessary?"

The woman sighed. "I'm on the 35th floor, that's why."

Another pause. Martina saw the lights coming on in the office building across from her. The scope and tripod were in place by the window, horizontal blinds pulled to the perfect tilt.

"We've got two, five minutes from now."

"Usual protocol?"

"Usual protocol."

While she waited for the inevitable "Coffee shop delivery" or "UPS" on the other side of the door, Martina pulled a red umbrella from the duffel bag, opened it, set it on the credenza by the window, and began focusing the telescope down at the street level where Chapel meets College in New Haven's Bishop Tutu Corner.

Chapter Thirty-Nine

The heavy steel door clanked shut and the room looked lighter. Maybe not a room, according to her definition of the word. Was it morning?

Kerry's stomach growled, and a growing awareness of herself and surroundings revealed chapped lips and a vague memory of drinking water at some point. Had he given it to her? Had someone?

Get up, her inner voice commanded.

Someone breathed in another part of the cell, she was certain of the sound. "Who's there?" she whispered. Now it was dark again. Where was the light from before? It hadn't been an actual light source because there was no reflection, and she couldn't make out anything specific. Had her eyes adjusted that quickly?

Assess, she narrated to herself. She moved her fingers, rubbed her hands together, wiggled her toes, shifted her hips, drew in a deep breath and reached up to feel her face and hair. No blood, no wounds readily apparent. She was still wearing the same dirty clothes, sneakers with no socks, and she could still detect a faint fragment of the gardenia-scented lotion she'd put on after a shower, whenever that was. Can I stand? she wondered. Should I?

Her hands fumbled around the floor. Cold,

smooth concrete. Not bricks. The surface was even and not porous. She crouched with both feet flat on the floor and felt around her body. Nothing.

Someone breathed again, this time louder. It seemed about ten feet away. "Is someone there?" Kerry said louder this time.

A voice sounded in the form of a moan. The pitch was low, but she sensed it was a woman.

"I'm ... here," Kerry said. "I'll keep talking. I know you're over there and can hear me. Say something when you feel ready." She waited. "Okay?"

Silence. Then a gurgling sound revealed someone trying to clear their throat.

"You don't have to speak, it's okay." Think, Kerry. "Can you knock? Like, knock once on the floor if you can hear me?"

Knock.

Kerry felt a tiny light in the center of her heart. I'm not alone in this creepy place. "Are you hurt?"

Knock.

"Bleeding?"

No response.

"Okay, you're not sure. Do you know how long you've been here?"

Nothing.

"More than a day?"

Knock.

"Are you—"

Throat clearing sounds. Then a soft, gravelly voice. "The sun's set six times," came the soft, gravelly voice, the voice of a woman.

"I can't see a thing in here," Kerry said, incredulous.

"You'll adapt."

Kerry sighed, taking this in. She blinked her eyes a few times. They weren't adapting at all so far. "Have you had any water? Or eaten?"

"Once a day a tall man brings me a sandwich and

bottled water."

"Does he say anything?"

"I asked a lot of questions the first day. Then," the voice cracked, and the woman sniffed.

Kerry placed her palms on the cold concrete floor. "What's that vibration I'm feeling?"

"BART train. There's a chime, too, on the hour."

"Does it repeat?" Kerry said. "Three chimes for three o'clock, four for four o'clock."

"One chime. On the hour."

A church, she wondered to herself. "Somewhere near Bernal Heights there are noon church bells every day, but not on the hour. I'd guess ... St. Paul's."

"That's the Mission," the woman said.

"That'd put us near 25th and Mission, but it's too quiet around here for that neighborhood."

A metal clang sounded from the other side of the cell. Kerry recoiled, expecting the door to open. It opened, but no light this time. Was there another door?

"Back here," her cellmate whispered. Kerry felt a bony hand grip her left sleeve pulling her away from the clamor. "No sound," the woman said.

Kerry obliged, instinctively curling her knees up to her chest with her back pressing against something solid and cold.

"Uh ..."

"Was that you?" Kerry whispered.

The woman put a finger over Kerry's lips.

"Mayyyyynaaaaa ..."

Mayna.

"May ... naaaa ... ack" the new voice cracked, ending in dry coughs.

I know that name. Kerry closed her eyes and slid one hand up to rub a sharp pain in her temple. Her cellmate's hand clasped around her elbow.

"What's the matter?" she asked.

Kerry opened her eyes, and to her surprise, she could see something – fuzzy shapes in the darkness. The woman's thin face and long, stringy hair, a sliver of light toward the ceiling and then, gradually, the shape of a boarded-up rectangular window.

"Mayyyynaaaa," the haunted voice moaned again, sending an odd vibration up and down Kerry's spine.

Chapter Forty

Grace knew the psychology of color and texture, the effect of nubby raw silk versus the certainty of shiny satin. It was 7:50 p.m. – just over two hours till the designated meeting. Her phone rang as she slid on a gray satin blouse.

Kathleen. About time. She'd left a message over an hour ago.

"Hello there," Grace answered.

"Hi, I'm sorry," Kathleen said, breathless. "Just got out of class. Are you home?"

"Just getting dressed."

"Good, I'm on Kensington now. Be right there."

Grace wrinkled her eyebrows. "You're on my street?"

"Well, yeah," Kathleen chuckled slightly. "You're home, right?"

"I mean, it's fine, yes, park in the drive, there's room. I'm just surprised is all."

Pause. "By what?"

"Pardon?"

"Surprised by what?" Kathleen persisted.

Grace struggled with her next words, applying the usual amount of caution to word usage indicative of her English heritage, while feeling frustration buzz in the center of her palms. She slowly walked down the stairs, while still talking. What was Kathleen doing here? "I've been wanting to talk with you this evening. I've completed my research, and—"

"Grace, I know that. I got your note. Remember?"

"What note?"

Pause. Then, "You left me a note that your formula was ready and to meet you at your house at eight." Kathleen pushed the doorbell. "This is me."

Grace jumped at the sound of it, grabbing the handrail and, in so doing, dropped the phone, which tumbled down the stairs and bounced on the wood floor. The doorbell sounded again. Grace reached a trembling hand to pick up the phone, all the while glancing around the room. She stood up to turn the door handle and smiled as large as her mouth would permit at the sight of Kathleen.

"Come in, quickly," she gestured and pulled Kathleen close, wrapped her arms around her and put her lips awkwardly to Kathleen's ear. "I never left you a note," Grace whispered, maintaining her grip around Kathleen's body. "Turn around, go start your car, pull up in front of the house and unlock the passenger side door. We're being watched."

Kathleen had parked what looked like a fifteen-year-old Honda at the end of the walkway. Thank God, Grace thought, deciding not to look behind her as she entered the vehicle. She got in and immediately put on her seatbelt and locked the door.

"What's going on?" Kathleen demanded.

Grace took a moment to breathe and collect herself and leaning to the right so she could see behind them. "That's good, it's a Sunday night so not much traffic."

"And why is that good?"

"Because if we're being followed, another car on the road will be more obvious."

"Jesus, Grace! I had a note thumbtacked to my

front door with my name written in a big black marker. I guess ... it scared me. Though now that I think about it, that's not really your style. But the handwriting, though—"

"How would you know my handwriting?' Grace turned quickly.

"Drawing on my white board the other day. You're a lefty. So's the author of this note." Kathleen pulled the crumpled page from her pocket and handed it to her.

I've completed the formula – meet me at my house at eight tonight. 147 Kensington.

"Where am I going, by the way?" Kathleen asked.

"Toward the university, someplace public with lots of people."

"I thought you said it would be easier to spot a tail if—"

"Tutu Corner, then left on College."

"We're on College," Kathleen corrected her.

"I mean, Chapel. All right, I did finish the formula, and the handoff is at ten. Tonight."

"Where?"

"I don't know yet. Someone will call me." Grace kept her eyes on the rearview side mirror and saw a car, about ten car lengths behind them, with smallish round headlights. An older car, European, she surmised. "Turn right here, quickly, no turn signal." She wrestled her phone out of her coat pocket and turned up the volume.

Kathleen obeyed and turned down a narrow residential street called Larkin.

"Good. Keep driving, not too fast."

"Do you see someone?"

"I'm not sure. I ... wait ... yes. The headlights. Damn!"

"Someone's tailing us?"

"Okay, let's do another turn to be sure. This time, two quick turns. This is Larkin, so ... at this stop sign, make a quick right, and then an immediate left. It's the same street, just a little jog along the way."

Grace stared into the side mirror as they turned left on the second half of Larkin. No lights yet.

"Here, pull over quickly and turn off your lights. The engine too. Quick!" One car drove past them, but it was a huge SUV. Not the old Jag or smaller vintage European she expected. "Now scooch down low, so your car looks vacant."

Kathleen pulled the emergency brake after turning off the engine and slid down with her head in the center console.

Grace, half lying across Kathleen's bucket passenger seat, bent her legs into Kathleen's chest and rested her head on the passenger door. At this angle, she had a clear view of the side mirror as well as any cars headed down this part of the Larkin. Two pedestrians walked arm in arm down the center of the street. A woman was laughing, her mate nuzzling her neck. "I think we're clear, I don't see the car."

"Did you ever?"

"Not specifically, no, but the headlights. I know that shape. An eighties-era Porsche Carrera or a perhaps a Jaguar." Grace sat up slowly, bending her knee on the edge of the seat. "We can't go home, you know," she said. "Neither of us."

"Ever?"

Grace shook her head. "Who knows."

Chapter Forty-One

Mayna, Kerry thought and shuddered. How could this be?

Her cell partner slid across the concrete and whispered. "They're coming. Pretend to be asleep."

Kerry quickly rolled to her left side with her face on her hands, eyes closed. Mayna. An old woman she barely recalled, but yet *did* recall suddenly and only now, from early childhood. A Southerner with an open face and stooped back, who always smelled like cinnamon. Mayna, she repeated to herself, chasing the shadow of a memory. There were two, she thought with sudden clarity, having no idea of what this meant. Two? Two Maynas? Two old women taking care of her? Wiping her mouth after a meal, walking among the shadowy hedges in Foxmoor Park. There were two. Two what?

Her cell partner's hand gripped her wrist. "They'll give you a sandwich and ram a pill in your mouth," she whispered. "Hold it on the roof of your mouth with your tongue and then pretend to swallow it, there'll be a flashlight on your face so make it look real." The woman slid away and collapsed in the other part of the cell as the barrel lock clanked open.

The cell *felt* darker than before. With a boarded-up

window, the perception seemed ridiculous. Only hints of beige and gray stretched across the dark concrete at certain times of the day.

Her cellmate, named Jodi as she had learned, hadn't spoken a word since they'd brought her back from the last round of interrogation. Kerry knew they'd beaten her. She hadn't seen anything, but the movements it took for her to change positions on the floor told of a body badly brutalized. She'd been monitoring her breathing for what felt like several hours – sleeping. This was good. But even so, she felt absolutely no closer to her end goal of escape.

CHAPTER FORTY-TWO

"Are you prepared for this?" Kathleen asked in a careful voice.

I will be, Grace thought. "Warehouse."

"What?"

Grace turned to her. "Warehouse is next." She observed Kathleen's confused expression. "Isn't that where you moved everything?"

Kathleen nodded.

"And didn't you tell me that Adrian made you move your office to a warehouse on the edge of town?"

"You mean the hood," she clarified. "Yeah, it's near Bridgeport."

Grace combed her fingers through her hair, flinching at the sound of pedestrians outside the car coming up behind them. "Okay. Let's back up a minute. Where are all your files? You did *keep* files, I hope?"

Kathleen nodded slowly. "Yes."

"And the clinical trials. You presumably have, like, notes, yes?"

Silence.

Grace closed her eyes and drew in a long, slow breath. "You didn't do ... I thought you said ..."

"We did them, yes." Kathleen cut in, her voice

louder now.

"Institution?" Grace demanded.

"Yale Medical School."

"Sponsor?"

"I don't know his name."

"Where's he from?" Grace pressed, surprised at how easily she'd slipped into the role of interrogator.

"Where, as in what city?"

Grace bit her lip. "What company."

"Adrian paid for everything himself."

"Okay ... so no sponsor."

Kathleen shook her head with a resigned shrug. "We had one, sort of. It was more of a verbal commitment."

"That means you didn't have one."

"But—"

"Investigator?" Grace went on.

Kathleen stared at the steering wheel.

"Moderator?"

"See, you have to understand ..."

Grace waved her hands back and forth in the air. "Look. Whatever you two think you were doing, it wasn't a clinical trial nor was it explicitly clinical research. You were experimenting on subjects."

"That's not fair!" Kathleen said. "Adrian put his whole life on the line for these trials. He personally took responsibility for everyone in the control group, and—"

"It's only a clinical trial if it's overseen by an accredited medical institution. If it has an impartial investigator. If it's properly funded and if you've got absolutely flawless documentation chronicling every stage, every reaction, every word the control group utters in response to the drug."

"That's if you intend to publish your findings," Kathleen replied, then lowered her head. "You and I both know that Adrian never expected to get that far."

"Regardless, you still need FDA approval to make it publicly available." Grace looked down at the floor mat of Kathleen's car. "Maybe he never intended for that either," she mumbled, glancing again outside the car. "Okay," she said with another heavy sigh. "Do you have *any* documentation?"

"The patient files are meticulous. Signed and notarized releases, extensive patient medical histories, weekly labs and screens, patient counseling—"

"Who did that?"

"Me, I'm licensed."

"As what?"

"LPC. I got my degree in social work, and I'm a Ph.D. candidate in clinical psychology. Adrian's my, well, internship."

God help you, Grace thought. But she knew Kathleen was amply qualified before even asking. She should apologize right now for the third degree. She understood Adrian, maybe better than anyone.

"If it had been you, would you have done it differently?" Kathleen restarted the engine.

"Yes. Maybe. Damn, I don't know," Grace admitted.

"I looked into getting a monitor, an investigator, and typically trials are overseen by Big Pharma itself, and they appoint an investigator of *their* choosing, who they know will essentially rush through the process, ensure the desired outcome, people they have stuff on, people they know and can be bought."

"That's a very bleak outlook."

"Come on, Grace, you live in the same world I do. You actually believe in the efficacy of drug trials?"

"Some, absolutely," Grace argued.

"We're not talking about fucking cough medicine, get real!" Kathleen closed her eyes momentarily. "These are anti-carcinogen cigarettes. Do you realize—"

"Of course I realize. Why do you think I faked the formula? They'll likely kill Adrian anyway, but we'll at least slow them down a bit."

Kathleen nodded, driving forward and turning at the stop light ahead. Grace watched her check the rearview mirror.

"See something?"

"I don't know, maybe nothing." Kathleen pulled up to a storage facility and parked and turned the motor off. "I'll be right back."

"I don't need all your paperwork, just ..." Grace called to her out the window.

"Don't worry, there's not that much anyway. It's in two big white binders. I know just where they are," Kathleen replied and headed toward the storage front door.

Grace instinctively slid into the driver's seat after Kathleen exited the vehicle. She began counting seconds ... ten one thousand, eleven one thousand, twelve one thousand. And she rolled down both front windows. What am I listening for, she wondered, but she knew she was afraid of everything right now and awareness would help control her fear.

Now they had an actual formula to deliver with patient records from what version of clinical trials they'd performed, in exchange for Adrian's life. She thought of her horticultural students now, her curriculum, her classroom. It all felt so far away.

Just then, she heard a *pop pop*, the distinctive metal sound, then three more in a sequence. Grace nimbly pushed the key into the ignition and backed the car out toward the street, never taking her eyes off the door to the storage building. A few more inches and she'd be on the street, driving away, safe from harm. Was Kathleen dead? How could she possibly leave now?

CHAPTER FORTY-THREE

She heard them mumbling to each other, her cellmate and the woman on the other side of the cell bars. Was it even English? Kerry had fallen asleep while they were talking. And now she heard Jodi's gasps of pain as she slid back to her place from the other woman's cell.

"What were you talking about?" Kerry pressed. "You were making a lot of noise over there."

"Come close," Jodi whispered with her hand outstretched. It was hard to make out, but her fist was closed. Kerry crawled toward her, painfully digging her knees into the hard floor, and reached up to feel for Jodi's hand. Awkwardly in the dark, their hands barely touched, and Jodi grabbed Kerry's hand with both of hers. She held her hand open and placed something cold in the center of her palm. A small object that felt like metal.

"She said to give this to you," Jodi said.

Kerry appraised the object with her fingers. A nail. "What the hell is this for?"

"Can you do it?" Jodi breathed.

Kerry stayed silent, wondering if she understood the situation correctly. They want me to kill our captor, she decided, and knew she probably couldn't do it, but a weapon like a nail evened the playing field a bit. The man would come with the tray in about half an hour, she decided, sliding the nail into her jeans pocket. What have I become?

Grace left the car half sticking out into the street when she turned off the ignition and crept out through the driver's side. Door wide open, she ran among the small sapling pines growing haphazardly in odd clumps in the front of the property. No more pops, in fact, nothing could be heard outside save for the steady drone of traffic noise from I-95.

I'm walking around in the dark, alone at night, in Bridgeport. Brilliant.

She rounded the entrance and peered cautiously first before moving another inch. The front door was propped open by something unnaturally blocking its closure. She took two steps toward it – a chair toppled on its side. Jesus, Kathleen, she thought, silently praying for a miracle. Then a thought infiltrated her mind, the kind of thought whose presence upsets the balance of every other thought or belief you might hold. Why hadn't the shooter come outside looking for her? Obviously, these were the same people who'd been tailing them all night, so they must have known they'd arrived together. So why weren't they coming after her? Unless they'd been after Kathleen all along, and not her after all.

Deep breath, she thought to herself and pushed through the awkward doorway. "Kathleen? Are you there?"

"Mmm, here."

Grace slapped her hand to her chest. "Thank God! Are you all right?"

"The binders," Kathleen replied. "They're in the gray cabinet."

Grace moved further inside. "Is there a key?"

"They're not locked. There's two large white binders. Go put them in the car and drive back to your house and wait for me there."

Knowing they weren't supposed to be going back

there, Grace instead stepped over the paperwork and toppled chairs toward the voice. Lying prostrate, Kathleen's head was turned to the right, and her upper back was moving up and down too quickly. She moved closer and saw a dark pool under her chest. "My God, you're shot."

"No, it's a flesh wound, just from my shoulder, I'll be all right. I'll call 911. Get those binders and get out of here, now," Kathleen mumbled.

Grace put her palm on Kathleen's back. She felt cold. "Did he place an ad?" she said gently.

"What?"

"He placed an ad for a graduate assistant, didn't he?" Kathleen looked up, searching her face.

"Are you sorry you answered it?"

"Not a bit," Kathleen replied. "What time is it?"

Just then, Grace's phone rang. Both women looked at one another and Kathleen nodded. Grace slid the green arrow to answer.

"Do you have it?" said the voice of Umbrella Woman.

"I will, by the time frame we agreed upon."

"You've got eight hours."

"Actually, eight hours twenty minutes," Grace retorted. "Unless something's changed."

"You have till eight tomorrow morning. Call this number. You'll get further instructions then."

"Is Adrian all right?" Grace asked unexpectedly.

The woman snickered. "Well, I wouldn't say that, necessarily." The line went dead.

Grace called for an ambulance. She then closed the warehouse door, sat on the floor beside Kathleen and put her paisley scarf up under her Kathleen's body to absorb the blood she had lost. She wondered how hard she'd need to push to stop the bleeding.

"Go!" Kathleen commanded. "Why aren't you leaving?"

"Be quiet and rest," Grace said dismissively. "People die from less than this."

"The more people who are here when they arrive, the more chance for questions and delays. We can't afford any more variables right now." Kathleen reached her hand up to squeeze Grace's wrist. "You know I'm right. Now get out of here and go home, take the binders with you. Please!"

Grace hesitated before rising to her knees. "You know what they'll do, don't you?"

"They won't kill him, don't worry. They need him."

"But if they release him and get his formula, they'll publicize it and take all the credit."

Kathleen forced herself to turn sideways and pulled herself upright, balancing on the good arm. "I've already thought of that. Can you bring me my backpack?"

Grace took off toward the car and returned in what seemed like a second. She placed the pack on the floor and unzipped it.

"Once you're sure he's been released, text me. And we're gonna do our own publicity."

"How?"

"Social media blitz," Kathleen replied with a grin. "Facebook, Twitter, blogs, leave that to me."

"But will you be, you know ..."

"From my iPad. I can do it from here or the hospital or wherever I am. It's been planned for weeks. Now go! Drive straight home and stay there. I'll text you to let you know where I am and my hospital room number and stuff."

Grace stood up and headed toward the door, listening for an ambulance. Where was the shooter now? Something just didn't feel right about leaving her there.

She started the car engine, and a chill went through her as she realized why.

"Kerry."

It was the mumbling woman from the other cell. Kerry heard Jodi crawl across the concrete to her. Judging by the time it took for her to get back, the other cell was about fifteen feet away, and their cell seemed about twenty or twenty-five feet long.

"Why are *you* here?" Kerry asked, not planning for it to sound so suspicious.

"I'm a witness. I saw the man kill someone. Now I'm what you'd call a loose end," Jodi replied. Kerry waited to see if there was more.

"He'll be coming again soon," Jodi confided. "There's a staircase down the hall on the right, and a door that's stuck, but you can push through it if you have the time and strength."

"She told you that? The other woman?"

"That's not all," Jodi continued. "She said you know the name 'Mayna'."

Kerry closed her eyes and saw lights behind her lids. Blinding lights and her neck felt suddenly hot.

"She said to give you this," Jodi said and crouched beside her, reaching out a hand.

A metal clang sounded against the concrete floor, the lock being pulled and the door opening. The scrape of metal against metal. It's time, she thought.

Like watching a movie of herself on a big screen, Kerry rose in slow motion and bent down to pick up what had fallen from Jodi's hands. A necklace of some kind, which she quickly crammed into her front pocket as she slid out the nail. With careful steps, she walked ten paces to what she remembered would be the space behind the huge metal door. Pressing her body flat against the concrete cell wall, even her heels touched the cold surface behind her. By the echo of his voice against the floor and ceiling, she estimated his height to be slightly less than six feet. Was she the kind of person who could plunge a rusty nail deeply into a stranger's eye? The question proved a worthy contemplation, which she continued to ponder as her right hand rose up toward the man's head.

Door completely opened now, a bright light from the hallway lit up the interior of the space, showing the man's outline, his tray held by both hands, and the woman in the secluded cell.

Her hair. Kerry blinked but couldn't pull her gaze from the woman's particular shade of light brown hair. The way it grew on her head. Something ...

Shaking herself to attention, with her right foot Kerry creaked the door closed, blocking out the light from the hallway.

"What the hell—" the man said, setting down the tray on the floor and turning with a jerk. Kerry kicked upward under the man's chin, causing a loud clap and cry as the man fell back. Both hands on the floor, the man pushed up to rise, when Jodi tackled him from behind. Nail in hand, Kerry reached down and, aiming for his eye, dragged the sharp point across the man's cheek and quickly stood.

"*Ahhggtt!*" The man shouted and grabbed Kerry's forearm, yanking her over his shoulder to the floor. His arms were thick, bare, and solid; there would be no chance of overpowering him. Using her only advantage – size – she curled her legs up to her chest and squirmed between his outstretched legs and rose behind him now. Jodi was in the doorway, she could just make out her silhouette. Kerry lifted her right foot and kicked the man hard in the side near his kidney, then kicked again, harder the second time. Jodi reached out for Kerry's hand and pulled toward the doorway. They both closed and shoved on the metal door and pulled the latch across the threshold, heading for the staircase. It was where they expected, but the stuck door had been propped open.

"What about her?" Kerry asked, looking back toward the cell.

"There's no time," Jodi said. Kerry looked into the open doorway and realized that they had but one choice right now.

CHAPTER FORTY-FOUR

Even in times of chaos, Grace Mattson lived an orderly life. It's how she'd been trained – as an Englishwoman, and as the daughter of a military commander. She awoke, panicked, at 7:05 a.m., as panic seemed to be the only common thread holding her life together lately. Her phone still showed no return call or text from Kathleen's number. She pressed redial again and heard it ring eight times with no answer.

Even so, she was prepared. Coffee, set on the brewer before bed, was filling in the carafe, while she took an abbreviated shower and toweled off her hair. As was customary, her bed was already made and clothes properly laid out upon exiting the bathroom post-shower, which shaved off precious minutes.

Taking the first sip, she sat admiring the four identical white binders. The bottom two, the originals, had been marked with a barely perceptible red dot in the center of the last page. And the top versions were, by any reasonable gaze, exact duplicates. Except that the contents of chapters three through ten were lab results from a different trial entirely – the clinical research for a nasal decongestant already on the market. How did she expect to get away with this? Because she knew what a clinical pharmacologist would look for: consistency between chapter titles and the table of contents, patient names, locales, and research assistants. Not individual lab results or specified feedback.

She checked her phone log again for Kathleen's number. Nothing since last night. She'd already called every New Haven hospital. And by her estimation, this fact left only three possibilities: phone was out of battery, the ambulance never came, and Kathleen was now dead from excessive blood loss, or else her 911 call had been intercepted and the ambulance that picked up Kathleen ... wasn't an ambulance at all.

Shoulder wound, Grace told herself. Not stomach, chest, no vital organs.

7:48 a.m.

Nothing looked out of the ordinary from the kitchen windows. She moved to the living room and looked out past the fireplace. Mr. Whidmore mowing his lawn once again before eight o'clock. Punishable by death, she thought. Upstairs now, she peeked between the slats of the vertical blinds up and down Kensington. No car with killers crouched under the dash, or men in trench coats reading a newspaper upside down.

7:59 a.m.

She sat on the fireplace ledge now, where she always seemed to find herself during critical moments in her life. Divorce. Appointment to Tenure. Neville's ...

Neville! She hadn't thought of him all night. He'd left no note as to his whereabouts. And now it was 8:01 a.m. Bugger, she thought, fumbling for her phone log. Umbrella Woman picked up on the second ring.

"I don't appreciate being kept waiting," the woman said in a practiced monotone.

"I'll speak with Adrian now, please."

There was a pause on the other end, followed by, "Perhaps you've misunderstood ..."

"Oh, I don't think so. I've got something you want very much, even need. And I'm prepared to give it to you when I've verified that Adrian's still alive."

"Bring what we want to the mini Chapel on south campus, nine o'clock. If you're not there on time—"

"Oh yes, of course, Adrian dies," Grace said. "Well, I think you're likely to kill him anyway so I either talk to him now, or you don't get what you want."

Grace started counting back from ten. After a moment of silence, she heard a rustling and then a familiar voice. "Grace."

"Are you all right?" she said, feeling her pulse speed up. His voice sounded odd, and his breathing was heavy.

"It's over," Adrian said.

As she drove, Grace pressed speed dial number three on her phone. Neville.

"Mother," Neville said after one ring. "To what do I owe the pleasure?"

"Hello, Neville."

"I know that tone," her son replied.

"What?"

"That's your 'I need a favor' voice."

Grace sighed, slowing down for a red light.

"What is it this time? Run a wire tap? Hack into the Pentagon? You seem to think I've got supernatural powers."

"I need you to follow someone."

"Who might that be?"

"Me," Grace replied. "I'm en route to campus. Know where Little Chapel is on south campus?"

"I believe it's called the Children's Chapel, but yes. That's where you're meeting them?"

"What, have you cloned my cell phone now?"

"Let's just say I know things."

"Good, that could be helpful. I'm driving my own car. After the meeting, I need you to follow them."

"Whom?"

Grace chuckled. "I didn't catch her name and address. She left me a note at the house. You said you saw her ..."

"Oh, right, of course. And what's the duration of this assignment? You looking for all-night surveillance, I suppose? I love the tacit assumption that I've got absolutely nothing better to do with my time."

You don't, she thought, but held her tongue. "Let's call it a treasure hunt, and I'm looking for where this step leads next."

It was likely that she was being monitored at this very moment, even while driving, and that her mobile signal was being monitored via satellite surveillance. So right about now, three blocks from campus, she'd need to scrutinize her every minute decision.

Parking. Faculty lot, or street? If street, left or right side? And on which side of the park? Bishop or Tower?

Paperwork. Should she carry the binders and the formula envelope with her, or keep them in the car until she verified Adrian's well-being?

Chapel. Inside, or out? Pews, or in the front of the altar? Would they be insolent enough to bring weapons into a church? Definitely yes.

Timing. It was 8:35 a.m. and the meeting was for nine. Should she go now and wait, or stay in the car wringing her hands for the next twenty-five minutes? They're probably watching me through binoculars, she decided, and pulled into a parking space on Bishop near Chapel. She stared at the white binders, three hours of painstaking treachery, and picked them up before leaving the car.

"Ms. Mattson!"

Good Lord, she thought, one of her horticulture students. The giggling blonde girl who always sat in the back chewing gum.

"You haven't had office hours in two weeks. Are you all right?"

The young woman stood head to head with Grace on the mowed lawn of the university chapel, wearing an oversized white frock and an ill-fitting hat perched on uncombed hair. The perfect picture of haphazard beauty tolerated only in youth.

"Not really, no," Grace replied honestly. "Would you excuse me?"

It was a rhetorical question asked only out of the relentless politeness of English breeding. Grace nearly shoved past her and strode across the large green expanse. Office hours, she thought. Am I still even a teacher here? With a quick glance at her watch, she observed the uncharacteristic emptiness of the chapel park and felt, suddenly, queasy. Beautiful, sunny day, a weekday no less, and not one student on the lawn. She stepped, cautiously, across the grass, slowly circumambulating the structure, watching each entrance for activity.

8:58 a.m.

Grace entered Little Chapel and paused to let her eyes adjust to the dark. Facing a vessel of holy water, she thought about dipping her fingers into the cool liquid, then her mind stopped midway. Neville! Where was he? She'd completely forgotten to check the lot for his car before leaving her own. Would he be there when she, or they, came out?

Somewhere up ahead, the clunk of heavy shoes echoed against the beautifully tiled floors. Grace looked up but saw no one. Heart thudding, she reached for the holy water and made a panicked wet cross on her forehead.

"Not a bad idea," came the woman's familiar voice, "in the circumstances."

Grace sucked in a gulp of air and slapped her palm to her chest. "Ms. Carrera. What a lovely blue you're wearing," she said, delighted by the woman's tiny facial twitch at the sound of her name. "Yes, I know who you are," Grace clarified.

Martina Carrera, Umbrella Lady, motioned for her to follow. "It's not a secret."

"No? Then why aren't you listed on the Herran-Quain website on the Board of Directors or masthead pages? I found you online somewhere else, on the—"

The woman stopped walking and turned to face Grace directly. "I'm many things to many people," she said, then continued walking. They passed through the length of the chapel, and up four stairs to another level. Every part of the décor looked beige – floors, ceiling, walls, even the scant furniture that pressed against the walls of the corridor. The woman stood, now in front of a tall door and knocked twice.

CHAPTER FORTY-FIVE

At the end of the hallway, Kerry and Jodi peered at the steel door, which they were warned would be stuck but instead had been propped open, almost waiting for them. And on the other side of it, a reflection of sunlight warmed a paint-chipped wall to an almost comforting sepia tone. Kerry stared at the strange hue, wondering how far they'd get, wondering when her next meal would be, and wondering about the last time she had felt at home.

"Come on," Jodi said, fumbling up the stairs. Kerry glanced up and then behind her. Bill Stine, the man she had loved for five years of her life, would be looking for her, to take something she didn't want to give and very likely to kill her. Jim Rex had planned to take over her apartment when she was out of town. How long had the plot been in service before execution? How long had she unknowingly been a pawn in Bill's larger scheme? Played the part of a loving wife while he was ticking off days on an invisible calendar, and to what end?

"Get back!" Jodi yelled, reaching to stretch her arm across Kerry's head and torso, while shots flew over their heads echoing like cannon fire in the narrow stairwell. Bits of paint and plaster clapped down over their heads. Kerry crouched, keeping her hands caped over her skull, thinking.

That woman. Why was she in a separate cell? Was she dangerous? And how had she come to utter that inexplicable word, Mayna? The name felt like buttered cinnamon toast on a snowy morning. Something protective, like a guardian. Not something – someone.

Jodi climbed the top stairs and peered left into a dark corner. A hand reached out and, in a split second, grabbed Jodi's shoulders, pulled her torso forward, turned her around and jabbed a pistol in her back.

Jodi screamed, and moved her arms up and then quickly down again. Kerry watched as though from a protective bubble, just observing the scene without intervening. Jodi's arms helped her to get her balance. In one motion she bent her body forward, throwing her hands up to yank her assailant off his feet, took hold of the back of the man's jacket and flipped him over her head.

Nice, Kerry thought, automatically retreating two steps. She weaved around the wrestling bodies, almost forgetting that there was a gun in there somewhere. The man, tall and fast, drew his fist up to Jodi's face and she tumbled back against a wall, slumping down a few inches. She recovered quickly and, just as the man turned his attention to Kerry, Jodi grabbed his ankles and pulled hard. The man's hands gripped Kerry's shoulders but she wriggled away as Jodi's foot immobilized the man's head. His arm, obviously practiced at this type of struggle, leveraged his body weight to roll sideways, where he faced Jodi and pulled the trigger. Kerry stood still, totally helpless. Jodi sank where she stood, then lowered to the hard floor in a slump.

"It's a flesh wound, run!" Jodi shouted. "Get out of here!"

And through some kind of strange logic, Kerry knew this was the right thing to do. She knew nothing about the woman Jodi, and now she was about to escape leaving her there to die. Would the old Kerry have done this?

The warehouse was long and dark, but this part of it had only a roof and no walls. Oddly quiet, no people, not even any ambient sounds, Kerry took off down the main corridor, feeling her way through the thick, stagnant air, through the confusion of her life as it had become. Slowly, she kept walking, now stepping out of the warehouse onto the tarmac, across a lot filled with parked trucks and trailers. Old Kerry would have analyzed the site, ascertained its function, its proximity to the rest of the city, main cross streets, landmarks, navigation so she could find her way home. Wait, where was that again? Would Byron her landlord recognize her or even remember her at this point? And was Jesse even still alive after Golden Gate Park?

More walking. Now, past the long parking lot and onto a dirt path with grass growing in random clumps along the edges. Groves of pine and eucalyptus jutted up from the distant horizon, with no ocean visible in either direction. Old Kerry would have wondered, now, what settlement of a seven-mile wide city wouldn't have an ocean view. But this new self, new person, only cared about the name creaking in the back of her brain like a squeaky rocking chair. A desperate itch, without nails to scratch it. Mayna was a woman, not a man. And not a thing, an object or a brand of some kind. An older woman with lovely dark skin, her nanny. Why couldn't she remember more details? Come on, Kerry, she thought.

She walked, still with nothing in her hands, no money, or ID, and no destination. Jodi was most likely dead, and they would be coming for her soon. But she walked languorously, drawing air deep into her lungs, pausing after every few steps to remind herself that she was still alive despite attempts otherwise. Based on the industrial smells, no traffic, scant buildings, she guessed that she was somewhere in South San Francisco. Maybe Brisbane or San Bruno. The road up ahead was a main street, likely leading to the highway. She looked up at the sky. Maybe 5 o'clock. Where was all the traffic?

A red Jeep pulled to the shoulder just ahead. A heavy set woman with long, smooth hair leaned out the window.

"Looks like you might need a ride," she said. The voice seemed friendly enough, no obvious signs of homicidal tendencies, the car looked well-maintained and besides, what choice did she have at this point?

Kerry reluctantly pulled open the passenger door and climbed up into the seat, barely looking at the driver. "Thanks," she mustered.

The woman drove on, turning to look every few seconds. "Not a great place to be out for a stroll," she commented. "Where you headed?"

"San Francisco Police Department," Kerry replied, surprised by her own words. At a red light, the woman turned to her. "Are you all right? I mean, do you need anything?"

"Water," Kerry said quickly.

"Sure. But I mean, like, medical attention."

Kerry lowered the sun visor and looked in the mirror. Who was that looking back? Black eye, blood crusted on the side of her head and lip, bruises on her neck and chin. Jesus.

The woman handed her a new bottle of spring water and pulled into a Burger King drive-through. She turned. Kerry drank the whole bottle at once.

"Grilled chicken sandwich, large fries, coke, and a diet coke."

Kindness, Kerry thought. She had almost forgotten what that was. She drank, and ate, and felt blood start to circulate through her body again, for the first time in … she could barely remember. Absent of any other signs of grief, tears fell on her hands and fingers as she ate.

CHAPTER FORTY-SIX

Grace breathed slowly to steady her thudding pulse and considered a number of scenarios. This was a chapel, right? Presumably, a member of the clergy would be on site at all times. Were they bound and gagged behind the white door? She hadn't heard any shots fired so far. And Neville ... the eternal wild card. Because the likelihood of him simply following directions and tailing the Pharmafia was unfortunately low. What was he more likely to do? Appear behind the white door with a big smile?

No one answered the knock at the door. Umbrella Lady stood completely still, barely breathing it seemed, not even blinking.

Grace felt the woman's anxiety. "Sure we've gone to the right church?" she said and snickered.

"Quiet."

"Maybe they're napping," Grace added, to which Umbrella Lady reached around to the holster on her hip and unsnapped it. She knocked again, and this time the door moved ajar. Was it open when she'd knocked before? The woman used her foot to push on the door, moving only a few cautious inches into the darkened room. She stepped through the doorway. Grace watched but didn't move, yet quickly recognized the T-shirt on a body slumped on the floor.

Kathleen.

She pulled a hand to her mouth to muffle a cry. Umbrella Lady looked back at her, and when she did, a hand reached out of the dark room from behind the door and seemed to karate-chop the gun out of her hand. Umbrella Lady went for her left ankle, obviously a backup pistol. Grace moved backward a few inches, unsure of what to do next. The hand behind the door reached out and grabbed the woman's arm, then shoulder, and threw her to the ground. She tried to get up, yet her assailant appeared prepared for this contingency, as his fist collided with her lower jaw.

"Uh!" The woman groaned and toppled over Kathleen and rolled onto the floor behind her. Grace moved into the room and surveyed the scene, her eyes landing on a suited man on the floor, Adrian, and another man wearing a clergyman's shirt collar.

"You okay?" Adrian asked her.

Grace stared at him for a moment, pointing at the plain-clothed man on the floor. "A priest? Minister?"

"He's alive," Adrian replied.

"And him?" she said pointing to the other man. "One of her ... goons?"

Adrian nodded, leaning over Kathleen's body.

"Is she ...?" Grace whispered.

Adrian reached down and touched Kathleen's neck for a long moment, then brought a hand to cover his face. "I owe her everything," he said in a shaky voice. "Let's go. We've got a lot of work to do."

They walked away slowly, though Grace could see Adrian's practiced eyes shooting left and right as they walked through the chapel grounds.

"Where's your car?" Adrian half turned to her.

She saw his face now, in the light. The whole right side looked purple and black, and his right eye was swollen shut and crusted. "I thought they might have drugged you."

"They did," he said. "We need to get out of here first, then I'll tell you everything."

"Tell me everything," she mocked, jogging to catch up with him. "Who do you think you're talking to? You tell me nothing. That's why we're here at this very moment. I risked everything for you. I thought I was saving ..." Her voice tailed off and emotion flooded her.

On the edge of the grassy path leading to the parking lot, Adrian turned and slid his arms around her shoulders. "Guard these with your life," he said, touching the white binders.

Grace shook her head. "I doctored them. They're fake."

"They don't know that. And they'll be coming for us." He looked out toward the street ahead. "They're already here."

"Shit!" Grace replied. Do they see us?"

"Lay down, here on the grass," he said pulling on her arms.

"What?"

"Quickly! Lay down on your back with your hands behind your head."

Grace obliged, secretly pleased that he had some trick up his sleeve. He sprawled perpendicular to her with his head on her belly, holding a page from one of the files in front of him as if reading. "Wait twenty seconds, then I'll look back," he said.

And by some divine providence, a horde of female joggers approached from the east side of the quad.

"Follow them!" Adrian said, jumping to attention.

Grace climbed back up and started running at their slow speed, gradually inserting herself into the middle of the huddle. Several of the runners exchanged glances but kept going. Adrian was a few feet behind her and looked wobbly on his feet. She turned and pointed toward Center Street. He followed.

"Is that your car?"

"It's on Trinity. But I've got backup," she gestured, looking toward the street and praying for Neville's support. A blue van screeched to the curb immediately in front of them as they reached the end of the grass. Adrian's arm blocked across Grace's chest.

"No, no, it's okay. You don't understand, it's Neville," she explained.

Adrian turned to her and glared wide-eyed. "Don't get in the van, Grace."

"Don't be silly, I called him."

The van's side door slid open. Neville Mattson crouched in the door jamb waving them in. "Come on, come on," he said, looking anxiously around the campus behind them.

Adrian took one step backward onto the grass, with his fingers gently pulling the back of Grace's blouse. "Don't turn around," he said softly. "Back up toward me and listen for my cue."

Grace disobeyed his directive and turned back. "Are you mad? It's Neville – I called him to meet us here. Don't you—"

"Who's driving the van, Grace?" he said quietly.

Grace peered into the vehicle behind Neville's head. It looked like a woman driving. A woman with neat, blonde hair. Hair very similar to Martina Carrera. "Oh, my God," she said under her breath.

"Two more steps back, you're doing fine," Adrian coached, now grabbing a deeper hold on the waist of her slacks.

"Mother, what are you waiting for? Pass me those chunky binders, whatever they are ..."

"Um ... the cars," she stammered. "I'm just trying to get a break in traffi—"

"Run!" Adrian yelled in her ear, jerking her toward him. She followed, struggling with the heavy binders, sprinting to keep up with his sudden lightning pace, still wondering how he was even able to walk.

"What about the van?" she shouted up ahead, just then hearing the screech of rubber tires against the pavement.

"They'll try to cut us off from Center Street." Adrian turned right at the next stop sign and paused to look back at Grace. "Pass me one of those," he grabbed one of the binders, crossed the side street to the other side of Carver, and held the binder over his head and dropped it on the sidewalk. The binder toppled half on its side with some of the typed pages exposed. Genius, Grace thought and smiled as he ran back to her. "Here, I'll carry this one. Follow me," he said.

"Mind telling me where we're going?"

"The Stu has a secret entrance somewhere on this street," he said and stopped. "Yellow Dye."

"What's that?"

"A clue, I guess. But—" he pointed. "There." He took off across the street toward a yellow house, with a Grateful Dead flag waving on the front porch.

"Down here," Grace said, looking down a steep staircase. Tires screeched around the corner toward them.

"Hurry," she said almost falling down the stairs. She grabbed the door and pulled. It clunked. "Locked."

Chapter Forty-Seven

"Can I help you?"

"Pete Stanton, please." Kerry scanned the front room of the SFPD precinct. "He's not here?"

The dispatcher typed something on her computer. "Detective Stanton's ... in a meeting."

"Tell him I'm here, please. Whatever he's doing, he'll want to see me."

The woman glared at her over the top of her glasses. "Your name?"

"Kerry Stine."

Kerry knew how she sounded, and also knew how she looked. Apparently, this was a compelling enough argument to get the dispatcher to pick up the phone. "Take a seat, please." A moment later, the dispatcher's phone rang. "Straight back and take a left," the woman said and pointed. "First, sign in here," she swiveled a clipboard and pen.

Kerry began walking on stiff, sore feet, worn shoes and dirty socks, and couldn't remember the last time she'd brushed her teeth or even the last known location of her toothbrush. She walked, dreamlike, almost floating, as she had on the road outside the warehouse. Walking and breathing, barely seeing the precinct crowded with vagrants and uniformed personnel.

Stanton stood in front of his desk, arms

outstretched, palms up, half smiling. Not a sneer, but not a happy smile either. Was there such a thing as happiness in the world of homicide detection?

"Much as I'd like to say you're looking well ..." Stanton raised a brow. "Can I get you something? Like a doctor?"

"How about a conference room."

Stanton pointed to the right. "Follow me," he said. "Anything else?"

"Water, a shower, food..." she half joked.

"In that order? Never mind, we'll get to that. Actually dinner, it's six o'clock."

She glanced quizzically at him. "Did you say dinner?"

"Sorry," he looked at the floor and seemed to blush. "I wasn't asking if ..."

Stanton kept talking, more like stammering, while Kerry couldn't help but smile in some deep part of herself. Was it a kind of paternal protectiveness thing, or maybe because he probably hadn't been laid in a year? He wasn't young, even that good looking by modern standards. His physique looked nondescript at best – medium everything. Brown hair with uneven, haphazard curls, blue eyes, very blue, his most distinguishing feature. She wondered now about his hands – what they felt like to hold, how they might feel around her shoulders. Did he know how to hug with both hands and arms, like a full body embrace, or did he do the man-hug thing?

"Kerry!" Stanton snapped his fingers. "Are ya with me?"

They were in a conference room, Stanton was seated, and in front of her a bottle of water and what looked like a blueberry muffin on a paper plate. How did he know she loved blueberries?

She sat carefully, and as she slid her chair close to the table, a woman, the dispatcher no less, walked in with a mug, a pot of coffee, and something under her arm. A tiny carton of real, cream, sugar packets, and a spoon.

"Mel makes kick-ass coffee and, well, clearly you need some right now."

Kerry chuckled, suddenly conscious of her hair. She sat, fixed the coffee the way she had before, in her old life. Cream, and a pinch of sugar, like one-quarter of a packet. Three quiet sips later, she opened the water and peeled the paper off the bottom of the muffin.

"Is it working?" Stanton asked.

"What?"

He pointed to the coffee pot.

"Yeah."

"Good." He leaned forward, folded his arms on the table. "Mind telling me why the phone number you left for me last time you were here was to a dry cleaning company?"

"I didn't know you," she replied quickly, barely even remembering the scam but happy that she'd done it. "Or trust you."

"Do you now?"

"Irrelevant. I no longer have a home, and I lost my cell phone, not to mention my wallet, purse, money, life."

"How about where you've been for the past few days?"

Kerry finished off the top of the muffin, wiped her mouth with the back of her hand and stood, reaching in her front jeans pocket. "Hold out your hand," she said.

Stanton raised his eyes to her fist hovering over him and held his palm up. Kerry dropped a long chain and pendant in it. "This is the key to how this all happened."

Stanton lengthened the gold chain and drew the pendant close, squinting. "It's a mizpah."

"How do you know about that?"

"Oh, they were a fad in the seventies and eighties, a

girl gave me one once."

"Now a girl just gave you another one."

"The key to your heart?" He tilted his head sideways.

Kerry sat and refilled her coffee mug. "The key to my past."

"Where did you get this?"

"Long story." She shook her head. "I was kidnapped."

"When?"

"Three days ago, and taken to a warehouse in South San Francisco, maybe Bay View or Hunter's Point. There were two other women in there with me. One of them gave this to the other woman to give to me. Kept saying this name I can't get out of my head."

"What name?"

"Mayna."

"Know someone by that name?"

Kerry closed her eyes and saw things, just as she had in the cell. Lights, moving images, thick fog, and a strange smell. "A woman."

Stanton leaned back and crossed his legs. "A woman named Mayna, and half of a necklace."

"My head hurts," Kerry admitted to him.

Stanton sighed. "Miss Stine ..."

"Miss Stine?"

"Okay, Kerry, you had a headache the last time I saw you. Migraines, you said. You've obviously been badly beaten, now kidnapped, you're likely dangerously dehydrated right now, malnourished, not to mention homeless."

"So?"

"So." Stanton paused, handing back the mizpah. "I want to help you, help you figure this out, figure out who commandeered your apartment, but first I need to know some things."

Kerry sighed, half expecting this. "Like?"

"Like who's Rosemary Castiglia and where is she now? Not to mention three other patients at the hospital you used to work at."

"They've disappeared too?" She barely remembered that part of her life now.

"No."

Good, she thought and sighed.

"They're dead."

Kerry's lids closed. "What patients, who?" she demanded.

"My assistant has the file. Wait, let me check." Stanton opened the door and looked around. "Manny," he called out, "where's Estevez?"

"Gone twenty minutes ago," the man replied.

"Sorry, no file," Stanton reported, returning to the conference room. "I'll find out the names for you, but I've now got four open cases on the books, and I think you are the only one who can help me. So ... should we maybe help each other?"

She nodded, thinking. Stanton genuinely wanted to help her. "You don't sleep much, do you?" she said.

"It shows."

"Uh-huh."

"Speaking of which, you need a place to stay. Wait here a minute." Stanton left and re-entered the conference room a minute later with a heavily-tattooed blonde woman wearing a 1950s dress. Classic, Kerry thought, always secretly jealous of anyone who had time to think about fashion. "This is Janice," Stanton said. "She'll help you get set up somewhere for the night."

"There's nothing, Detective," the woman said. "I'm sorry."

"What about the safe house, or the—"

"The Lucchese trial, we're putting up five witnesses right now. I'm sorry." The woman left the room, and Stanton looked defeated.

"Come on, I'll get you something to eat, and we'll think of something."

CHAPTER FORTY-EIGHT

"Where are we going?" Kerry asked from the front seat of Stanton's black SUV.

He shook his head. "What are you hungry for?"

She shot him a look.

"I'm ... I'm sorry. I meant—"

"What?"

"Why can't I ever say the right thing around you?"

"Because you care what I think about you," she replied honestly, hiding the hint of a smile.

"And why is that?"

"Tuna melt and fries," she said, answering his original question.

"Ah!" he snapped his fingers and pointed to a neon sign ahead. "Mel's Diner and, correct me if I'm wrong, but that could be a parking space right out front." He drove on, eyeing the space. "My God," he looked at her, "that never happens. You're my good luck charm."

Stanton turned off the engine and walked around to open her door, not to be chivalrous, she surmised, but because he considered it part of his job. She followed him inside and watched him pick the last booth on the right, farthest away from any table. Interesting, she thought, adding this to her invisible list.

"Are you supposed to arrest me?" she said the instant they sat down.

"Not much for small talk, are you? Thank God you're not a doctor."

"Well, are you?"

Stanton shook his head and took off his jacket. "I have no evidence that you've committed a crime. Though I've got enough people who say you were involved with a missing patient to hold you for questioning."

"Is that what this is?"

A male server wiped down their table, put out napkins and silverware and two menus.

"So why do I care what you think?"

Kerry stared down at all four pages of the ginormous menu. She shook her head pretending to be annoyed, but she liked the ease of their banter, almost flirting but not really. Enough to make her forget the last few days of her life, and almost feel like a normal person. "Because you're lonely," she said without looking up.

Stanton knitted his brows, attentive.

"And because I don't fit any of your existing female stereotypes."

He angled his head sideways and smirked. "How do you know I'm not gay?"

She laughed aloud. "Don't be ridiculous. Your hair, not to mention your clothes, your watch, your car."

Stanton examined his watch, and Kerry couldn't help but smile.

"Gay men are meticulous in appearance. You look like you're twenty minutes late."

"For what?"

"Everything."

"You're right, I am."

"See?"

The server returned and Kerry observed Stanton's

manner while placing his order and wondered. The server brought out two coffees and two ice waters. They both drank silently, and Kerry wondered, suddenly, how she might look in a 1950s dress like the woman Janice at the police precinct. She could tell Stanton respected that woman, as he hadn't looked her up and down despite her visible and prominent cleavage. Was he not that kind of man, or was Janice simply not his type? What was his type?

"What's the last thing you remember about your last shift at the hospital?"

"Castiglia's chart was missing when I went to check it."

"Did you report it?" He used an interrogation voice.

She nodded. "I told Nurse Redfield, my supervisor on that shift. She was right there."

"And?"

"She blamed me for it," Kerry replied.

Stanton sipped the coffee. "Why?"

"Aren't you gonna ask me if I took it?"

"Why would you?"

Kerry thought about this.

"I assume you'd take someone's chart if you wanted to hide something about their medical history," Stanton surmised. "Like lab results, for instance. So the question then becomes why would the shift nurse want to suppress Castiglia's chart, and from whom?"

The server set two plates on the table. Kerry eyeballed Stanton's burger and fries.

"What?"

"I've been conditioned not to trust the police," she said.

"Where did that come from?"

"You seem like ... you're on my side. Like you believe what I've told you."

"Maybe I do, maybe I don't. But that's okay," he

said biting into a French fry, "make me work for your trust. I like a challenge."

Kerry bit into the tuna melt and closed her eyes. She sipped the ice water and then devoured the rest of that half of the sandwich. "Sorry," she said, "guess I was hungry."

"Let's get back to the necklace," Stanton said.

"Jim Rex, the man who broke into my apartment ..."

"Your brother-in-law."

Kerry put the sandwich down. "I just can't get used to that."

"Sorry."

"No, you're right, or that's the story anyway. I don't know if I believe that they planned it around a training I was supposed to go to. But regardless, he came to get this." She pulled it out from under her shirt.

"Did he say anything to you about it?"

"Rex? He asked me if I remembered. Something I had as a child. He said a lot of things I didn't understand, but he meant to confuse me, talking in riddles."

Neither spoke for a few minutes, digesting not only the food but the ideas circulating around the table. Mel's Diner was typically crowded, Kerry thought, serving typical tourist food that everybody liked. A successful marketing scheme.

"Do you remember much about your childhood?"

"I try not to. It gives me headaches."

"Migraines actually." Stanton tipped his head to the side, which was becoming his trademark.

Kerry shrugged, unsure of where he was going with it.

"Probably nothing there you need to look into."

"No need to be sarcastic."

"None of my business, right?" he pressed.

Kerry shrugged, not sure how to answer. Stanton slammed his mug on the table. "Bet your ass it's my business," he said.

"My childhood? In what way?"

"Look, these men are killers. We're talking about a man who orchestrated a five-year marriage as a sham, for some higher purpose. Your friend, the homeless man, Jesse? Dead."

Kerry closed her eyes.

"Your cell mate, Jodi? Likely dead. What about the three missing patients, who are also dead by the way? Are you seeing a pattern emerge?"

"Stop it!" She wiped her wet eyes on a dirty napkin.

"I want to know what elderly hospital patients have to do with all this," Stanton added in a gentler voice.

"It's where it all started."

Jesse, Kerry kept thinking as they walked out in silence to Stanton's car. Was it true? Had they actually found Jesse's body? She went through every step of that night in her mind, the scene at Golden Gate Park. Then Stanton touched her arm for the second time tonight, she noticed.

"Hey," he said, breaking her from her thoughts. "You've got a lot to think about. If you want to be alone, I'll get you a hotel room."

She kept walking.

"If not, well, I've got a spare futon on my sun porch. It's painfully bright in the mornings and overrun with plants."

Kerry nodded with a tacit, 'I'll take it'.

Stanton turned from Geary onto Hyde Street past the Asian Art Museum and then east on Mission to 4th Street. He turned into the Target parking lot and pulled up to the front door. Without looking at her, Stanton reached over her legs into the glove box.

"Sorry," he said pulling something out. "On my birthday this year, I saw this on the ground outside a little mom-and-pop bookstore in the Mission. The store was closed so I couldn't turn it in there, so I decided the money wasn't mine, it might have been someone's paycheck, and so I couldn't spend it – only give it away." He unfolded the hundred-dollar bill and put it in her hand. "Should be enough for a toothbrush and a change of clothes, yes?"

Kerry searched his face and tried to swallow the lump in her throat. "Keep it up, Detective, I might start to like you." She opened the door and stepped out. He was smiling. "You'll be here when I get back?" she said with unexpected fear in her voice.

"I'll be right here," he reassured. For some reason, she believed him.

CHAPTER FORTY-NINE

How was it, Kerry wondered, that a gritty homicide detective was the only trustworthy man she'd ever met? You don't even *know* him, her inner voice argued. A hundred dollars, for a professional bargain shopper, could go a long way. She made a quick mental list.

Phase 1: Toothbrush, toothpaste, deodorant, razor, soap, shampoo, mascara, lip gloss.

Phase 2: Underwear, yoga pants, T-shirt, handbag.

Total: $72.79 with some cash to spare.

At the checkout line, Kerry felt someone's gaze on her from behind. She tried hard not to look back. Breathe, she told herself, you're completely paranoid. The cashier moved quickly without a word of friendliness. Fine, she thought and held out the $100 bill. She tore the tags off the wallet and purse and stored the change inside, moved out of line and immediately turned to check the direction of the stare. Stanton, she sighed with relief.

"Gum," he explained, holding out a pack.

"Are you my bodyguard now?"

"I think you need me."

"You were spying on me shopping for underwear. What kind of pervert are you?"

Stanton walked directly beside her with his right hand on her back, talking while simultaneously scanning the parking lot. "I especially enjoyed your selection process of bras," he added, unlocking the passenger door. "Black, pink, black, pink, white, then back to pink, then black."

"You should be arrested."

He laughed. "You're right." The black SUV was still parked just outside the front door. Even so, he covered both sides of her on the ten steps out, as if he expected gunfire.

"Not taking any chances, huh?"

"Clearly you being alive is a liability to someone."

In the shower, Kerry replayed the way Detective Stanton had said the words, 'I'll be right here.' He'd put no particular emphasis on any of the words, yet they weighed on her now like lead. Had Bill ever said that, or even felt that sense of protectiveness toward her? No, she decided, enjoying the novel sensation of shampoo on her scalp. She'd been in there twenty minutes already. Much of the planet was in a drought while she took her time exfoliating her skin, shaving her legs, over-conditioning her hair. Toweling off, she realized she'd completely forgotten pajamas. Damn it.

"Detective?" she called through the closed door, sensing he was within earshot.

After a long pause, strategic she was certain, he spoke from the other side of the door. "Can't you bring yourself to call me Pete? How about Peter?"

"I don't have any pajamas," she said opening the door a crack, still wrapped in a towel.

"And somehow you think I'm the pajama type? Hold on." He vanished and returned a minute later with folded sweatpants and an oversized T-shirt.

"Perfect."

"Get changed and then come and sit for a minute.

Are you a wine drinker?"

Stanton had changed out of street clothes into what looked like sleep pants and a faded Miles Davis T-shirt. He caught her looking at it. "My music collection includes the Dead, Vivaldi and everything in between. I'm a broken stereotype, just like you."

"How am I even a stereotype in the first place?"

"You've got this studious look about you, for one thing."

Kerry poured a glass of wine from the open bottle of Chianti on the kitchen table. "Well, I *am* broken, then, because I'm not in the least studious."

"No? Do you read the Wall Street Journal? Do you stay up late pondering the nature of the universe?"

"No. Neither of those," she replied.

"That's okay because that's not what studious means." He took a sip and moved further out on the couch as she sat on the other end. "You're a thinker. You don't laugh constantly as a way of masking social nervousness. You don't blurt out every single thought that comes into your mind either. You sometimes answer a question with just your eyes. That's what studious means."

"So let's hear my faults, since you're so keen on observation."

"You're kind of stuck up," he said.

"What?!"

Stanton tried to muffle a laugh. "How about telling me what's really on your mind."

Kerry looked deeply into the bottom of the glass. "Are those three patients dead because of me?"

"I'll tell you one thing about them. They all had advanced stage lung cancer. What was Castiglia being treated for?"

"Same thing. But somehow, she was getting better. She had relatives back East, and when she came back from that trip, Connecticut or New York, her tumor was about half as big."

Stanton blinked and nodded. "Did you report this to anyone?"

"Of course. We asked her about it but ..." She sighed.

"What?"

"She pretends that her English isn't good and she can't understand people. But I've heard her on the phone. Her English is perfect."

"So why pretend? Is she afraid of doctors? Probably not atypical for that generation." Stanton pointed at her neck. "I see you're still wearing it, the mizpah. Hoping it'll help you remember something?"

"Hoping, yes."

CHAPTER FIFTY

A young woman with a bandanna on her head pulled open the Stu door at the bottom of the stairs. Grace exhaled and took a step forward. The girl's palm went up.

"What's the name of your senior project?" she said directly to Grace.

"Greek history," Adrian chimed.

"Who in particular?"

"Hercules," he added.

"Come," the woman said and opened the door wider. She stared wide-eyed at Grace. "Do you require protection?" she said to Adrian.

"Shelter."

"For how long?"

"One night."

"Food and amenities?"

"Yes," Grace answered for him.

The girl studied each of them closely, one then the other. "Wait here," she said finally and disappeared into the dark background.

"Have you been here before?" Grace whispered.

Adrian shook his head. "I've known about this place. It used to be a sorority hideout a long time ago and ended up as a sort of safe house in the sixties. I suspect all the ivy leagues have some variation, or at least did."

"Where'd you get the password?"

"Kathleen gave it to me, probably thinking I might need it."

The girl approached out of the darkness. "Come," she said and led them from the entrance down a narrow hallway lined with tiny lights on the floor and ceiling, which illuminated a path to a larger room with larger lights, this time in blues and greens, strung across the ceiling in long lines like an upside-down swimming pool. The large room had long tables, enough space to easily fit a hundred people and only two dwellers eating in silence at separate tables.

"Food will be ready for you here in fifteen minutes," the girl said, passing them and walking toward another room.

Grace looked back with raised brows at Adrian.

"Don't say I never take you anywhere," he joked.

The next room, much smaller and almost square, had red and white lights along the floor and a large chandelier hanging in the center. "Showers are here," the girl said and pointed. No stalls, but showers and drains, and one wall with benches, folded towels, and white robes hanging from hooks.

"Extra clothing in here," the girl opened an armoire that seemed to materialize from inside the wall. Inside were drawers and clothing hanging from padded hangers.

"Where did all this come from?" Grace asked.

"Private donors, university alumni, mostly. People who have stayed here before."

An hour later, they were both cleaner, well fed, and lying on the same futon in what resembled the smallest room of the labyrinth.

"Where was her computer?" Grace asked about Kathleen.

"A laptop I trained her to take home every night.

Should still be in her backpack."

"And why are we sleeping in the same bed if we're the only ones in this place?"

Adrian rolled onto his back. "Maybe there's only one bed."

"Well, you needn't think you can take advantage of me," Grace said, leaning on her side to face him.

"I can barely move, so I think you're safe."

Grace got up to hang her bathrobe in the wardrobe. "What are we doing here?"

"Figuring things out. Hiding. Who from? We don't know."

"No," she said, "we know. We're hiding from a multimillion-dollar corporation that thinks they can make a lot of money from your magic cigarettes and don't want to be cut out of the deal."

He smiled. "That's right."

"What are we going to do?"

"Cut them out. It was Kathleen's idea, really."

"What?"

"Social media."

"Like Twitter?" Grace was somewhat familiar with what she'd deemed the un-Facebook.

"All of it. Twitter, LinkedIn, Instagram, Google Circles."

"So what's the plan?" Grace watched Adrian's eyes close.

CHAPTER FIFTY-ONE

Smoke. There's smoke everywhere, but her breathing feels normal, the air smells normal, and her eyes don't sting. Is it fog? It's San Francisco, her subconscious mind told her, Fog City. Fog is a certain color, like whitish. Even if it was darker in color, it wasn't the same; not even remotely similar to smoke from a fire. What's on fire then? The images were moving too fast. Moving, changing shape before her eyes, as though she'd been drugged and time was moving at the wrong speed.

Little girls' hands, holding and clenching, then slipping away from each other, larger hands, much older hands, pulling them apart and carrying away one little girl by snatching her up from the waist like a bag of groceries. Screaming, no, crying, like little-girl crying. Why was she crying, who was she? Then like in a movie, all movement in the landscape stops, absolute silence, interrupted by the *clop* of a man's heavy dress shoes walking in slow motion, carrying away that little girl. In the fog. In the smoke. A necklace falls to the ground, a gold chain on the hard ground, half submerged in a puddle, a match in color to the flames in the background. Now silence again except for the muted sounds of someone crying. That little girl.

"Come here, darlin'," someone says from nearby, but no one is visible. An invisible old woman with the most comforting voice she'd ever heard, a voice like hot milk and honey, a voice that could induce sleep and safety with one word. Now an image of the old man's hands wrapped around an old woman's throat. "Mayna!!" A little girl screams, standing watching the gnarled hands around the old woman's neck. A long arm swats her back, then returns to the neck. "*No!* Mayna, Mayna, Mayna ... Mayna ... Mayna."

Now another old woman sits in a wheelchair coughing, her eyes are watery, not from crying but from coughing. She's wearing a light blue hospital gown that's open in the front and untied. Her skin is wrinkled and dotted with age spots, her hair short and slicked back behind her ears. Wire-rimmed eyeglasses worn on top of her head fall and bounce on the floor when she coughs again. She's moving in slow motion, looking up at a doctor who's handing her a cigarette. She blinks, takes the cigarette, and he lights it for her. As she sucks the smoke into her body, a light goes on in her chest, like something glowing. With every drag on the cigarette, the light gets a tiny bit larger. Now her face begins to look younger, her hair is blonde, and the skin on her chest is even textured and tan. The old woman rises from the wheelchair as a young woman and hugs the doctor and kisses him on the cheek, walking away in slow motion. One step, then another slow step, walking. Strong.

"Kerry, it's a dream. Wake up." Stanton. His hands were on her shoulders, not grabbing, just touching, almost holding. Kerry opened her eyes.

"Where am I?" she asked stupidly. The room was dark, some light filtering in from Stanton's kitchen. "Could you turn a light on?"

Stanton clicked on a lamp on a table next to the futon, then propped up her pillow. She watched him sitting on the bed, his hands on her arm with a familiarity that didn't match the little time they'd spent together.

"Some nightmare," he said, shifting an inch closer. "Wanna tell me about it?"

"I like being here, like *here*," she said looking around the room. "Is it okay?"

Stanton smiled. "It's my house, of course it's okay."

"I mean, isn't there a policy about—"

He shook his head. "No. Well, yes, but, tell me."

Kerry drew in a deep breath. "There was a fire. I saw smoke but didn't smell it, or feel any heat from it."

"Fog maybe?"

"That's what I thought, but no. I did see fire at one point. A little girl crying, two of them actually, holding hands and being pulled apart by an old man. And a necklace fell on the ground, in a dirty puddle."

Stanton nodded. "Bet I know what that is."

"And an old woman wearing an old-fashioned house dress, with a smock over it. I called her ..."

"Mayna. That's what your cell mate was saying."

"Mayna." Kerry tried the word out to see how it felt saying it. "An old, old – my head hurts."

"Keep talking. I'll get you some aspirin in a minute."

"Mayna is an old woman in my dream with a sweet voice. She's trying to take me from the old man, then his hands are around her throat. I'm watching him do this." Stanton's hand tightened around her forearm, and she realized she was crying.

"Do you remember her?" he said softly.

It was the simplest of questions, but one she wasn't sure she could answer. "It's like my body remembers her but not my mind." Kerry stopped talking and closed her eyes, chasing that imagery again, the slow, liquid place where things moved the wrong way. "She was my nanny, growing up I think."

"And the other little girl?" Stanton sounded as if he knew the answer already.

Kerry's cheeks felt wet and cold before she even realized they were tears. "My ... my ..."

"She was your sister."

Kerry didn't hide the sobs at hearing this. Her body slowly leaned forward onto Stanton's broad shoulders and her arms clasped around his torso. "How do you know?" she muttered into his chest.

He was still holding her, stroking her hair with one hand. "Earlier at the precinct, you said something. Something like you *knew her* or something. The girl in the cell. And that she'd given you the mizpah, or gave it to the other one who gave it to you. Just seems sorta natural, two sisters separated in childhood and the only thing left between them is that necklace. Two halves of a whole."

Kerry pulled away and took in Stanton's theory. The necklace. Jim Rex. A fire. An old man who put her in a big black car. The sister she never saw again. They were just words and phrases so far, thoughts she didn't own. But her body knew the truth. The buzzing in her palms, the warm feeling in the center of her chest.

"What's her name?"

Blinking the tears from her eyes, the name came into Kerry's mind without even searching. "Kate," she almost said as a question. She nodded. "Kate," she said again.

"Do you remember anything about her?" Stanton said very slowly, very carefully. "And was that her in the cell?"

"She said 'Mayna' over and over ... I think it had to be. And I remember her hair. The color."

"Was she still alive when you broke out of there?"

"I think so, barely."

Stanton rose and moved into the kitchen. Making coffee, Kerry surmised, though the clock read 3:42 a.m. She followed him. "Do you have a bathrobe?"

"Back of the bathroom door," he called out from the kitchen.

It smelled like him. Not an odor, specifically, but a kind of general smell. Clean, a little sweet, like fresh air and sugar. She wrapped it tight and tied it around her waist. "There was something else in the dream."

Stanton turned around, leaned against the counter and crossed his arms.

"Another old woman." Kerry climbed up on a dark wood barstool and laid her palms on the granite counter. She paused before talking again, sorting out her thoughts. "It was Rosemary Castiglia."

"You recognized her?"

"No. Well, not really. It didn't really look like her in the dream, I don't think she wore glasses. But I know it was her. I feel it. She's the beginning of this whole nightmare. I mean," she chuckled, "the nightmare that's become my life."

Stanton poured two cups of coffee and sat on a stool across from her. Kerry looked around and smiled. "It's like a diner in here."

"I designed it this way."

"You designed this kitchen?" she said, somewhat shocked.

"We'll get to that. Finish your story."

Kerry sipped the hot coffee. He'd stirred cream and a tiny pinch of sugar into it. Was he a mind reader now? "She was in a wheelchair looking really old and frail and horrible. There was a doctor standing over her and he handed her a cigarette, and lit it for her."

"Nice treatment for lung cancer. Okay."

She shook her head. "No wait, it wasn't that. He was, sort of, helping her. He lit the cigarette for her, and every time she took a drag, I saw a little light in her chest gradually get bigger and bigger."

"Her cancer, no doubt."

"No!"

Stanton stared. "No what?"

"Every drag on the cigarette made her stronger, and younger. Her hair went from gray to blonde. Her skin from mottled to supple and tan."

Stanton rubbed his hands on his chin, scratching the razor stubble. "Sorry, I need to shave."

"Do you usually at three in the morning?"

Kerry looked out the living room windows, as a tinge of dove gray lightened the dark landscape.

"So you think Castiglia's still alive?"

"I know it. I've always known. She went to New Haven to supposedly visit some family, and she came back, and her tumor was almost gone. I told Nurse Redfield about it and she said she'd seen the ... "

"What?" Stanton pressed.

"The chart! Maybe that's why her chart disappeared." Kerry got up and paced the kitchen floor, holding her coffee mug. "What if she had some kind of experimental treatment in New Haven, came back and told her doctors about it, suddenly her tumor's one-quarter its original size and, well," she raised a brow, "that's not gonna make SFMC look very good, is it?"

"Interesting theory, Miss Stine. I'm impressed that your brain can work that well this time of day. I think we'd better start looking for our missing patient." Stanton got up and Kerry sat still, watching him.

"Why didn't I remember any of this until now? How could I have forgotten it?"

"That's easy. There are lots of memory-blocking drugs on the market. Propranolol, about a dozen varieties, not to mention the mind's natural ability to shield us from painful truths."

"I need to go back to that warehouse. I think you know why," Kerry said with a plaintive look.

"Okay," he agreed, too easily.

She was still looking at him.

"What – now?"

"Are you going back to sleep or something?"

"I'm lucky if I can go to sleep at all. Now that I'm awake and drinking coffee, no chance."

"Well, it's early, there'll be no traffic and it'll be easier to find it now that it's getting light out."

"Um, it's pitch black out there. What makes you think you can even find this place again? You've been through quite an ordeal, don't forget. You're probably not thinking straight."

"I don't know how, but I know I can find it again. At first we thought, Jodi and I, that we were near Bernal Heights based on the sound of church bells and the frequency at which they went off. But we heard no cars or street noise, so I knew we weren't in San Francisco proper."

"Church bells. So not St. Paul's?"

She shook her head. "Already thought of that. There's tons of traffic and life there, we would have heard something, car horns, screeching tires, street noise, people talking. We heard nothing outside. Not even birds. I think it was Bell Episcopal Church."

"Where's that?"

"Bayview."

"Bayview? No way. And you think you were down by San Bruno?"

"Listen," she insisted. "That bell tower is incredibly high, and there's nothing around to mask the resonance of the bells. I think we could have heard it from there."

CHAPTER FIFTY-TWO

After a surprisingly good night's sleep and more than adequate breakfast, Grace felt the strong coffee activate her brain cells.

"Do you know what you're looking for?" she whispered to Adrian, sitting beside her on a Bridgeport/New Haven local transit bus.

He shook his head. "What I need is on her computer, and they took that when they took her backpack. It was on her when they brought her to the chapel."

It was an odd moment to smile, thinking about Kathleen. But Grace felt like there might finally be something she could contribute to this process. "She had another one."

Adrian spun around toward her. "What?"

"A backup," Grace replied.

"You mean a drive or something?"

"A backup laptop. She kept it in the warehouse above one of the ceiling tiles. She thought she was pretty slick, but I saw her when I came in behind her once."

"And you're sure that's what it was?"

She nodded. "I asked her about it, and watched her put it up there."

"How do you know it wasn't her regular

computer?"

"What did her everyday laptop have stuck on the outside, like all over the top?"

"Stickers, palm tree stickers I think. And surfboards."

"Right. This one was black. So if you had a plan of what to do after the trials, I think it's safe to assume that her plan is stored on that other machine, where no one but you or her would ever find it."

"She never told me about another laptop."

Grace nudged him and rose. "We're here." The warehouse was barely a block from the bus stop, which by her estimation would give them a bit of time to assess the safety of getting in there. It was early still, barely 9 a.m. on a Sunday, and the street was deserted. The front door was still propped open.

"Um ..." Adrian said.

"Nothing you can do now. It's already been ransacked so doesn't much matter at this point."

"Jesus. My files!"

Grace entered first, heading directly to the back of the main room. She dragged a chair from the round table and stood on it, then the table itself, it to reach the ceiling tile.

"Be careful."

"Watch the door," she replied, pushing up lightly on the ceiling tile. It hit something and couldn't rise properly, which could only mean one thing. She gently slid the tile to the right, pulled the computer with one hand and felt Adrian's arm around her waist as she reached with the other hand. Adrian grabbed the machine, helped her down to the table, stepped off the chair and plugged in the power supply.

"Did you two work this out together?" Grace asked him.

"We didn't get a chance. She came up with

everything and they took me before she could tell me about it. She'd already been drugged when they brought her to the chapel."

"Do you know with what?"

"Sodium Pentothal or something similar. People think it's a truth serum, but that's been debated for twenty-five years. Thanks to my bad teeth and constant dental work, it doesn't really work on me anymore. Here we go," he said as the computer booted up. Palm trees on her wallpaper, Kathleen had an icon on the desktop that read "Oxen."

"That's it," Adrian said. "Wait, what is that?" he asked about the small box that he popped up.

"It's password protected," Grace said. "Well, don't look at me," she shot back at Adrian's bewildered gaze. "I barely knew her."

"But you'd spent a lot more time with her lately, and she likely set this up recently."

Grace tapped her fingers on the desk and shook her head. "Bronchioloalveolar carcinoma. Too long."

"And too obvious," Adrian replied.

"What's your product name?" Grace moved her chair directly behind the computer and sat up tall. Adrian sat beside her. "Did you hear me?"

"Yes."

"Well?" Her fingers were perched on the keyboard ready to type.

"It's not that simple."

Grace sighed and slumped back against the chair. "People have died because of the work you're doing. Do you realize that? And you're afraid to tell me the name of your product? Do you want me to sign a fucking non-disclosure agreement?"

"I have s—"

"I was kidding! If you don't trust me, Adrian, who are you going to trust?" Grace ignored him and started typing random words in the box hoping to get lucky. Palm, palm springs, Kathleen, lung ...

"Oxium," he whispered. "That's the product name. And please consider that highly classified at this point."

"Whatever," she mumbled and typed it in the box. Incorrect. "Does she use Twitter or have a blog or anything?"

Adrian snapped his fingers. "Yes, and she was always on my case because I never read her blog entries."

"Good, we can search it. Was it WordPress, or Blogger?"

"No idea. I don't know anything about blogs."

"No problem," she said. "What's ... what *was* her last name?"

"Leavenworth."

Grace opened a new Internet Explorer browser and typed "Kathleen Leavenworth blog WordPress" into Google. She scanned quickly through the list. "Here we go, I think, biogirl. Sound familiar?"

Adrian nodded. "Yep."

"The full ID is biogrl737." Grace typed it in the password box and clicked Submit.

A folder opened. Adrian read the files aloud. "General, Plan, Order, Execution, SM." He looked up.

Grace shrugged. "Social media?" She clicked to open the folder. "Facebook, Twitter, Reddit, Instagram, Snapchat, Pinterest," Grace read out. "Was she organizing a petition or something?"

Adrian shook his head. "Her idea was to protect me by making me a public figure." He rose and started walking around the warehouse.

"You mean going public with your findings?"

"Not formally," he clarified. "More like informally. Like starting a buzz on Twitter about the product, you know, getting people talking about it, asking questions."

Grace typed the Twitter URL in a browser and entered biogrl in the search box. Thirty-seven biogrls came up, and only one with a '737' suffix. She clicked to open the account. "Here she is on Twitter, got a nice following so far too – 247. So ..." Grace thought for a moment. "The right message to all those people might get them to retweet to all *their* followers, and it keeps going from there."

"Viral," Adrian said under his breath.

"Right. She's got it all mapped out here. After Twitter, finding a new treatment volunteer and posting daily findings, like in a log, on her blog but also interviewing the volunteer live and posting videos on YouTube. How are you feeling today, that sort of thing." She turned around to Adrian, who was leaning against a three-high file cabinet. "Are you sure you're ready for this?"

"No. But it's the only way. Getting my name out to the public is a great way to keep myself alive."

"Oh, she's got more here, too. Have you seen this?"

"Not yet."

Grace smiled as she read. "She's got a meme going, that—"

"A what?"

"Like a slogan, or a saying, song, that spreads across cyberspace." Grace kept scrolling on the page. "My God, she's written a rap song with contact names of who could record it and put it on YouTube and a product page on Facebook. But not just uploading it. Look at this ... it's a precise timeline of events and when to launch." Grace sat back and nodded. "She's a bloody genius."

CHAPTER FIFTY-THREE

"So where do we start?"

Grace glanced out the front door. "I need to pick up my car."

"At your house? Forget it, it's too dangerous."

"It's at the chapel," she replied. "What about Kathleen's car?"

"Never had one."

"She most certainly did," Grace corrected him, "an old blue Toyota or something, we drove around in it."

"Looks like there's a lot I didn't know about her. Where is it now?"

"I drove it back to my house last night and parked it out front, and it was gone the next time I went out front. We need to rent one then, more inconspicuous anyway."

"Agreed."

"Why don't you take care of that and maybe bring back something to eat?" she said.

"And you'll while away the hours leisurely surfing the net?"

Grace pointed to the laptop and opened her eyes wide. "This is going to save your life."

"Okay, okay, I believe you."

"You haven't got a phone," she remembered. "Is

there a landline in here?"

"Somewhere," Adrian scanned the interior.

Grace pointed to a black and gray console phone on a file cabinet near the far wall. "Good. Then you take mine. It's charged."

Grace went to the phone console, picked up the receiver to see the number, and programmed it into her phone. "Here, just press redial if you need to call."

"I'll be back soon," he said.

"I should think this is about a two-hour task," she said facing the computer again.

"Rental car and dinner? Probably twice that."

"Better get started then," she said, "and close the door on your way out."

A moment after she heard the door thud closed, Grace desperately craved a cigarette. Years ago, they'd helped her focus, and she needed that now more than anything. And it surprised her how little importance the past few days seemed to have, despite being on the run and spending a night in a fraternity safe house. I can't go home, she thought, and my son's working for the pharmaceutical mafia. Excellent.

She clicked to open a document in the Oxium folder entitled "Social Media Plan.docx". It looked like a long Word document.

Headlines. One to title the first blog post, then a different title as incremental teasers on Twitter. Then connect to Reddit and add Pinterest, Instragram, maybe LinkedIn. Then a new Facebook product page.

Twitter, product name: Oxium.

Slogan: *Smoke the Ox for the lung detox*

"Love it," she said aloud, nodding. Reading further, she found Twitter hashtag suggestions:

#smoketheox

#smox
#smux
#adriancalhoun
#magiccigarettes
#thenewalbertschweitzer

Lord, she thought, that's all he needs.

Next, send a story idea or tip to *tv@huffingtonpost.com*

Another Twitter teaser, this time *Wh?re's Adrian Calhoun* with all previous hashtags, as well as *Wh?'s Adrian Calhoun*, this time with a link to a blog post with his picture and bio.

A YouTube video of Adrian being interviewed about his development of Oxium, but he turns around, flinches, says, who's there and the camera turns off, to make it seem like he's a target and in danger and, therefore, somebody important.

Twitter again: Adrian Calhoun abducted or kidnapped? Let that conversation evolve for two or three days and start gathering some #wheresadrian momentum.

A public clinical trial called #nanotrial with a new stage-4 lung cancer volunteer, daily feeds on YouTube and the blog. Send news story of this to all news channels, Huffington Post, BBC World News, CNN, etc.

Grace quickly scanned the final stages, including interviews with Sanjay Gupta, Christiane Northrop, and other leading health officials, where Kathleen hoped for a public feud between the Surgeon General and Deepak Chopra. Wow, she thought. Nothing like aiming high.

Within an hour, she'd written two blog posts and a succession of teaser headlines for publishing them on Twitter. She knew it was all hype and bloated the facts, glamorizing what she knew had been most likely a series of short cuts, people working for free, ill-informed volunteers and a hell of a lot of luck.

Even so, she thought, it all did sound very impressive.

Adrian was a pioneer who'd never had a successful relationship in his life, never held a job for more than a year or two, never set down roots anywhere, married, had children, bought a house. What had she accomplished in all that time? House, job, career, a husband who left, an estranged son, small teaching stipend, and a greenhouse full of dwarf orchids.

Tick, tock, she reminded herself. Adrian had been gone for two hours already, and she knew it would be at least two more. She had to get everything written, polished and ready. By the time he got back, his life as he'd known it would be over.

Part Four

CHAPTER FIFTY-FOUR

Grace awoke with her face pressed to the cold desk and the smell of Mexican food.

"Mmm, Chi Chi's," she mumbled, listening to what had to be Adrian rustling a plastic bag. She pulled herself up and immediately clicked Control-S on the desktop. "Did you complete all your assignments?"

Adrian was biting into a burrito held together with thin paper and small white napkins. "I borrowed my neighbor's car, went to an ATM, stopped in at my apartment for a—"

"Your apartment? Are you insane?"

"Stealth mode, I promise."

Grace pulled out a foil-wrapped burrito and a small paper bag of tortilla chips. All the times they'd gone to Chi Chi's, sat in the red, dumpy café with yellow plastic seats arguing about plant morphology or the amazing adaptability of the human species, she never would have guessed that one day they'd be trapped in a warehouse planning a media heist as a life-saving measure.

"Well?" she said, taking the first bite of a chicken green chili burrito," I've been doing my homework too."

"Why do I feel this sudden sense of dread?"

"You should." She took another bite. "After we push the green button, so to speak, there's no going back and your life will never be your own again."

He scoffed. "Is it now? Was it ever?"

"Geez," she frowned. "I didn't even scare you a little?"

"Grace, I just love you." Adrian set down his burrito.

"Uh-huh."

"And I'm sorry for the unthinkably few times I've told you that."

"It is unthinkable."

"You're one of those rare people who knows not only how to care for people but how to make them feel cared for."

"I see you stopped at the bar on the way here."

"I'm serious."

"Sorry." She took her hands from the keyboard and put them in her lap. "I'm not going anywhere, you don't have to be afraid."

"Who said I'm afraid?"

"Well, aren't you?"

Adrian was chewing. "Yeah. What a ride."

"Ride?" She raised one brow. "You must be mistaken because it hasn't even started yet."

"That's comforting. What did you write while I was gone?"

"All of it. Do you understand? All the delusions you had about going public, applying for FDA approval, we're doing it, but just backward."

"Not the names of the control group, I hope."

Silence.

"Grace? Come on, I'm responsible for their well-being."

"No, you're not. You *were* responsible for the health of their lungs and the size of their tumors for a very limited duration."

Adrian shook his head. "We're giving out their

names? For God's sake. What value could that possibly have to the media?"

"Visibility. Transparency. Authenticity. That's what media *is*. But we're getting another volunteer anyway. I placed an ad on Craigslist and in the newspaper offering a thousand bucks to any stage-4 lung cancer patient who will talk to you for ten minutes."

"Um ...why?"

Grace took a pile of sheets off the printer. "We're planning to conduct a sort of mini-trial with this patient X, filmed and then posted on a daily YouTube feed."

Adrian walked cross-armed around the room. "Kathleen devised this?"

"This is just the beginning." She handed him the stack of pages.

"Too Good To Be True?" he read aloud from one page. "A Cigarette That Cures Lung Cancer."

Grace nodded. "That's right. Yes or no? Right now."

Chapter Fifty-Five

"How can you see anything in here?" Detective Pete Stanton sighed, squinting his eyes.

"It's perfect," Kerry whispered. "It's not even daylight yet. If they're here, they won't be ready for visitors."

"Where else would they be?"

"Who knows." Kerry closed her eyes for a second, trying to remember the layout of the building's interior.

They approached the outer door of the warehouse, the only door on that side of the twenty-foot tall, steel monstrosity. The high rib-steel metal exterior was likely reinforced to sustain gunfire. Maybe originally a military structure, she wondered, but why so far from the Presidio?

Pointing ahead, Kerry narrated. "Up ahead is a door. If it's propped open, we're fine. If not, we'll have to find another way in,"

Stanton was on her heels as she moved toward the clunky metal door, and saw its outline separated from the doorway. "It's open," she whispered.

"I'm right behind you."

Kerry turned and, even in the dark, she detected the outline of Stanton's face. Even here, it felt slightly comforting. "Only one way down there and it's a narrow hallway."

"Well, this time you've got me, and I've got this," Stanton held up his loaded 9mm pistol.

"I'll go first, I know where I'm going." Kerry slipped soundlessly through the doorway and down the short flight of stairs. She barely heard Stanton behind her. The first door on the left would, or should, be closed. Ten steps now, five, yes, door closed.

Deep breath.

The second door led to their cell and had a creaky, rusted-out barrel bolt. The door was open. Wait, she thought. "Did you notice any cars in the lot outside?"

"No," Stanton whispered back.

"The door's open."

"Someone's still here then," he said and inched past her. "Let me go first this time. Flashlight?"

Kerry pulled the mini Maglite from her jacket pocket. Stanton aimed it flat against his chest, pushed the "ON" button on the bottom, lifted it enough to cover it with his palm and moved one foot into the cell, swirling three fingers' worth of light across the floor.

"No one's here," he whispered.

Kerry tapped his elbow and pointed toward where she knew the other cell was. Stanton took two steps to the right and let more of the light illuminate the interior.

"Kate!" Kerry whispered. "Talk to me. Are you here?"

Stanton took five more steps and Kerry followed, then stopped. "Did you hear that?"

Stanton stopped and held the pistol facing up.

"Ohhhh," a moan sounded, but muffled like a person buried under a stack of blankets.

"Kate," she said in a regular voice now. "It's me."

"Mmm," was the response from the far part of the

room in the other cell.

"It's her," she said coldly moving past Stanton. "Give me more light."

He shone the full spectrum on the far cell and, by then, Kerry was at the bars. "Kate, get up, please," she said, wiping unexpected tears from her face. Something moved in the far back corner, then scrapes of skin and clothing on the concrete floor. Kerry peeled the flashlight from Stanton's hand, and he grabbed her wrist.

"I'm okay," she said, shining the light on a face she hadn't seen in many years.

CHAPTER FIFTY-SIX

The fair, freckly complexion took her back to a song they used to sing while playing hopscotch on the gritty sidewalk outside their house in San Francisco. Narrow bridge of the nose, high forehead. Without realizing it, Kerry had come forward and intertwined her fingers with the woman's among the cell bars.

"Kate," she half whispered, half cried. "They hurt you. Why?"

The woman shook her head slowly, as if she was using her ears to assess something, then slowly drew the cold air into her lungs.

My God, she can't see.

Now Kerry stared into the cloudy blue eyes and knew what she'd unconsciously determined a moment ago. "I knew it was you before, you know, when I was here, when the three of us were here."

"Then I'm sure you know she's dead," Kate said in a cold monotone.

Kerry nodded before considering the woman wouldn't actually see her nod. Would she sense it, or hear the micro movement of her hair brushing against her shoulders?

"They dragged her back in here after she was shot, then put her body in the trunk of a car out front and drove it away, somewhere."

"When did they leave?" Kerry said.

"A few hours ago. They'll be back soon, I expect."

Kerry had been holding Kate's fingers tightly. "Sorry," she said and loosened her grip.

"Who's the guy?" Kate asked.

"A police detective. He's ... helping—"

"Pete Stanton," Stanton said and moved closer to the bars, then looked quizzically back at Kerry who just shrugged. "We need to get you out of here," he said, walking the length of the cell.

"There's a button on the wall," Kate said. "Should be right outside the door you just came in. I hear the man press something there that clicks."

Stanton went into the hall, still holding onto the edge of the door. "I feel it," he said. "I can't press it with one hand, though. Kerry, hold this door open."

Kerry obliged, liking the sound of him saying her name. Or more like the vibration of it on her skin and body. With one hand, she held the door ajar, while Stanton used both of his thumbs to press the button. It made a metal *thunk* and the cell bars separated at the center by fifteen inches.

CHAPTER FIFTY-SEVEN

In Stanton's car, Kerry and Kate sat together in the back seat.

"Someone tell me where I'm going," Stanton called back.

"I want to take you to Gina's," Kerry said softly. "Do you remember her?"

Kate laughed aloud as if the question were ridiculously obvious. "Of course. Though I haven't talked to her in a few days, so she'll be worried sick about me."

Kerry replayed Kate's words back in her mind a few times. "Did you say ... a few ... days?"

"While I've been here, I mean."

"I saw her several days ago," Kerry recalled. "She said nothing ..."

Kate placed her hand on Kerry's arm and gently squeezed. "She said she tried."

Kerry let the tears rain down her cheeks now and didn't care how vulnerable it made her look. Even in front of Stanton.

"It's a lot to take in, I know," Kate said softly.

"What the hell happened to you?" Kerry said, confident that Kate would understand the subtext of the question.

"I lost my sight in the fire. The fire you

supposedly don't remember."

"I remember," Kerry said, "or enough anyway." She blinked more tears from her vision and half expected her temples to start throbbing again. But they didn't. Not today. "I've heard of carbon monoxide causing blindness, but not fire."

"Smoke inhalation complications can cause it."

"Huh?" Kerry replied.

"You don't believe me," Kate surmised. "Do you think I'm not me? And some kind of vitreous clone? Go ahead, quiz me."

"No," Kerry said, quietly resigning from the conversation.

"You're right not to believe."

Kerry looked at her again. Kate was holding something in her hand, something gold and shiny. The mizpah. Kerry reached two fingers into her jeans pocket, then remembered she'd bought yoga pants at Target and therefore didn't have any pockets. Her hand instinctively moved to her neck, and she pulled the chain to the outside of her shirt. She leaned forward and put the pendant part in Kate's hand – it clinked against the one Kate was already holding. "So the one you gave to our cellmate to give to me was ... mine?"

"Yes, I kept it all this time, and this one's mine," she added, raising her palm and opening her fist. "Jim Rex was looking for this, that's why he came in the first place – to find this. Or more accurately ... these." Kate pointed to their surface – two jagged puzzle pieces that fit together.

Kerry took off her necklace and stared at the pendant, trying to make out the tiny words inscribed on the front. "What is it?"

"Press them together and look at the back."

Stanton pulled the SUV to the curb outside Gina's apartment and wondered why there was an available parking space. "I'll wait here, I've got plenty to do," he said, reaching to pull his laptop from a bag on the floor of the back seat. "Be careful," he added with a fist out the window.

Kerry looked down, touched his hand, sensed the shape of a cell phone and instantly slid the object up the sleeve of her shirt.

CHAPTER FIFTY-EIGHT

Gina Varga opened the door to her posh Pacific Heights apartment, and Kerry saw the three of them – she, Kate, and Gina – all crammed in a canoe in shallow water. She knew, somehow, that it was Tomales Bay in northern Marin County. She wasn't remembering exactly, or was she? Gina was hugging Kate now; Stanton in his car at the bottom of the stairs; Kerry buried somewhere deep inside her head.

A wooden house, a beach house with a rickety pier.

It definitely was a wooden house, built on stilts, tall and angular in shape, with tall windows. Almost every room had both a bookcase and balcony overlooking Tomales Bay on the east side and the Pacific off in the distance to the west, occupied only by wind, fish, and occasionally loons. An endless gray driftwood pier pressed outward into the bay from the driveway. It always amazed her how ominous that pier looked from inside the house but how welcoming, warm, and oddly smooth it felt on her bare feet in summer.

Gina ushered them into her living room, adorned with brightly colored flowered fabrics. Red flowered sofa, yellow flowered chair. Kerry had always wondered who would buy these. Gina asked some perfunctory questions, like where they had been, and Kerry continued on the pilgrimage in her head. Did I really live there, she asked herself, but there was no question. How else would she know these things, remember parts of this house? But the most driving question of all: where had these memories been before now?

Mitchell Stine, her father, whom they called Munny, loved two things besides her and Kate – wood and books. He built the house in Inverness. *Inverness?* The name blinked instantly to the forefront of her mind from somewhere deep in her neurons. He'd built it over the course of two summers with his three older brothers, whom she had never met. There were bookcases and shelves in every single room, and real wood on the walls and ceilings. And not rough cut lumber either but custom finished, two-inch-thick, beautiful honey-colored pine boards. A creaky double staircase led to her parent's loft bedroom, and she and Kate slept in what they called the bubble room – a second bedroom on the main floor that had the optical illusion of being curved – walls that curved up, a slightly domed ceiling. And yet, from the outside, you could see that they were all perfectly level, ninety-degree right angles.

Kerry snapped her attention to the present at the sound of a familiar name.

"She died a long time ago."

"Mayna?" Kerry asked.

"Well, I'm glad you're still with us after all," Gina said.

Kerry reached over to squeeze Kate's hand. "What do you remember about her?"

"Everything," Kate replied.

"I ..." Kerry tried to get back to the Inverness house. She pictured the bay and the row boat they used to play in. She saw an old woman crouched near the pylons, with a rope coiled around it and one of her hands. "She was out—"

"She was a servant," Kate said in a harsh tone. "There's nothing wrong with it," she added, facing Kerry now. "Lots of families had them back then."

"In San Francisco?"

"Mayna had been your Daddy's nurse when he was a baby," Gina said. "He was sick, and she later lived with him in the house after your mother died."

"She took care of us, but she also cooked, cleaned, pretty much ran the place," Kate added.

Kerry examined the geometric pattern in the rug and continued to wonder whose reality they were talking about, and where it had been all these years. "Why didn't I remember any of this?"

"You weren't supposed to," Gina said quietly, eyeing both her and Kate.

"Why not?"

No one spoke in what felt like a vacuum devoid of sound, thought, and movement. Kerry broke the silence and walked around the living room, stepping on creaky wood boards, again taken back to the Inverness house. It was calling her.

"Remember the treasure hunts?" Kate asked her.

She remembered.

"Daddy said there was something he'd buried for us, hidden somewhere in the house."

"And we never found it," Kerry added, sitting now on the other end of the sofa. Why didn't they ever find it, as hard as they'd looked? Every weekend, almost, started with him asking who was in on the treasure hunt. Then, as easily as the word Inverness had entered her brain, another thought came in its place. It was never buried there in the first place.

"It wasn't in that house," she said aloud now. "He buried it in Inverness."

Gina's eyes widened, and she'd stopped shaking her crossed leg. "You remember that house?" she asked.

Kerry nodded. "That ... I remember. He built it with his brothers, and there was wood on all the walls inside. He was a woodworker."

"Well, in his spare time he was," Gina added. "Primarily, he was an architect. He designed ships."

Kerry leaned against the couch cushions. And then wept freely in front of two people she had known deeply once, and barely seen over the past decade. The ease of her tears lately more than just surprised her. She was becoming someone she barely recognized, someone free with their emotions. "They told me," she said to Kate, "that you died in the fire." The sobs made her voice and hands tremble. Kate moved close and held her. "But I didn't remember you anyway, even if they hadn't told me. As if something happened to my memories."

"Yeah, something happened to them all right."

"Kate!" Gina snapped.

"No," Kate argued. "That's enough. I won't lie to her now."

"This is not the—"

"He, Munny, inherited something from his family," Kate said directly to Kerry. "Something ..." she caught herself, "... valuable." She shook her head. "More than just valuable."

Kerry wiped her eyes, interested, but not knowing who to believe at this point. "So there really was a treasure all along?" she said in a small voice, a child's voice that didn't feel like her own.

"There was. And you were right that it was never in the mansion. But the men who wanted that treasure didn't know that."

"Who?"

"I heard Munny refer to them as The Consortium at one point, but I never knew exactly who or what they were. They had him, the house, all of us on surveillance and they set the house on fire and watched on camera to see if, in a frantic moment, he would give up its location and grab it before the whole place burned to the ground."

Kerry swore she could smell smoke right now in some part of her head, or nose. "Consortium," she repeated Kate's word.

"Men in fancy suits. Museum curators, supposedly. All from different cultures and walks of life but with one common purpose. They were treasure hunters."

While Kate talked, Kerry watched as Gina stood in slow motion and moved to the window, gripping the back of a chair.

"They'd arrange meetings," Kate went on, "at the house when Munny was there alone, drug his drink and ransack the place."

"How do you know this?" Kerry asked.

"Mayna told me," Kate said. "It happened more than once too.

She could almost hear her father's voice right now. He called her Keys back then. "Did he die in the fire?" Kerry asked, again from her childhood voice. But wait, her grown-up brain reminded her. He couldn't have.

"He died of a heart condition," Gina said from the windows.

"You know that's not what happened," Kate shot back.

"They killed him?" Kerry paled. "But why kill him before they found the treasure? Obviously, they knew it wasn't in the house, right?"

"He died because of that treasure," Kate said. "He died to protect the secret so we would find it."

Gina stood at attention near the entrance of her living room closest to the kitchen. "I told you," Gina pressed, "you lived with him and Mayna after the fire, and he died of a heart condition a year later. You lived with Mayna after that."

Kate was holding the necklace. Kerry watched her and Gina, wondering about this Consortium of hit men. Were they watching her now? "And what about Jim Rex? And was Bill, my husband, part of this scheme?"

Kate aimed her head toward the floor, and Gina looked out the window. "Answer me, someone, for God's sake. I was married to the guy!"

"I don't know," Gina answered.

"Maybe," Kate replied.

"And none of them knew it was in Inverness?"

"One person did," Kate said, nodding.

Mayna, Kerry thought. The only person Munny ever trusted.

"She was as much family to him as we were."

Kerry sighed and rubbed her face and her temples. "Whatever Nigel or his men did or tried to do to my memory, I remember everything about that house."

Gina's eyes snapped to attention and she took two steps closer, then seemed to catch herself for being so obvious. "Would you ... remember how to get there?' she said carefully.

Kerry remembered an endless drive on a road overlooking the open ocean, which had to be Highway 1, because Inverness was south of Bodega Bay. "Give me your necklace," she said suddenly, taking Kate's necklace and holding it beside her own so the two halves of the mizpah fit together. She squinted to see the engraving on the back. Kate's half had the numbers '2530' arranged vertically, and on Kerry's half 'Drkes Lndg.' "I think it's ... an address," she said astonished by the realization, then startled out of the moment by the sound of clapping from somewhere behind Gina.

Chapter Fifty-Nine

"Well done, young lady," mocked the old Englishman who had helped Kerry escape from the hospital.

"Nigel," Kerry said and shot a death stare at Gina. "*You* set us up."

"Get up, girls," Nigel commanded with a gun in his hand, pointed at her and Kate. "We're going for a little ride."

As Gina locked her apartment, Nigel took out his phone and pressed a single button. "Take care of the detective in the black SUV downstairs," he said and winked at Kerry.

Five minutes into their journey, Nigel's phone rang. "Yes," he answered, listened, then turned to Kerry. "Looks like your detective friend's a bit smarter than we expected."

Kerry smiled to herself, pleased that her telepathy had worked.

Nigel insisted Kate sit with him in the front seat, Kerry and Gina in the back. Kerry knew it wouldn't help their situation to call her any of the vile names she'd been thinking, so she asked her something constructive instead.

"So, Mata Hari, what's the heirloom?"

"*Daddy* never told you?" Gina snipped back at her.

"Only that there was something and we had to find it."

Gina bit her lip and looked out the window for a few silent moments. Kerry watched her make eye contact with Nigel from his rearview mirror. "You might be surprised to learn, then, that you're a direct descendant of ..." she cleared her throat, "Sir Francis Drake."

"The pirate?" Kerry said, incredulous, then laughed. "Kate, you know about this?" she added after a moment.

"Yes."

"Related how?"

"Your father's side," Gina answered. "Grandfather's grandfather." She waved her right hand in the air. "The point is, there are some who believe in the existence of something called the Drake Jewel."

"I've heard of it," Kerry said, trying to remember where.

"It's just a legend," Gina added.

"Not just," Nigel corrected from the driver's seat. "It's a formidable legend based on irrefutable historical fact. It was presented to Drake by our beloved Queen Elizabeth I upon his safe return from circumnavigating the globe."

"Well, is it a legend or a real jewel?" Kerry said to Nigel.

"Oh, very real, young lady, said to have been housed in the National Maritime Museum in London."

Kerry looked at Gina, suddenly curious about her use of the word 'legend'. "What type of jewel? A ring?"

"It's a pendant," Nigel replied in a professor-voice. "There was talk early on that its original incarnation was as a choker-style necklace, but later became more known as a pendant that Drake was said to have worn on his belt as his chief adornment."

"One side is a locket," he went on, "with a mini-portrait of the Queen on the outside painted by Nicholas Hilliard, with a cover that contains an etching of the Queen's avian emblem – a phoenix."

"How old is it?" Kerry asked.

"Fifteen-nineties I think, though that's debatable, to say the least."

Kerry, riveted by Nigel's story, looked outside as they crossed under the last spire of the Golden Gate Bridge. She checked Gina's frozen expression.

"And quite ornate, mind you, which would have been very typical for that period in history. The pendant is surrounded with a diamond shape of 18-carat gold and rubies. From the pendant hangs a cluster of small, uniform pearls, likely Tahitian-based on Drake's travels, and below that, a very large, and I do mean *large* natural cultured pearl."

"You've seen this?" Kerry asked him.

"Only in pictures, I'm afraid. Now, much more interesting than any of this is the intaglio-cut sardonyx cameo of two faces," he explained. "One of an African male superimposed over the face of a European – we don't really know if it's male or female. This could mean many things – different cultures made to represent Drake's globe-trotting, if you can call it that. Or else the wide colonial stretch of the monarchy's imperialism over other cultures. It can be interpreted a number of ways and has been, over the past four centuries."

Kerry watched as they continued to North Bay – high green hills, tall trees. I know this road, she thought. Of course, having lived in San Francisco all these years, she had been here many times. But this was different. Okay, she thought, her brain working to assimilate this new information. A treasure, passed down in her lineage to her father. "You said it's in the Maritime Museum," she said looking at

Nigel.

"Well, it is, in a way," he snickered.

Gina turned to her. "Nigel and his posse of treasure hounds think it's a fake."

"And the real one's buried in some beach house?" Kerry said. "Ridiculous."

"That's what I thought," Kate added.

"No, no," Nigel cut in, "it's actually quite plausible. Drake, you see, was a pirate. Well, actually, more of a privateer, which just means his pillaging adventures were financed by the monarchy as a means of expanding the empire. As such, he amassed quite a few enemies, as you might imagine. Speculation suggests that, in what became his typically paranoid state—"

"He had a duplicate made," Kerry said.

"Very good. And had to have it completed very quickly and hidden away somewhere."

Kate closed her window in the front seat. "She's wondering what it would be worth now."

"How do you know?" Kerry protested. "Actually I was—"

"Twelve million." Nigel turned his head slightly to the right and leaned back. "And that's dollars."

"Jesus," Kate mumbled. "No wonder."

"And that's no doubt the reason why we were separated after the fire, and why the lie was created to convince me that you were dead," Kerry said to Kate.

"So we wouldn't put the necklaces together and find it ourselves?" Kate surmised.

Kerry nodded. "Have they come looking for it before?"

"From me? Well, easier to steal from a blind woman, surely. But they've supposedly been watching you."

"Watching me? Who?" Kerry demanded.

Nigel waved his hand. "No need to go into all that

now. We've seen the two halves of the necklace, that's what's important."

"Byron," Kate blurted.

No, Kerry thought.

"I'm warning you," Nigel said.

"Your new neighbor, the cute guy down the street," Kate added, giggling.

"Damen?"

"Think about it," Kate said. "Byron, your landlord, had access to your apartment any time you were at work."

Kerry pictured Byron fumbling around her jewelry drawer and bedroom. It was almost funny. "You mean to tell me you had people, numerous people in my house all looking ... for this?" she touched her neck, "and you never thought I'd be wearing it? Not even Jim Rex who's a convicted criminal?"

"Enjoy the moment," Nigel jeered. "How'd you find out about Mr. Rex? Your detective friend, no doubt."

Stanton, Kerry thought now. Would he be following them up here like she'd mentally instructed him? Maybe they hadn't known each other long enough to enable telepathy quite yet.

"Where was it?" Gina asked.

"Hanging from the bathroom mirror in plain sight," Kerry mocked. Kate snickered from the front seat. "How 'bout the jar of flour on the counter? A trap door under the toaster?"

"As usual, young lady, you seem to be missing the point," Nigel said.

"Not likely," Kerry shot back. "You think that by knowing where I would hide something of value will give you insight into where Munny might have hidden the jewel." Kerry concealed a secret grin, enjoying the metallic feel of the necklace around her neck.

Kerry was glaring at Gina, when a muffled cry came from the front seat. Nigel had the butt of his

9mm touching Kate's jaw. "I don't suppose you know much about gunshot wounds, do you?"

"Nigel," Gina snapped. "Don't be stupid."

"In the movies, you see, they always put the tip of a silencer on someone's temple, not a bad idea for discretion as there's less sound and less bleeding that way, and your victim dies instantly. That same pistol aimed at the jaw, however, at a slightly upward angle has the most remarkable effect of horrific pain, with death trailing by several seconds, maybe longer."

Gina glanced out the side window. "You might want to put that down. There's a woman in the next car screaming and staring at you with a phone in her hand."

"Really? That one?" Nigel asked, turned, and pointed the pistol at the car.

"No!" Gina screamed.

And at that very second, Nigel swerved in front of the white sedan and tore down the next exit ramp on the right. Rubber tires and metal clunked over two curbs and bounced left and right before four tires thudded finally on uneven pavement.

Kerry instinctively gripped the bottom of her seat to keep her head from hitting the roof.

"So, the older Miss Stine, you may want to reconsider your position."

"He'll do it," Gina said flatly.

"I don't need to know now, when we get there," Nigel added.

A sick thought came into Kerry's mind now, thinking of the word Kate had uttered in the warehouse cell. "How did you know it wasn't hidden in the house?" she said, looking first at Gina, then Nigel.

"It was Mayna's idea to hide it there in the first place," Kate said. "She knew all along."

"But how did you know?" she pressed, now

asking all of them.

Just past signs for Bodega Bay, Kerry noticed Gina had her eyes glued to the landscape. She pulled Stanton's spare cell phone from her purse and typed "2530 Drake Landing, Inver" in a single text message just before pulling out a tube of lip moisturizer for cover. Please please please, she thought, don't reply.

"Inverness 4 miles" the sign read. A slate-blue farmhouse on a wide corner struck something in her memory. Had she been in that house? Even the house next to it looked familiar. I know the way, she realized now, watching Nigel drive past the correct turnoff.

"It's back there," she said pointing with her head. Of course, they'd find it so delays would be pointless. Nigel kept driving. What could he be up to, she wondered, when he turned down a road on the right and parked in a small, private lot. The sign read "vacationrentals.com".

Nigel picked up his phone and dialed. "Yes, this is Mr. Baker, and I'm here with my family to see the Drakes Landing property. What week? Um," he turned his head, "when do we need it, love?" he paused. "Right, second week in August, that's right for two weeks. I'm in a black car, shall I follow you there? Yep, right, thank you."

"Nice scam. Am I your daughter or your wife?" Kerry asked and made a disgusted face.

"You and you," Nigel pointed at Kate and then Kerry, "have one job when we get to that house. I'll stall as much as I can, and Gina will entertain our property manager."

They'd be turning off Sir Francis Drake Highway onto Drake's View Drive, a left on Douglas, right on Dover, left on Sunnyside, right on Behr, and left on Drake's Landing. How did she remember after all this time?

Nigel parked on the sandy edge and motioned them out toward an elderly woman in a flowered housedress. Kerry tapped three times on Kate's elbow at the end of the pier.

"Mmmhmm," Kate replied, "I can smell the water."

"Do you remember anything about this house?" Kerry asked.

"Do you?"

"Everything."

"Well, you may not anymore," Kate replied.

Gina and Nigel went up ahead. Kerry held Kate's elbow and walked her down the length of the pier. She held tighter to her sister's arm and walked slower, each step a careful move into their collective past.

"I have so many questions. Like why you seem so strangely tolerant of all this treachery."

"I pick my battles carefully and there'll be time to explain," Kate answered.

"Do you really think it's still here, or was it ever?"

Kate snickered. "I never believed in any treasure. He always ended the game with a little box of chocolates, as if that was the treasure. Mayna, before she died, told Gina about how we had to have both necklaces to ever find what he'd left for us."

"Girls?" Nigel called in his tourist's voice. "Come up and see what you think. It's perfect!"

CHAPTER SIXTY

Grace heard Adrian shift positions on the floor where he'd been resting his eyes for the past hour. By now her fingers were tingling from so much typing, her left butt cheek had fallen asleep and her stomach was growling. She heard the wind outside, a tacit reminder of the lateness of the hour and how little time was left.

"Are you awake?" she called to him from across the room.

He gave an affirmative groan.

"Where are the backups to your documentation?"

"Right in front of you," Adrian replied. "Kathleen's hard drive."

"The main drive, or a separate drive? Or you mean a jump drive?"

Adrian sighed, rubbed his eyes and sat upright against the wall, thinking. "Should be in a folder on the desktop called Ox. Will we need those?"

"I'm sure, since we no longer have the white binders."

"But will we need to ...?"

Grace sighed and reminded herself to count to ten before answering. "Yes, Adrian, we need them. Whether it's a newspaper asking about them or a pharmaceutical company, venture capitalist, whatever. You've got to be able to prove that your formula works, and not just by test subjects."

"Just find my control group then."

"They're still alive?"

Adrian wrinkled his brow. "Why wouldn't they be?"

Instead of answering, Grace checked traffic on Twitter and saw that she had seven new followers.

"What?" Adrian said, reading over her shoulder now.

"I'll show you." She clicked on Damienbtt, a new follower. "This guy's now seeing all of Bio Girl's new tweets and only started following her after I posted a link to the first blog post." She clicked again. "Take a look here. An oncologist and an Xtreme rock climber."

"Is that significant?" He eyed her nervously. "I know, I'm clueless about technology."

"It's okay, this part's just math. Our new friend Damienbtt is a longtime Twitter user and has 455 followers, and—"

"And he's following us? Wow."

"Right!" Grace replied. "So if we were to add up all the people who follow all of his 455 followers, we're talking exposure to—"

"Tens of thousands of people, my God. And that's just one for today?"

Grace nodded slowly, the number just now starting to sink in. "Right, and we've actually got seven new ... wait ... eight new followers now."

"Jesus."

"I'm just finishing the third blog post now, and I've created a Facebook fan page."

"Where?"

Grace didn't bother telling him that Facebook fan pages are actually on Facebook. Instead, she pulled up the page showing a horizontal banner with a picture of people smoking. On top was the phrase

"Smoke the OX" and on the bottom, "An Unlikely Cure", with the word "Oxium" on a pill bottle on the right. Under the banner were a *Like* button on the left and a *Message* button on the right. Adrian started pacing again, sighing loudly.

"What? What's the matter now?"

Silence.

"You gave me the go ahead," she argued, knowing he was not trustworthy in his present state of mind.

"I know."

"You tried to do this yourself six months ago."

"I know."

"Well, weren't you prepared for this?"

"I guess not."

She watched Adrian lean against the wall and slide down into a crouch, hands in his hair. "What will happen now?"

"We wait," she said. "I've done the launch, now it needs to move itself."

"What will that look like?"

She smiled and pointed at the screen. "Retweets."

"On Twitter." He nodded. "Like forwarding an email?"

"No. You forward someone else's tweet to all your followers."

"Will we know?"

"You can see when someone retweets one of your tweets if you turn on that notification in your account. Once that starts happening, we can send a direct message thanking people for the follow and ask them if they want more information."

Adrian crossed his arms. "Kind of pushy, don't you think?"

"If you're selling workout videos, yes. But this is a potential cancer cure. Mainly, I want to hear people talking about it."

"What else can we do?"

"Search engines," she replied. "I've already got us

hooked into Google, Ask, a few others, but also using the engines themselves for auto-complete."

Adrian shrugged.

"If from this computer I Google "cigarette that cures cancer," then you could go to the Kinko's down the street, Google the word "cigarette" and it could auto-populate the rest of my previous search but in your search box, sort of like asking "did you mean this? Or this? And if you keep going to different computers and ..."

"So the search criteria builds on itself," Adrian surmised.

"If you want to work on that, I'll create my own Twitter account. A new one," she added, "hook up with an oncology Twitter community and start forwarding biogirl's posts. Wait," Grace said scanning her emails, "we've got one retweet, yes!"

"Who? And how many followers do they have?"

Grace grinned at him. "You're getting it, that's good. Let's see." She clicked the user account. "Ah," her voice sank.

"What?"

"Hmm. Well, could be good actually."

"A doctor?"

"A DJ, as in radio. Also a blogger, though, and he retweeted my second tweet, 'Someone you love has lung cancer? Please RT and pass it on!'."

"And he did."

Grace had clicked on the DJ's user account website, where he had links to radio podcasts. "Oh, no way, talk radio. Even better."

Chapter Sixty-One

Adrian stood over Grace's shoulder as she typed.

```
Privately funded clinical trials? WTF IS
this guy? #adriancalhoun #lungcancer #oxium
#magiccigarettes
```

After hitting Send, Grace turned to get a full look at the man whose life she had just changed. "You look ragged." She shook her head.

"Can't imagine why."

"No," she countered, squinting, "It's good. This is good. Now we need a picture of you and not your med school picture from twenty years ago, either." She watched as Adrian's five-star ego took over.

"Like a candid shot?"

She considered the question. "More like one of those Annie Liebowitz portraits, black and white, bags under the eyes, no makeup, distracted visionaries. Know what I mean?"

"No, I don't," he admitted. "But the light's good outside for a black and white right now."

Five-star ego, she thought and followed him outside.

CHAPTER SIXTY-TWO

"You two, go," Nigel said under his breath. "Gina, watch them. And here," he pulled Kate's fold-up walking stick from inside his coat. Kerry snatched it and unfolded it, sliding the flexible handle into her sister's grip. Gina glared at her.

"I don't need it here," Kate said in response. "I know every inch of—"

Kerry nudged her and led the way through toward the main entrance to 2530 Drake's Landing. Gina trailed behind them eight feet, watching their every move. "Are we getting warm?" Kate joked.

"Doubt it."

"Now you sound like me," Kate noted.

Kerry brought Kate into the living room of the house, and let her eyes scan the familiar space. "Do you really think—"

"What, that he hid something here?"

Kerry nodded. "I'm just like him, you know."

"Really?"

"In his mind, everything had to be done right. Woodworking's based on precision, and he was an architect ..." Kerry said thinking aloud.

"And...?"

"It means he didn't do anything haphazardly. Everything meant something in relation to something else." Kerry stood back a few feet and looked upward, pointing. "You can't see it now, but you remember the twin staircase that we used to run up and down, racing all the time?"

"To the loft. I always won," Kate smiled.

"The staircases, they're like two halves that meet and come together."

"Sounds like a bad song," Kate said.

"Or how about a necklace?" Kerry smiled and ran up the left staircase and stopped. "They don't join at all, though, it's just a landing." She leaned down to feel under the carpet and knocked on the floor softly. It sounded hollow, like it should. She rose and looked down the steep angle of the stairs and caught sight of a black vehicle parked on the far side of the sandy berm.

Stanton, Kerry thought. Thank God. She instinctively glanced at Gina to see if she'd seen it, but Gina had her eyes locked on Kate.

"Do you remember the boxes he used to make for us?" Kate asked, cautiously climbing the stairs.

"Yeah, with trap doors."

"Well," Kate said, "his boxes had secrets. Sliding panels, handles that weren't really handles."

Think Kerry, think! What am I looking at? A wooden landing with carpet and a small two-shelf bookcase above.

"Darling?" It was Nigel's ingratiating voice directed to Gina. "Bring Katie down here, would you?" he said as a command. "I want her to meet Mrs. Reed."

Gina moved to the bottom of the staircase. "Come on," she said, grasping Kate's elbow and walking them toward the front door. Kerry remained in the spot between the two staircases, absorbed in her father's design, wondering, quizzing herself the way Munny would have if he had been there. A bookcase, she thought. They're all over the house.

All over the house.

Okay, why? Because he loved to read. Was there any other reason? Come to think of it, she remembered there being bookcases in almost every single room. She started in the loft where her parents' bedroom had been and wondered – when is a bookcase not a bookcase?

Her fingers trembling, she reached up and touched the top of one of the books on the top shelf, expecting it to pull down like every other book she'd ever pulled off a shelf. It didn't budge at first, heavier with a strange, gluey sort of weight. Pulling harder now, she saw that the book was somehow attached to the book next to it, wait, to all the books on the whole shelf, about ten in total. Pulling harder and keeping her eye on the front door, Kerry leaned to the right to peer out of one of the first-floor windows and saw Gina, Kate, Nigel and an older woman in a circle. Returning her gaze to the bookcase, the entire row of books collectively pulled forward, and behind it was a long, recessed cubby. She frantically reached inside the far left side, dragging her bare fingers across the horizontal wooden length. The wood was unfinished and rough.

And it was empty.

Hurry, she reminded herself, running now from room to room checking each book shelf, trying not to be noticed by Nigel or Gina peering in every few minutes. Then she realized what she'd forgotten – the non-bookshelf upstairs had a recessed part to the front cover as well – the part attached to the book cover façade. She returned to the first bookcase and pulled the façade down again, this time angling her fingers awkwardly up and back.

Where was Stanton, she wondered now, feeling suddenly vulnerable and wondering if he'd packed his reserve pistol on his ankle holster, and if he thought that would somehow be considered conspicuous. She touched each finger to the inside front of the bookcase and, just then, felt something that didn't feel like wood.

"What are you doing in here?" It was Kate at the foot of the stairs. "We could hear you running around on the creaky floors. Have you found something?"

Shit, Kerry thought. "I thought so, but no," she lied.

Kate stared back with a cloudier version of the most beautiful blue eyes she'd ever seen.

"Hey," Stanton, in the front doorway, called up to Kerry. "Take your sister and wait in my car," he said, pointing, and slowly approaching them. "Now," he said in a more insistent voice.

Kerry went down the stairs and took Kate by the elbow toward the back door.

"I wouldn't if I were you." Nigel, in the front doorway now, stood with an arm wrapped around Mrs. Reed's neck and a gun shoved into her rib cage. The old woman whimpered with eyes tightly closed. "Don't think I won't," he said to Stanton, while Stanton kept his gaze on Kerry.

"Go, go, now," he shouted. Kerry and Kate swung out the back door toward the parking lot. With one hand on Kate's arm, Kerry very carefully switched her handbag from the left to the right shoulder.

"Get in the car," she commanded to her sister.

"Only if you do," Kate replied.

"I'll be right here," Kerry reassured and lowered Kate into the back seat and closed the door. She moved away from the car to stand on top of the dirt hill and saw Stanton with his arms out, Gina off to the side, and Nigel still restraining Mrs. Reed. Stanton bent down to put his gun on the ground.

Damn, Kerry thought. Now what?

"Let her go," Stanton demanded. Nigel just smiled,

pushed Mrs. Reed violently to the ground and headed down the driveway toward the pier. Where is he going? Kerry wondered, and watched Stanton reach down. His backup, she thought, laughing to herself and observing the scene from the hill near Stanton's car, where Kate was sitting safe. Gina kept hold of Mrs. Reed while Stanton pulled what looked like a .32 caliber pistol from an ankle holster, aimed at Nigel who was running, and fired a shot.

"Ah!" Nigel sank down and rolled over the bulk of his own legs, tumbling on the pier toward the edge of the water. From her distance, Kerry saw blood gushing out of Nigel's leg.

Stanton moved carefully toward Nigel, gun held out, motioning for Gina to move away from Mrs. Reed. Kerry gave a nod when he glanced back toward the house and car. Stanton kicked Nigel's gun from his hands into the water and watched it splash on the other side of the pier.

"This is Detective Pete Stanton," Stanton said after pressing redial on his phone. "I need a car and an ambulance at 2530 Drake's Landing in Inverness."

CHAPTER SIXTY-THREE

Walking the narrow strip of carpet from the First Class restroom down to Coach, Kerry watched Stanton fidgeting in his seat. Left leg crossed over right, then right over left, unbuttoning the second button on his Oxford shirt and loosening the tie she wasn't sure why he'd even worn. He reached up to wipe his glistening brow, then spotted her eyes on him and wiped his hands on his pants.

"I'm sorry," Kerry said squeezing past the well-dressed woman in the aisle seat.

Stanton glared apologetically at her. "I'm sort of afraid to fly."

"I can see that," she said gently and held one of his hands, still looking in his eyes. It was a tactic, she knew, and probably unnecessary at this point.

"Estevez confirmed," Stanton said.

"She's alive?"

Stanton nodded.

"Text?"

"Yep."

"Did he talk to her directly?"

"Yes, but he got a door pretty much jammed in his face."

"What did he say?" Kerry pressed.

"Just asked to speak to Rosemary Castiglia, I

guess."

"And?"

"The man said she couldn't come to the door, then an old woman shouted something from behind the door and he slammed it shut."

Kerry inhaled deeply. "So we have the address now, right?"

"Oh, yeah," Stanton nodded. "He did the UPS scam."

Kerry rolled her eyes and laughed.

"Said Robert and Claire Castiglia from New Haven had sent her a package, and he needed to confirm the address."

"Nice. How'd he get the New Haven address in the first place?"

Stanton smiled. "Estevez has, let's just say many talents."

Kerry nodded. "That usually means he's been in prison."

"Not answering that question," he said and pulled a crumpled page from his jacket. "Castiglia, 795 Chapel Court, New Haven."

"So Rosemary's alive and probably at home right now," Kerry analyzed, "and we've still got no idea who smuggled her out of SFMC."

"That's right," Stanton affirmed, "but whoever was treating her in New Haven is likely at the center of the three other lung cancer patients ... who all died within a twenty-four-hour period."

Kerry thought for a minute. "You said they were all late stage terminal, right?"

Stanton nodded and gripped the edge of his seat as the plane bounced out of its usual pattern.

Kerry watched him close his eyes and swallow. "Do you know, I mean, are you allowed to tell me how they all died?"

Stanton drew his head close to her ear. "Trace amounts of chloroform on the nose and mouth. So peacefully, they just wanted them out of the way."

"How could you determine that outside of an autopsy? And what family would grant permission for an autopsy on a terminal cancer patient?"

"Well," Stanton sat back with a smug look. "For one thing, basic forensics analysis caught traces of something green on the nostrils and mouths. Aside from that, relationships are as important to police work as evidence."

Kerry smiled. "You know someone."

Stanton tilted his head. "Well, I might have a personal friendship with a magistrate. And in this case, I might have explained the possible connection between these victims and—"

"Don't you still need permission from the family?"

"Not in the case of a capital crime."

"How do you know it was, necessarily?"

Stanton shook his head and put his palms up. "Sure, three people, complete strangers, all died from being smothered by chloroform inhalation. Could happen. But regardless, even if it's suspicion of a capital crime, you can get a court order to impose an autopsy." He studied her face. "And how would you know about autopsies, Miss Stine?"

Kerry chuckled. "Like every TV show is about that. People are fascinated by death."

"Really," he said as a statement.

"Aren't you?"

"No."

"Don't be ridiculous! You're a homicide detective."

"Doesn't mean I'm fascinated by death. I just like finding answers that other people can't find. And no, I don't do crosswords, and no, I don't do them in pen. I just like reading between the lines."

"So you like making assumptions."

"You are very argumentative to—"

"What do you read between *my* lines?"

Stanton breathed deeply and stared at the seat in

front of him. "I think you ... and your sister grew up with a lot of secrets. And now you're looking for the missing pieces. Aren't we all?" he added lightly.

An official *ding dong* accompanied red lights on the ceiling panel of the plane, and the seat belt sign flashed. "Crap," Stanton muttered. "Turbulence."

Kerry slid her arm under his elbow and clasped his hand tight. "I'll protect you," she whispered.

Stanton blinked, then leaned his face close to hers. "No one's ever said that to me before." He squeezed her hand tighter. "I like it."

Chapter Sixty-Four

Grace had placed the ad in The Hartford Courant, Craigslist, and on the community bulletin board in Atticus, linked to her cell phone. Adrian had rented them a hotel room at the Courtyard Marriott three blocks from the university. It was a perfect location.

Grace kicked off her slippers and stretched out on one of the two rock-hard double beds, the laptop open at the foot of it. "Got one more subscriber," she said.

"To the blog?" Adrian said from the other bed. He sat upright, ankles crossed, dark eyeglasses hanging below his wavy, too-long salt and pepper hair as he read from a pile of papers he'd taken from one of the trials' binders.

"Fourteen so far, not bad for twenty-four hours."

Adrian stopped reading.

"I'm uploading your picture from my phone," she said, half expecting him to leap off the bed to see it. He stared at the white wall in front of him. "Aren't you curious?"

"No."

"Why not? Do you object to this?"

"Yes, yes, if you really want to know," Adrian climbed off the bed, "I object to all of it! That picture isn't really me, not as I really am. It's ... some kind of media machine that Kathleen devised and you are engineering."

Grace sighed and rolled her eyes. "And you've got absolutely nothing to do with it? How did you expect all this would go down? I mean, after you concluded that the medicine actually works. You'd – what – walk into Pfizer and say, boy, have I got something for you?"

Adrian, on the edge of the bed with his legs crossed, drew a deep breath and silently looked at Grace. "I know someone."

"At the FDA?" Grace asked, widening her eyes. "Since when?"

"Not to cut any corners, just to get the project in the pipeline, so to speak."

Grace's phone vibrated just then. She and Adrian stared at each other. "Get it," he said. "The ad."

Jesus, she thought, that was fast.

CHAPTER SIXTY-FIVE

"Are you sure about this?"

Kerry allowed herself to remain lost in the imagery, just how she'd always envisioned New England. Tall canopies protecting orderly, uniform homes, perfectly manicured yards, color-coordinated mailboxes positioned near the street like little sentries. "Yes, I'm sure," she replied dreamily.

"Why?" Stanton persisted behind the wheel of their rented sedan.

Kerry knew what he was asking, and also what he wasn't.

"I mean, what would make you look in the newspaper the minute we got here? Who even reads newspapers anymore?"

"Just logic I guess," she said. "Go to a new place and first check the newspapers and the Craigslist/Miscellaneous category. You can learn a lot about a place that way."

Stanton was listening, then wrinkled his brow at the sound of the British woman's voice saying, "Turn left one hundred yards."

"Can't – I – turn – that – thing – off?" he said with gritted teeth.

"Like going to Brooklyn, for example. It would be unlikely that you'd find an ad there for 'Goats – Five for Twenty Dollars'. But you *would* find something like 'Fully Authenticated Andy Warhol Sketch Pad'."

Stanton nodded. "That's good investigative thinking."

"Don't bother," Kerry shot back. "I'd never join the PD."

Stanton laughed aloud. "Who said anything about that?"

"You were thinking it, admit it."

He leaned his head to the side. "I've *been* thinking it. Now what about the newspaper, though, what would make you look there?"

It was an honest question. Why had she put two quarters into a newspaper box at the airport and bought a Hartford Courant? "I don't know," she admitted. "I guess it just seemed ... logical." She laughed as she said it that word again. "We're here looking for the family of a lung cancer patient, so I checked the Classifieds under Services and then Health and Wellness."

Stanton nodded but said nothing.

"You act like you don't believe me."

"I guess I just don't get what led you there."

"A hunch?" Kerry suggested.

Stanton snapped his fingers. "Now that, I understand."

The GPS lady spoke again, directing them to turn right at the lights up ahead.

"And that's why it caught my eye. One thousand dollars just to spend ten minutes talking to someone—"

"But you said it specified only last stage lung cancer patients, right?"

Kerry nodded. "What are the chances of that? There's just ..." her voice trailed off, "... something ... about ... I can't say, really."

Stanton grabbed her arm and squeezed gently. "You okay over there?"

This neighborhood now had tall trees and deep green dark hedges surrounding every home and perimeter, very English looking. No, she wasn't okay, not completely, though she didn't know why. There was something about this place.

"Have you been here before?" Stanton's eyes were on her now.

The dark hedges weren't just surrounding each property, they were protecting them, creating an aesthetic barrier, a buffer. She couldn't take her eyes off them for some reason. "Yes," she found herself saying.

"When?"

She turned to him now. "What?"

"You just said you've been here before."

More green hedges now, cobblestone driveways, gardens lined with slate. My head hurts, she realized suddenly. "I don't know."

CHAPTER SIXTY-SIX

"Haha!" Stanton said smiling, as he pressed the 'Mute' button on the GPS. "Now ... Temple and the next right should be Church, right?" Stanton asked. Kerry was rubbing her temples. "New Haven Green?" he tried again.

"I don't feel well."

Stanton turned onto the park entranceway and veered into a spot outside the tall monument. He turned off the engine. "What's the matter with you?"

Kerry looked at him now but couldn't seem to speak. I can't go with you, she thought, trying to think in a volume that he might hear, so she wouldn't need to speak or retreat from the comfort of her head. But there wasn't comfort there either, was there? Only a tightness and the familiar sickening vice grip on both of her temples.

Stanton was dialed in, as usual, unclicking his seat belt and turning sideways. He picked up her hand and felt the pulse, pressing his fingers into her skin. Kerry stared at the glove box.

"Hmm," he kept pressing. "I see the problem now. You have no pulse because you're actually dead. Or else you're a vampire. Wait ... I feel it ..."

Had she been in her right mind, she would have laughed, at the joke and the inappropriate timing of his comedy attempt. He felt her forehead, and then the glands in her neck. "Say something. You can talk, right?"

"I can't go with you," she said.

"Where?"

"There," she replied. "I mean, I feel a little sick. You go, investigate, I'll wait here."

"I can do that," Stanton said, "but you're the one who called and talked to them. Don't you think ..."

She couldn't hear him now over the sound of her own sobs. Where were these coming from? And the sudden nausea? My God, she thought, I'm gonna throw up on him. I'll never look at him again. Was this how a nervous breakdown started?

Stanton had put both his arms around her body, drawing her head and torso into him. "I'm right here," he reassured.

"I don't know," she tried to say, then stopped and succumbed to whatever inside her was intent on spilling out. She let the convulsion of sobs release. Her body went limp under Stanton's grip.

"Look what you've been through in the past month or two," he said. "Maybe it's just catching up with you. It's understandable."

"It's not that," she said, leaning back to rub her stomach. "I feel sick, suddenly, as if I ate something bad."

"Since when?"

Kerry shrugged. "Since now. When we got here." She caught sight of two people walking toward the stone steps surrounding Bennett Fountain in New Haven Green. A middle-aged man, academic type, and a well-dressed woman, fifties, stylish gray hair, long trench coat.

Her temples throbbed now and her vision blurred.

"Do you need to go to a hospital?" Stanton stared, with wrinkled brows.

"No."

"Want me to get you some medicine? Is it a migraine?"

"No."

"Jesus," he sat back against the car door. "Nothing I hate more than feeling helpless. Tell me what I can do."

Kerry swallowed, almost as if to ask her roiling intestines and throbbing head for just five minutes with these people. Five minutes to see if either of them were the root of everything that had happened – to her life, to her job, and to these helpless cancer patients who she couldn't help but think died because of her.

She suspected, only now, that Nigel was involved with Bill and Jim Rex to get hold of her half of the necklace as a means of finding what had been buried in the Inverness house. But what about how her job had literally unraveled in the space of one day? Had they done that too, all part of their master plan? Or was there something else, some other reason why Rosemary Castiglia's chart and body had vanished one day into nowhere? Something told her that the two people on the steps right now might give her at least one of those answers.

As Kerry clicked out of her seat belt, she noticed something about the woman, the way she was standing, the way her coat draped over her shoulders. The shape of her jawline. Why was it familiar? How could it be?

Stanton opened the door for her and tried to help her out, but she shook off his grip, then caught herself. "I'm sorry," she said.

Stanton put his palms up and waited for her to close the door.

"Good afternoon," Stanton announced as the two strangers approached. "I'm Robert Middleton, and my wife, Melissa. She's feeling a bit unwell at the moment," he put his hand gently on Kerry's head.

"You okay?" he said quietly.

Kerry looked up and nodded, not because she felt okay but because this was the role she was supposed to be playing. She could do it for five minutes, couldn't she?

"I'm Adrian," the man said, "this is Grace Mattson."

All four people shook hands and stood in a semi-circle. Kerry didn't try to stop the tears now. "I'm sorry," she said looking directly at the woman. She blinked to get a closer look at the woman's strangely familiar face. "I don't know what's ... I ... know you," she said, almost astonished by the concept. She didn't consciously recognize the woman and nothing about her face specifically reminded her of anything, or anyone. Or did it?

The woman gave a slight smile. "I don't believe we've met before. I ..." the woman stopped and lowered her head to look closer at Kerry. "I'm sure this is a terribly upsetting time for both of you." She looked now at Stanton. "You're the one who's sick, I presume?"

Stanton nodded. "Today's a good day, though," he said in a chipper voice.

"Well, maybe we can make it even better. Shall we sit down?" Grace said, pointing to the nearby steps. Kerry followed and pretended to pay close attention to the woman's story about an obsessed scientist who developed a cigarette that cures lung cancer, and they need a volunteer to test the medicine live on YouTube.

"Honey," Stanton said, turning to Kerry. "What do you think?"

"I'm gonna be sick."

Stanton rose. "Okay, let's go," he said pulling her arm. "She's a bit out of sorts today," he explained to the two strangers. "Maybe we should—"

"Maybe we should cut the crap," Kerry

interjected. There was dead silence all around, except for the wind coursing through tall pines on the park perimeter. "We're not who we said we are," Kerry explained, wobbling slightly as she rose. "This is Detective Pete Stanton from the San Francisco Police Department. Homicide."

"I apologize for the deception, Doctors," Stanton said. "We had, we *have* our reasons."

"Such as?" Adrian asked.

"Rosemary Castiglia," Kerry jumped in and watched the two strangers exchange desperate glances. "I see you recognize the name. Well, she was, I mean is—"

"She was Patient X," Adrian said. "The first in the control group. How do you know her?"

Stanton nodded, thinking. "Okay, so that explains why when she came out here to 'visit family'," he said making quotation marks with his fingers, "she got home and her tumor was half its size."

"There were eleven more, twelve in the whole group. They all—"

"How many from San Francisco?" Stanton demanded.

Adrian cleared his throat and glanced at Grace. "Rosemary ... and four more," he said, staring intently at Stanton now. "Why?"

"Castiglia's okay," Stanton replied.

"What do you mean 'okay'?" asked Adrian, moving a step closer.

Stanton turned toward Kerry, who nodded soberly at him. "The other four," he said, "are dead."

Adrian stared. "Dead? I've kept in close contact with all of them ever since they got back, I'm in touch with their doctors and part of their treatment plan. My clinical research wasn't some underground—"

"Oh, come *on* Adrian, it was underground." Grace interrupted. "You were in a warehouse, they tried to kill you, for God's sake. They're still trying."

"Who?" Stanton asked.

Grace leaned in a few inches. "A group of researchers, as they call themselves, contracted by a consortium of pharmaceutical company execs, who investigate false claims of supposed miracle cures, scare or buy off the doctors involved, package it up as a new invention by their own companies, file for patents, and make themselves billions of dollars. It's been going on for decades."

Stanton listened to Grace while monitoring Kerry in his periphery. He scanned Adrian's face. "Did they find you?"

"They kidnapped me, forced Grace to give them our formula," Adrian answered.

"Well, you got away obviously, though not easily by the looks of that scar," Stanton gestured to Adrian's forehead.

"We gave them a faked formula," Adrian said, "which they may or may not still have at this point and it will take them half a year to figure it out."

"I like that," Stanton nodded. "So you're going the YouTube route to sort of go public on your own."

"Grace thinks it'll be harder to kill a celebrity who's a household name," Adrian said, squeezing Grace's hand.

"Are you?" Stanton asked.

"He's being interviewed by the Huffington Post later today," Grace said, "and I think we've found our YouTube volunteer." She turned to Adrian. "We got another call from our ad on our way here."

"I can help get you police protection at the very least," Stanton said in a more official tone, "connect with the New Haven PD, tell them your story, and see if they can track down your kidnapper."

Adrian looked at the ground. "They killed my assistant, Kathleen Dwyer," he said quietly.

Stanton shook his head. "I'm sorry. You're not

safe here out in the open. Come with me."

Kerry had wandered up ahead and waited in the passenger seat of Stanton's car, watching Grace approach. Her walk, the way she drove her hands deep in her trench coat pockets, the familiar angle of her jaw. Grace opened the driver's side door, sat, and closed the door.

"You're English," Kerry said, wiping her eyes on her shirt cuff and no longer caring who saw her.

Grace stared at the passenger door, unmoved.

"Were you born there?" Kerry pressed.

"Manchester," she nodded.

Kerry looked up and breathed, framing her next question in her mind first. "Have you ... ever lived anywhere else? I mean besides Connecticut?" She watched the woman close and then open her eyes as if she'd just made an important decision.

"San Francisco," the woman nodded. "Twenty-seven years ago ..." she continued, with an odd stare. "I suspect that's about how old you are now."

"That's exactly how old I am," Kerry replied, squinting now, processing the subtext, and barely breathing. Stanton and Adrian had moved from the stone steps to under a thick canopy of trees, which the wind was bending now at thirty-degree angles. "My father was Mitchell Stine," Kerry said carefully, still not completely certain this conversation was happening. "Everybody called him Munny."

The woman, still staring now, seemed to struggle to process something. "I didn't," she said softly. "I called him Mitch."

"You ... knew him then." Kerry's mind wouldn't slow down now, and though she was sitting she felt suddenly out of breath. She had a perfectly clear picture of Mayna standing in her typical house dress in the kitchen of the San Francisco house, a dish towel in one hand. Had it not been for their different races, she might have been her own mother. Had she always known? Kate wasn't born till three years later, so the timing seemed, right now, at least possible. Could Grace be her? No. It was too random. This Englishwoman no less, across the country, a complete stranger. It wasn't possible. "How did you two know each other?" Kerry asked finally, getting back to basics.

Grace drew in a deep breath and seemed to shake off her previous eeriness. "I was doing my residency at SFMC," she said in a more regular voice, "and my roommate, Cassandra, was taking one of your father's classes at UCSF. She was an architecture student." Grace drew in a long breath. "Her car was totaled in an accident, so for a while, I dropped her off at school on my way to the hospital every evening. They give residents all the crappy night shifts that nobody one else wants," she added under her breath. "This one class, Aesthetic Theory I think, got out at eleven and sometimes they all went to this bar afterward, and one time I went with them and met ... your father." Grace sniffed and touched the corner of her eye.

Kerry watched this display of stifled emotion. Had she loved him? It seemed obvious enough now. Of course, the story could be easily checked, but she didn't need to check it. Her body knew. The migraine and nausea had disappeared somehow. She breathed heavily into the moment, and then returned her gaze to the woman's familiar blue eyes.

"Were you in love with him?"

"I might still be," Grace said easily. "I've never loved anybody else."

"Not Adrian?"

"Oh," she shrugged, "I love Adrian, yes, of course. Like family. No, not like family, he *is* family. But that's different."

"After I was born, Munny and his housekeeper,

Mayna, raised me themselves, I hadn't realized that," Kerry said in a dreamy voice, "really until now. How hard that must have been for him."

Grace nodded and closed her eyes. "Indeed."

"Why didn't you stay there?" Kerry asked matter of factly. "If you were in love with him."

The woman pulled in a long breath and again wiped tears from her eyes. "Well, if you're really who I think you are, we've got a lifetime of questions to work out with each other, that being one of them."

Kerry recalled the events of the past month, the past two months, the hospital, it all came flashing back and somehow seemed to make a tiny bit of sense in this particular moment. She felt something loosen in the center of her chest just then, and she reached out and grabbed the woman's hand. "Yes," she said, still looking at the familiar face and turning the word *mother* over and over in her mind.

CHAPTER SIXTY-SEVEN

"Did you call the intern?" Grace asked from the hotel room double bed with her eyes still closed.

Adrian groaned from the bed next to hers and slowly rolled over. "Don't you ever rest?" he complained.

"It's a fair question," Grace said, coming out of the bathroom a few minutes later, having brushed her teeth, washed her face, hands, and pulled the plastic brush through her hair, which was still damp from last night's shower. "There's the question of confidentiality and getting an NDA signed. Also, an intern could be a minor, so there's—"

"What are we doing?"

"What?" Grace looked down at Adrian's face to make sure she'd heard him correctly. He's horrible in the morning, she reminded herself, remembering so many late study nights and conversations when they'd been working together on what they had called *fringe horticulture* and other species cultivation that would one day be used in biotech's fringe medical remedies. It had been important work, at the time, and they had both agreed to live like eighteen-year-olds in and out of hotels, pulling all-nighters, when they were way too old for such things.

"What are we doing here?" Adrian sat up and

folded his arms behind his head.

Grace sat on the edge of her bed. "I'm protecting you."

Raised brow. "You're my bodyguard? How much weight can you bench press?"

"I might surprise you," she said.

"No interns."

"No?"

He shook his head. "Not at this stage. I think it's too risky, and by the time we bring in a new person, orient them on the project, the history, the requirements," he waved his hand. "They always have so many questions."

"Shouldn't they?" Always the devil's advocate.

"We don't have time now. We've got a willing volunteer and really just a few days to administer the serum and check his levels. I'm thinking IV at this point. There's no time to make actual *product* and properly ventilate, yadda yadda. Just take the liquid form and see what happens."

"You've used the liquid form in some of your trials, right? I remember Kathleen saying so." She walked back into the bathroom.

Adrian nodded and flung back the bed sheets and rose. "We ran out is the truth of it. At one point, all we had was the liquid form, and we were halfway through."

Grace sighed and closed her eyes.

"No, we didn't continue the same trial after changing forms. I concluded the results we'd measured so far with the inhalation method, and started another one with the IV."

"Miraculous," she said, pulling on clothes from behind the bathroom door.

"You don't have much faith in my judgment, Grace." Adrian paused for the comment that never came. "Confirm or deny?" he pressed.

Grace exited the bathroom fully dressed, moving

quickly through the room to find her purse and phone. She looked briefly at him, then continued her investigation. "I'm not going there right now."

"Where?"

"That conversation's a landmine. I'll be at the warehouse getting set up."

"Is there coffee downstairs?"

"Don't rush," she said, ignoring the question. "Call me when you're ready and I'll come and get you. I want to check Twitter, and the blog hits, and get a sense of who's watching us at this point."

Grace returned to the Courtyard Marriott an hour later, carefully balancing one of those cardboard drink trays on one of her flattened palms. She kicked the bottom of the door with her toe. Please, please don't be in the shower, she thought.

"Hi, honey, I'm home," she joked as Adrian pulled open the door.

"Awww, you brought me a venti cappuccino." He kissed her on the cheek and took the drink tray from her hands.

"We're all set up for Milton Genovese, who will meet us at the warehouse tomorrow," Grace said.

"Tomorrow? We need to—"

"I know, I know. He'll be in the area all day today and can come by anytime we want to give us a baseline for all his vitals."

Adrian nodded, blinking.

"Did you shave all that stubble?" Grace realized that he too had noticed the level of domesticity between them. Sleeping a foot away from each other, sharing the same room, same space.

"I did. And I'm being interviewed by the Huffington Post this afternoon. Someone named Sheila will do the interview via phone. Make sure my phone's charged at three o'clock," he reported back and smiled.

"Not surprising." Grace sat cross-legged on the floor, nursing her coffee. "I've just checked biogirl, and we've got forty-five new followers to the Twitter account and fifteen new blog subscriptions."

"Jesus." Adrian put his coffee down. "In one day this happened?"

"Well, almost two days. And the Twitter search hits have become #smoketheox to #smox to #smux."

"How many ... I mean how many hits or search hits or whatever you call them?"

"A lot. They don't show the totals like Google does, but I kept scrolling down and it was more than just a few pages. Anyway, the video camera's set up and we've got it for a week, I paid in advance. And I arranged with my friend in radiology to get two MRIs done."

"But we'd have to admit him first, wouldn't we? And get concurrence from his primary?"

Grace smiled.

"You've got friends who do complimentary MRIs? What are you, the mafia or something?"

Grace paused to arrange the right words. "I have a friend in radiology whose mother is sick."

"Let me guess," Adrian said and smiled. "Emphysema?"

"Yep."

"So she's granting you use of an MRI—"

"Twice. Two of them, including slides and the flattened images," Grace moved her hand in a circle.

"In exchange for Oxium for her mother? Sure, whatever she needs," Adrian replied. "Though it might be a while."

"Might be sooner than you think," Grace said under her breath.

CHAPTER SIXTY-EIGHT

Time to Quit? Maybe Not.
The Huffington Post
By Sheila McClaren

(New Haven, Ct.) Everything you've ever believed about cigarette smoking is about to radically change, thanks to a man being hailed as Dr. Miracle.

With more letters after his name than can fit on a business card, Dr. Adrian Calhoun is small town, but not small time. Originally from a tiny dot on the New England map known as Saco, Maine, Calhoun has spent the past twenty years quietly researching one of our civilization's most efficient killers, while beefing up his already bloated resume. Why? He's got a cause. What's the cause? Among other things, fighting lung cancer.

But with degrees in microbiology, virology, and horticulture in addition to his M.D., you might be thinking, "Why lung cancer?" It's a fair question, considering his collegiate rallying against the ever powerful tobacco lobby, which Calhoun still considers to have unequivocal congressional control. But Calhoun's obsession is larger than that.

Tracing back to the loss of his mother to the disease eighteen years ago, Calhoun began experimenting with cellular modifications to not only tobacco plants but other substances known to counter the toxic effects of nicotine. When asked about these 'other substances', Calhoun refused to comment.

Ever heard of Oxium?

If not, don't worry. You will. Whatever his motivations, Calhoun, a resident of New Haven, Ct. incurred significant personal cost over the past five years to develop what people are calling the answer to our prayers – a cigarette that not just slows but may even reverse lung cancer.

Calhoun describes his somewhat underground clinical trials as not just a means of protecting his invention but also a "prudent way of protecting the safety of (my) control group", which originally included eleven Stage IV sufferers of small cell lung carcinoma (SCLC). A later control group included just six adults suffering from non-small cell lung carcinoma (NSCLC). Calhoun closely monitored the effects of patients inhaling Oxium every hour over a two- and four-week period, and in every case, there was at least a 35% decrease in primary tumors.

But Calhoun has a long way to go, says Dr. Jesse Goodman, FDA Chief Scientist and Deputy Commissioner for Science and Public Health. "Filing for a new drug application is the tip of the iceberg," says Goodman, including a long list of institutional and medical review board approvals needed to begin the process. Asked about the efficacy of so-called 'back room trials', Goodman dodged the question and pointed to the fact that most trials are performed first on rats.

Other factors that could affect the conclusion of Calhoun's research and the ultimate availability of Oxium to worthy candidates include the over-regulation of the pharmaceutical and biotech industries over the past several years. This compounded by the costs of lengthy clinical trials and the risk of low market return could slow the process even more. There's always a possibility of accelerated FDA approvals for life-threatening illnesses like HIV that have no viable treatments, though this bureaucratic shortcut has received strong criticism and is considered a perilous gateway for other FDA applicants wanting a faster process.

Whether Calhoun intends to take down Big Tobacco or Big Pharma, he's got a solid idea backed by two decades of experimentation and research. "As to the future path of Oxium," says Goodman, "time will tell".

Chapter Sixty-Nine

"Ready?" Grace said and watched the elderly man in front of her nod. She reached over his head and pressed the REC button on the digital camera.

"Could you state your name, please?"

"Milton Genovese," the man replied in a gurgly voice.

"How old are you?"

"Seventy-five."

"And how did you come to be here with us today, Mr. Genovese?"

"To be a guinea pig," he said and chuckled, then coughed. Grace closed her eyes momentarily. "I'm here to take a new medicine to heal my lungs."

"And it's your choice to be here?"

"Yes."

"All right then. Pulse is seventy-two," Grace said and recorded the number on the spreadsheet open on her laptop. She threaded the blood pressure cuff through the metal end and slid the cuff onto Mr. Genovese's arm. After inflating and deflating it, she announced, "One twenty-five over seventy-five."

"Is that good or bad?" the man asked.

"We're just taking a baseline today, so we have something to compare your numbers with after we begin treatment. Do you remember your weight from your last doctor's visit?"

"About one sixty-five," the man replied. Grace recorded the number and slid a digital thermometer into the man's mouth. One second later, the object beeped. Grace pulled it out and announced "Temperature ninety-seven degrees."

Just then, the door to the warehouse barged open. Grace immediately pressed STOP on the camera and put a reassuring hand on Mr. Genovese's shoulder.

"What are you doing here?" she called out, somewhat annoyed at the interruption. "I was going to pick you up."

Adrian approached and walked up to the older gentleman and extended his hand. "I wanted to meet our newest patient," he said with a car salesman smile. "I'm Dr. Adrian Calhoun."

"This is the man who invented your miracle cure, Mr. Genovese." Grace secretly rolled her eyes at yet another display of what she considered grandstanding.

"Wow, I'm honored to meet you, and I guess I'll just say thank you. I'm in your hands." The man smiled. Grace leaned down to whisper in his ear. "You can go now, sir, and we'll see you for the first treatment tomorrow. Two o'clock, right?"

The man grabbed both sides of the chair and slowly pushed himself to a standing position. "See you then."

Grace motioned for Adrian to walk him out, and as she checked her watch, she tapped her fingers on the laptop cover knowing who was likely on the other side of the warehouse door.

Chapter Seventy

"Is that really you?" Grace heard Adrian say outside the door. A wide grin inhabited her face.

A moment later, she caught sight of Adrian leaning down to hug an old woman in the doorway. "Come in, please," Adrian said and held the door while the old woman walked into the large warehouse room. Adrian took her arm. "Can I help you? Can I walk with you?"

"You can," the woman said, "but I don't need it. I'm fine."

Adrian and the woman approached Grace, who came around to greet them. "This is my partner, Grace Mattson."

"Hello, Rosemary, can I call you Rosemary?"

"Certainly, yes. It's nice to meet you finally."

Adrian stepped back a few paces and crossed his arms. "How long have you two been planning this little visit?"

Grace snickered and winked at Rosemary Castiglia. "I called and asked her if she wanted to talk about your treatment on YouTube, and—"

The old woman turned to Adrian and grabbed both of his hands. "Of course I would, Dr. Calhoun, it's because of you that I'm even standing here. Because of you, my tumor's gone."

Grace held her breath while watching Adrian wipe sudden tears from his eyes.

"I came here to thank you, and to tell the world on YouTube what you've done for me."

"Okay, so you're clear on what's going to happen now?" Grace said. "Dr. Calhoun will be filming us, and I'll be asking you questions, which you should answer as honestly as you can. Do you have any questions before we start?"

The old woman listened and nodded. "I'm ready."

Grace set a cup of water next to Rosemary, sat opposite her, and suddenly wished she'd touched up her makeup before nodding to Adrian.

Adrian held up three fingers, then two, then one, then pointed at Grace and pressed the REC button.

"I'm Grace Mattson and I'm here talking with lung cancer patient, Rosemary Castiglia from San Francisco, California. Rosemary, how old are you, dear?"

"Seventy-nine."

"And when did you first hear about Dr. Adrian Calhoun?"

"I replied to an ad in the newspaper the end of last year about a doctor looking for volunteers for a new lung cancer treatment.

"And where did you go for this treatment?"

"Oh, I don't remember exactly. It was," laughs, "an old warehouse that we pretty much used as a smoking lounge."

"A smoking lounge?" Grace chuckled politely. "Can you explain?"

"Dr. Calhoun was testing a new cigarette that cures lung cancer."

"Tell us how that worked."

"Well, we all showed up at eleven o'clock, there were six of us, the doctor and his assistant took our vital signs, we signed a lot of paperwork, they hooked us up with monitors, and we smoked these funny cigarettes, one after the other."

"How many did you smoke during one treatment?" Grace asked her.

"About five or six. Then they'd test our vitals, we'd smoke a few more, and then come back in a couple of days."

"How many times a week did this happen?"

"Three, to start, then during the second month, twice a week, and once a week for the third month. Then we started the cycle again a few months later, but in a different place."

"Okay. How long had you smoked and about how much?"

The woman snickered and shook her head. "Three packs a day, sometimes more, for about thirty years."

"And how did the cancer manifest? I mean, what kind of—"

"I had tumors in both lungs, small cell carcinoma. It was stage three when they discovered it."

Grace leaned back and sighed, thinking. "These cigarettes. What were they like? Did they taste like ... tobacco?"

The woman paused. "Not really, they sort of tasted like coffee, and sort of minty but not like menthol. I think he said there are herbs in them."

"So not an unpleasant taste then?"

"Oh, no. Very pleasant," the woman nodded and smiled at Adrian behind the camera. "I liked them."

"Okay. So tell us how you felt after smoking a few of these cigarettes."

The woman breathed deeply and closed her eyes. "I felt calm. They made me very, very calm."

"Did they have any adverse side effects? Did they ever make you sick? Or dizzy? Or any side effects that came a few days later?"

"Yes."

Grace and Adrian exchanged glances.

"Can you describe them?"

"I slept better than I'd ever slept in my life. And I had more energy during the day. I've never been the outdoorsy type, and, well, I'm old. So I got tired easily and usually went to bed by about seven at night. After I started treatment, I could stay up late with my husband, watching Letterman!" she said with a cackling laugh.

"What types of treatment were you getting from your regular doctors?"

"Well, we tried chemo, I had two rounds of radiation, and the cancer still came back. So then I got these injections, which were horrible. I had sores in my mouth, constant diarrhea, terrible insomnia and I felt nervous all the time."

"Were your tumors shrinking as a result, though?"

"No. I was considered terminal when my husband saw the doctor's newspaper ad. It was like a miracle. Those cigarettes saved my life."

CHAPTER SEVENTY-ONE

HBO LIVE

Real Time with Bill Mann

Guest: Adrian Calhoun

Mann: You've heard of him, you've read about him, you follow him on Twitter, you've probably seen him on YouTube, so you know my next guest is the Anti-Christ to lung cancer. Please welcome the innovative Dr. Adrian Calhoun.

Calhoun: Thank you.

Mann: Were you ever a smoker?

Calhoun: (Laughs)

Mann: What's so funny?

Calhoun: That's your job, isn't it? To make me laugh?

Mann: You've got me confused with Letterman. My job is to say the wrong thing and make people mad. What's yours?

Calhoun: (sighs) I have so many, I have to think about it.

Mann: Making the world a better place?

Calhoun: Sure, I'm a hippie, I admit it.

Mann: When were you born?

Calhoun: 1955.

Mann: And you're from ... Maine, right? Portland?

Calhoun: Saco. It's near Portland.

Mann: I've actually been to Saco believe it or not. How many people lived there when you were growing up?

Calhoun: Less than a thousand, I imagine.

Mann: So were people healthy in Saco, Maine at that time? I mean, what was your impression of what made a healthy person back then? You got an undergraduate degree in biology, then a master's in virology, and then you went to med school specializing in pathology and oncology.

Calhoun: (Nodding)

Mann: I mean, wait, how many degrees is that exactly?

Calhoun: Laughs.

Mann: No, seriously, you're a healer. Right?

Calhoun: I like to think so, yes.

Mann: Were you always one?

Calhoun: I used to kill a lot of bugs when I was little.

Mann: That's it, you're going to hell! Wait, wrong TV show, sorry. But, I mean, who do you hope to heal by getting Oxium manufactured? You lost your mother to lung cancer, was that part of it?

Calhoun: (Pauses) Part of, like, the journey? Sure, of course. Though I was studying cancer before my mother got sick.

Mann: So she smoked cigarettes at home when you were young?

Calhoun: Everyone did. In the sixties, you almost attracted more attention if you didn't smoke. It was as ubiquitous as drinking spring water is now. None of us had any consciousness about hydration. Hell, the majority of illnesses pre-1900 were caused by dehydration.

Mann: That's interesting.

Calhoun: And there weren't always a lot of

options as there are now. You had alcohol of course, which is dehydrating, coffee and tea, also dehydrating, and then sugary drinks like sweet tea, lemonade …

Mann: Oh, and one of my all-time favorites, buttermilk. I've tried it. It's good.

Calhoun: So is chocolate and ice cream. Life is hard, and food is a wonderful salve. So things like fat, salt, sugar not only taste good but can make you feel pampered and indulged. A quick fix, and there's nothing wrong with that.

Mann: And cigarettes?

Calhoun: Well, sure. They release dopamine, which makes you feel calm, relaxed, relieved.

Mann: Does anybody else hear a looming 'however' in that sentence?

Calhoun: Sure. Within seconds of inhaling a lit cigarette, the poisonous toxins in carbon monoxide gas enter your bloodstream and start wreaking havoc on every one of your vital organs. So the combination of nicotine and carbon monoxide gas raises your blood pressure putting strain on your heart and blood vessels. Compound that over the quantity and longevity of your habit.

Mann: I used to smoke, for more years than I'd like to admit. So I can vouch for the fact that cigarettes make you feel good. Then, the relationship sours and they start to make you feel like crap. So what's your remedy?

Calhoun: Well, just to be clear, Oxium is not a cessation aid. But it has been proven to mitigate the effects of lung cancer.

Mann: COULD it help with addiction?

Calhoun: It's possible, sure. Oxium contains a variety of plant extracts and herbs that—

Mann: Plant extracts? Did you say marijuana?

Calhoun: (Laughs)

Mann: I swear I heard you say marijuana, sorry.

Calhoun: No, there are no cannabis extracts in Oxium, but I know what a fan you are of it. And rightly so. Cannabis is very medicinal.

Mann: For things like lung cancer?

Calhoun: It helps with the nausea caused by chemotherapy, it's also anti-inflammatory. But it's the specific combination of herbs and extracts in Oxium and the amounts of each substance and the synergy that they collectively create that makes it a potent anti-carcinogen.

Mann: That's intriguing. What's in it?

Calhoun: Sorry, that's not public knowledge yet.

Mann: Oh, come on!

Calhoun: Sorry.

Mann: Okay fine, be that way. Let's talk about something even more controversial than cigarettes. Tell me what you think is wrong with the pharmaceutical industry.

Calhoun: (Snickers)

Mann: Was it always this way? Fifty years ago? A hundred years ago? I mean, did the most corrupt and powerful political lobby start out with good intentions?

Calhoun: I think that's a reasonable assumption, yes. I mean, the people who are in charge of making medical decisions, requirements, standards in our country, like the Surgeon General, they're doctors, for the most part. They have to have an actual medical degree from an accredited medical school in order to perform their jobs. And you don't go down the grueling, lonely path of medicine just for fun. You do it because you feel compelled to heal sick people. Because you can't picture yourself doing anything else.

Mann: So what happened?

Calhoun: Health is an efficient cash cow, that's obvious. Everybody will pay for it, people are willing to pay a lot, and it's easy to market. Like war.

Nobody likes the idea of war, but it's like caffeine for the global economy. But that's not what it's about.

Mann: So you think what started as a noble purpose a century ago is only about money now?

Calhoun: No. I think what funds the pharmaceutical industry isn't illness. It's fear. What's the most universal thing there is, among all of us sharing this planet? We're afraid of dying, and we want longevity more than anything, and we're willing to sacrifice other amenities so we can pay for it.

Mann: Like high cholesterol, for example.

Calhoun: Exactly. Regardless of what we eat, how much we exercise and how clean we live, our organs work less efficiently as we get older. The way we metabolize food. The way stress works its way through our bodies. We get slower, weaker, and it's easier for disease to inhabit a weak host than a young, vital one.

Mann: What about medicines like Abraxane for lung cancer? That's an FDA-approved anti-carcinogen.

Calhoun: Yes, it's FDA approved and widely administered.

Mann: What's wrong with it? Or let me ask you this ... why is Oxium a better choice for lung cancer patients?

Calhoun: Well, it's not a choice at all, at the moment, because it hasn't been FDA approved or formally manufactured. But, the question I always ask with pharmaceuticals is about the side effects of the medication. Medication changes something in your body, and those changes can trigger other changes. That's a basic given of human biology. The problem with many of the most powerful prescription medicines is that while it's attacking a disease, it's also killing off your body's natural immunities to not only that particular disease but other diseases, which can create a long-term imbalance, which just creates its own vicious cycle of more imbalance.

Mann: And you intend for Oxium to be inhaled through the lungs, right?

Calhoun: Well, yeah, though I hope it will be available in a number of forms. But the idea is that inhaling the smoke from Oxium will be the most efficient delivery mechanism to the parts of the lungs that are most critically affected. A pill that gets absorbed through the bloodstream is also efficient, and systemic, but just takes longer. And there's more chance for complications that way.

Mann: So what's next for Adrian Calhoun, the man who's invented a cigarette that cures cancer? You need a benefactor, right, to help you manufacture your product?

Calhoun: Well, there are a few steps in between there, but ultimately yes.

Mann: My assistant's reading some emails that have come in during this broadcast. People are writing, "Way to go, when can I get some," and here's someone who's asking why the cure is in cigarette form, as that definitely wouldn't help with the addiction of inhaling something into your lungs.

Calhoun: It's a good point, and as I said, it's not a cure for addiction. Although ... the herbs in the formula will help to heal and strengthen the lungs, and calm the mind so it definitely could have a positive effect in that direction.

Mann: And here, a gentleman named M. Sharma, who says he's from a San Francisco-based pharmaceutical company, is interested in learning more about your cure. Looks like today might be a good day for you, Dr. Calhoun, and for lung cancer patients everywhere. Thank you for being here today.

Calhoun: Thank you.

Chapter Seventy-Two

"Pete," Kerry whispered. "Wake up, we're landing."

A flight attendant walked past and told the man next to them to raise his food tray.

"Ma'am," Stanton said to the flight attendant, "this woman drugged my drink. I'd like to have her arrested and taken into custody as soon as we land."

Kerry laughed and shook her head at the flight attendant, who smiled and kept walking. "Why didn't you ever take a pill before this? You just suffer every time you fly?"

"Pretty much, or for long periods I just wouldn't go anywhere."

"That's horrible. There's so much to see in the world."

"Well," he smirked, "there is now. Don't let me forget, I need to call my boss when we land."

"You told him you were leaving, right?" Kerry said.

"Well, the arrangement was for four days off. I'm gonna tell him I have the flu and can't fly due to my ears being too blocked to handle the pressure. I'll tell him I have a note from a doctor here."

"What a scammer."

"It's worth the risk, believe me."

Kerry inched closer to him. "Really?"

"Well, I can't remember the last time someone asked me to go anywhere with them, for one thing, let alone England. I'm gonna take as much time as I want right now."

Kerry leaned in and kissed Stanton's cheek, then toppled clumsily onto his lap as the plane's wheels touched and bounced off the ground. "Welcome to London Gatwick Airport."

"Don't you wanna check in to the hotel first? I'd really love to sleep a bit more, to be honest."

"I can imagine. You've got a few more hours on that anti-anxiety pill. This won't take long, I promise, and we'll get you a nice cappuccino on the way."

"What is this secret errand that we're doing?" Stanton asked, hoisting their luggage into the "boot" of a taxi.

"Greenwich," Kerry instructed the driver.

"Royal Observatory today?" the man asked.

"Eventually, but we're starting at the Maritime Museum," Kerry said and then turned toward Stanton. "We're going to see a jewel in a museum."

Stanton perked up. "Wow. I've always wanted to go there." Stanton turned sideways and flopped down on Kerry's lap and closed his eyes. "Night-night."

"If you see a coffee shop, could you stop?" Kerry asked the cabbie.

"Oh, yeah, best in town's round the corner."

A man named Marcus walked down a grand, curved staircase to meet them, right on schedule. Kerry had already fed Stanton two Earl Greys, so he was standing appropriately upright and politely shook the man's hand as a greeting.

"Miss Stine," the man said and shook her hand, then clasped his hands behind his back. "I'll admit I was surprised by your query."

"Really?" she said, suddenly conscious of her handbag.

"Well, you not only requested a private tour of the Drake Jewel but a private audience." The man leaned in toward Kerry. "Are you intending to steal it?" he asked with a smug chuckle.

Stanton looked at Kerry, then at the man, then took another sip of his tea.

Kerry knew that, in the game of poker, part of the game is knowing when to keep your mouth shut. She did, and they followed the dapper old man up a grand staircase and down the Antiquities hall of the Special Collections wing. They passed through a security checkpoint disguised as "greeters" wearing disarming light blue suits. But Kerry knew better. "Hello, hello, hello," she said to all three of them. Stanton turned to look at each of them as he walked past, looking appropriately confused.

"Here," the man Marcus instructed and motioned them down a narrow, dimly lit hallway. "You've come at the right time of day, we're about to close." He checked his watch. "Sorry, we are closed actually, so we're the only ones here. Are you sure you're not up to no good?" the man said with a sly grin.

Kerry smiled and took the man's elbow. "In fact, I'm up to something very good."

"Not sure exactly what that means, but okay. It's down here, follow me. There's really no need to talk softly, but we all do it as sort of paying homage to the past, so to speak. We walk slowly, keep the lights dim, as if the ghosts and spirits guarding these monuments of history might be disturbed." Marcus stopped walking and pointed at a deep alcove, with brown painted walls, a white ceiling, a minuscule light shining downward, and a tiny gold pin from which hung a striking pendant. "Here," he pointed.

Kerry stared at its long shape, the diamond form made up of luminous gold ornamentation interposed with large, dark burgundy shaded rubies. The two faces in the center – one white and one dark – were surrounded by ovular trim and encased in more gold. Hanging from a tiny ring on the bottom of the jewel was a cluster of tiny pearls delicately strung together, and below that – a single tiny ruby stone ... and an enormous teardrop-shaped Tahitian white pearl. Kerry, her eyes affixed, realized she was hardly breathing.

"I can barely see it. Can't you turn the lights up?" Stanton complained.

"I'm sorry but I'm afraid not," Marcus replied. Normally on a sunny day, there's plenty of ambient light from the skylights to illuminate the actual piece, even reflections that light it up so it sparkles from time to time. Now, Miss Stine, you were very precise in your request to the Director. Would you like a few moments to ..."

"No, it's all right. Let's go into a conference room so we can talk."

Marcus put his palms out as if to surrender to his confusion, and turned toward the outer room. "It's down here, and yes, it's brightly lit, Detective."

Stanton nudged Kerry. "You told him I'm a detective?" he whispered.

"Why not?"

The conference room was small, round, and just what Kerry had hoped for, resembling a police interrogation room. "What are these used for?" Kerry indicated the fainting couches.

"Oh," Marcus reflected, "mostly for old ladies whose rheumatism is acting up and they need to rest for a few moments."

Stanton sat in a burgundy leather armchair, while Kerry put her handbag on the round table. "I have something to show you." Marcus came to the table and Stanton kept watch. "Actually, it's something I want to give you."

Kerry unzipped her large handbag and pulled out a large, crumpled piece of blue fabric and set it in the center of the table. The weight of the fabric *thunked* against the heavy wood surface.

"Go ahead," Kerry said, looking directly at Marcus.

The old man hesitantly approached the blue fabric and turned to her. "It's not ticking, is it?"

"There's nothing harmful in there. But it's something you'll be very interested in."

The man gently unwrapped the folds of the fabric and picked up the object to pull back the final layers. It was something shimmering, gold and silver, with several other colors. He abruptly turned back toward Stanton. "Would you flick on that other switch, please?"

Stanton obliged and returned to the table, staring at Kerry. "My God," he said. "Are you kidding me? It was *there* all along!"

"What kind of ... joke ... young lady ... "

"It's no joke, sir. My name is Kerry Stine and my father was Mitchell Stine from San Francisco, a well-documented descendant of Sir Francis Drake. The story of Drake making a duplicate of the jewel before it was brought here in 1585, sir, was true. This is the real one that's been buried in our summer house in Inverness since 1965."

Marcus held the object in his trembling hands for a moment, looked deeply at Kerry, and then set it down on the fabric.

"May I presume that you've got the proper documentation that goes with this outlandish claim, my dear?"

Kerry pulled a 9 x 12 manila envelope from a compartment in her handbag and handed it to him. "Everything's here, along with authentication papers, documentation on the insurance rider from Lloyd's of London and a contact name there, my mobile number and email if you want to contact me." She turned toward Stanton and looked at the door. "Ready?"

Stanton looked helplessly at both her and Marcus.

"You can close your mouth now," she said to Stanton and helped Marcus into a chair.

"I ... um ..." Stanton muttered.

"Yes, sir, I concur with that sentiment exactly," Marcus said and burst into a wide grin.

"Am I to understand that you are donating this artifact, whatever it turns out to be, to us,

Miss Stine, without any ..."

"This is where it belongs and no one needs to know otherwise. No scorn or scandal will come to the museum."

"You mean for housing a fake heirloom for the past four hundred years?"

Kerry nodded at Marcus, zipped her handbag, opened the door, and walked out.

"Our cab's still here, good."

Stanton shook his head. "That's all you have to say at this moment?"

She laughed. "You think I should've sold it to Sotheby's for twelve million dollars?"

"Or something! You certainly could have."

"No," she said and took his arm. "I have what I want."

"Is that so?"

She knew he knew what she meant. "Carlton Hotel King's Cross," she told the cab driver and smiled.

Acknowledgements

My heartfelt gratitude goes to the people who provided me love, support, encouragement, expertise, consultation, energy and care while bringing this story to fruition.

To Lee, the person I trust more than anyone – for your love, cheerleading, reality checks, and extraordinary patience - you are such a gift.

To my amazing parents for your constant love and encouragement, for teaching me to dig beneath the surface, and to believe in myself.

To my sister, one of the wisest people I know, who always gets it, no matter what it is.

To my faithful and insightful readers - Missy, Gail and Kadi, for your intelligent questions, smart feedback, and excellent attention to detail.

To Natalie Goldberg for your book, "Writing Down the Bones," which launched me on this path.

To Beth Barany, my writing coach, for your savvy advice and guidance.

To Emma, for showing me how I want to be when I grow up

To Paulette Burns, my fourth-grade teacher, who read the entire Chronicles of Narnia aloud to our class and, thus, birthed my unending love of stories.

To Judy Avila, writing companion and role model.

To the master storytellers - Arthur Conan Doyle, Agatha Christie, J.K. Rowling, C.S. Lewis, J.R.R. Tolkien – your characters have become part of the mythology of my life, giving me constant companionship and inspiration.

To Jayne and the folks at Rebel for your support, encouragement, expertise, kindness and patience throughout this process.

And to Olivia and Cassidy, the sparkliest stars in

the sky

You are all part of my family and my village...THANK YOU.

About the Author

Lisa Towles has had over fifty short stories published in literary journals, and she spent twelve years as a journalist, columnist and art reviewer covering the fine art scene in New Mexico. In 2004 she received two journalism awards by New Mexico Press Women's Association for two art reviews published in a weekly magazine.

Lisa is a former Board member of Southwest Writers (New Mexico), and a current active member of MWA, Sisters in Crime, and International Thriller Writers. Her website is www.lisatowles.com, and she maintains four blogs, including a writing blog called Digital Raconteur.

Lisa was raised in New England and lived in Exeter (U.K.) and Albuquerque, New Mexico before relocating to the Bay Area. Lisa works in the tech industry and is in the process of getting her MBA in IT Management.

Also by this author writing as Lisa Polisar ...

Knee Deep, Blackwater Tango, The Ghost of Mary Prairie, Escape: Dark Mystery Tales

Non-Fiction: Straight Ahead: A Musician's Guide to Learning Jazz and Staying Inspired

And for more from this author ...

Please turn the page for a preview of *Ninety-Five*

NINETY-FIVE

CHAPTER ONE

It's Sunday morning, I have no idea what time it is and the silence is entirely wrong – for this place. I jerk upright too fast, and my head spins, and my half naked body feels clammy with a sudden panic. Looking ... looking ... Why am I not in my bed? I'm not even in my room; it's ... David Wade's room down the hall (wtf am I doing here?) I surmise from the Drake and Sia posters on the wall. Maybe a fire drill went off and I slept through it, with only a smoking shell of a building left in a sog of wet carpet and dripping walls. But I don't smell smoke. Maybe everyone's still sleeping.

Or maybe they're all dead.

As I lift the sheet to see my alarming bare hairy legs, the door opens. I scramble to cover myself, like a prostitute caught in a congressman's hotel room.

"Good morning, sweetheart." It's Wade, smiling. Bastard.

"Fuck off," I reply in a chalky voice.

He sits on the opposite bed, sizing me up, fumbling with a cacophonous paper bag. "How do you feel?"

I half laugh half cry at the question. "How do you th— what am I doing here? Are we, like, married now or something?"

He starts tearing open sugar packets and cream containers and pouring them in a disastrously tall cup. "I think I'm gonna throw up," I say and slap my palm to my mouth.

"Calm down, Zak, this is just what you need, believe me. Drink."

"I feel like I need a blood transfusion, or at least my stomach pumped. And what's wrong with my throat?"

"How's your head?"

"I just answered that," I shoot back with a loathing for David Wade that I'd never felt before now, certain, it seems, that he has everything to do with this Sunday dystopia. I dutifully start sipping what smells like instant calm and comfort – English Breakfast Tea, light and sweet. My stomach stays neutral, so I draw in a deep breath and settle back against the pillows, wondering where my clothes are, waiting for answers.

My esophagus feels like it's lined with broken glass. So I sort of spill the tea down my throat by leaning my head back, half-listening to Wade's story of a party, a bar, and how I apparently drank something that was intended for someone else. I feel my hand start gripping the sheets. Focus, I say to myself, you're fine, this is temporary. Drink, breathe, repeat.

"Today is Sunday, October 20th, confirm or deny?"

"Confirm." Wade smiles.

"Where are my clothes?"

"No idea."

"How did I get here?"

"I brought you."

"From where?"

"Fountain of Time."

"What? Hyde Park? I've never even been there."

"Well, apparently you have," he says, with mock attitude.

Fucking Wade, I'd like to strangle him right now. Okay, think like an investigator, I tell myself. "Who was supposed to drink what I drank, and what was it?"

Wade settles back now on the bed, leaning against the wall, still facing me. "Question one, I don't know for sure." He pauses.

"Question two?" I press.

"Tamango."

I only know this drink from reputation, or at least until today that was true.

"What's in it? I mean, is there ..."

"No, nothing that would cause permanent damage," he replies, reading my thoughts.

I'm walking now in boxer shorts and bare feet around David Wade's room, and it's surprisingly clean in here for a dorm room.

"I need some clothes, do you have any ..."

He moves to the closet and starts tossing out things – long sleeved T-shirt, sweat pants, black socks, telling me all the while about Tamango's frightening list of ingredients, only two of which are actually known to man – 85% grain alcohol and roselle leaves, in addition to a mysterious concoction of purportedly hallucinogenic African herbs.

"I feel like I've seen my entire body from the inside out. I seriously remember the color, the texture of my blood, muscles, organs, even cells. Is this – typical?"

"Last night was an accidental glimpse into what we're not really supposed to see. If you want a real glimpse, and a guide to show you around, come back here tonight at midnight."

"No thanks, master of the opium den, throw your own life away if I care. I'm gonna clean up and try to feel normal."

"Try all you want," he says as I move to the door, "but I will see you at midnight."

"Fuck off, I'll see you in hell."

45516930R00181

Made in the USA
Middletown, DE
06 July 2017